M000300992

DARKNESS UNVEILED

(SKY BROOKS WORLD: ETHAN BOOK 2)

EMERSON KNIGHT

MCKENZIE HUNTER

This is a work of fiction. Names, characters, businesses, places, events, and incidents are either the products of the author's imagination or used in a fictitious manner. Any resemblance to actual persons, living or dead, or actual events is purely coincidental.

McKenzie Hunter

Darkness Unveiled

© 2017, McKenzie Hunter & Emerson Knight

McKenzieHunter@McKenzieHunter.com

ALL RIGHTS RESERVED. This book contains material protected under International and Federal Copyright Laws and Treaties. Any unauthorized reprint or use of this material is prohibited. No part of this book may be reproduced or transmitted in any form or by any means, electronic or mechanical, including photocopying, recording, or by any information storage and retrieval system without express written permission from the author/publisher.

For notifications about new releases, *exclusive* contests and giveaways, and cover reveals, please sign up for my mailing list.

ISBN: 978-1946457-85-1

ACKNOWLEDGMENTS

First and foremost, I'd like to thank McKenzie Hunter for allowing me to play in her world once more. What a fun place to be, with a rich mythology and full of complex characters I loved to spend time with. Darkness Unveiled was particularly challenging to write. I don't know how I would've completed this book without my beta readers and Stacy McCright, who consistently kept me from straying off the path.

I'd also like to thank Gloria Knowles, C. Hindle, and the most supportive group of authors I could ever ask for: John P. Logsdon, Orlando Sanchez, Shayne Silvers, and Benjamin Zackheim.

Lastly but most important, my thanks to you, the reader. Fans of McKenzie Hunter and SBS have been very supportive of Ethan's POV, and I couldn't feel more fortunate. Without you, I wouldn't be able to do what I most love to do, write. You're the best!

CHAPTER 1

*P*repared for an awkward conversation, I parked my white Audi R8 in front of Murphy's Pub, across the street from Josh's high-rise condo. Actually, the condo was mine—an investment property I leased to my brother because it helped me keep tabs on him, and it was close to the pack's club, which he managed. Managing a nightclub played well to his strengths—and his weaknesses. Once a floundering nightspot that appealed almost exclusively to the supernatural community, the club was now a premier attraction for the Chicago social elite and drew plenty of celebrities, rock stars, and professional athletes who appreciated Josh's hands-on approach to customer satisfaction. His attentiveness, however, was a double-edged blade. The club provided the pack with a number of valuable connections, but his participation in the festivities was becoming an obsession—especially lately. His increased appetite for recklessness was not just limited to partying.

Josh was a powerful witch, serving the Midwest Pack as a blood ally. Personally, I didn't trust magic. It was seductive and unpredictable, which is why I didn't want him training Sky, but he thought otherwise. She had a natural ability to borrow magic and use it. He wanted to know how she was able to convert dark magic to natural magic, and training her gave him a chance to explore her ability. He wanted power—always more power—but their sessions had led to predictable mishaps. He was drawing attention to himself, and to the pack, and he was putting her safety at risk.

I turned off the engine. Before I could open the door, I saw her walking on the other side of the street toward the condo building. A further glance revealed her Honda Civic parked nearby. *Perfect timing.* I hesitated, waiting in my car while I considered the ramifications of what came next. At the best of times, my brother was sensitive to what he perceived as my intrusive, overbearing attitude. Over the last year, I had done my best to give him the space he wanted, to let him make his mistakes and learn from them, but putting Sky at risk was a line I needed to cross.

She didn't want my protection, either.

After Sky had watched Josh destroy the Gem of Levage a year ago, Sebastian had invited her to join the Midwest Pack, the most powerful pack in the country—against my objection. She still hadn't made a formal decision, but she seemed determined to lead an independent life. He was going out of his way to ease her into joining us, using Steven and Winter as connections that served both as protection and encouragement. I didn't want Sky to join the pack. I'd told her so, and she'd kept her distance from me ever since. She didn't understand my objection. It wasn't personal. I wanted her safe, but there were risks to joining the pack—dangers I didn't feel she could properly anticipate. She didn't know enough of our world to make that choice, and she didn't want to. She wanted to remain on the outside looking in, but that wasn't possible, either. Once she formally declined or Sebastian withdrew the invitation, her relationship to the pack would largely come to an end, but I would always be there to protect her, even from a distance.

Deciding my chances of talking sense into either of them together were almost nil, I opted to pick up some steaks in the natural foods store next door. A short time later, I approached my Audi with a grocery bag in one hand and my key fob in the other. When I pressed the fob, unlocking the door, the corresponding double chirp was engulfed by the sound of an explosion from the building behind me. I turned to see the windows blown out of Josh's condo on the twentieth floor. The vibration from the explosion triggered an incongruous chorus of car alarms from the parking garage and vehicles parked on the street. I dropped the grocery bag and ran toward the building as the doorman backed away from his post, his attention fixed upward toward the source of the explosion. He didn't bother to stop me as I slipped inside past a group of panicked residents hurrying out of the building.

Inside the lobby, more anxious residents emerged from the elevators to be directed toward the exit by a uniformed concierge. "Please exit the building in a calm, orderly fashion," he pleaded in a strained voice. Not trusting the building's power, I entered the stairwell and ran up to the twentieth floor. I emerged from the stairwell to find my brother—apparently unharmed—outside his door, partially surrounded by his frightened neighbors.

"I left the gas stove on." He smiled, the full measure of his considerable charm on display as he soothed their anxiety with a deep, humble sincerity. "My bad," he pleaded, splaying a hand over his heart.

Concerned for Sky, I roughly pushed through the neighbors and past Josh without a second glance. Relief washed over me when I found her safe, sitting upright on the dark gray couch. She appeared shocked, staring at a dozen small cuts on the backs of her hands. I rushed to her, kneeling as I took her hands into mine. "Are you okay?" I asked, examining her. She nodded. Gently turning her wrists, I saw more cuts on the back of her forearms. Judging by the location of the cuts, I assumed that she'd been able to cover her face with her hands just before the explosion occurred. In her shock, she seemed to have forgotten her animosity toward me.

"I think I blew up your condo," she said, her expression blank.

I stifled a relieved chuckle as I examined the damage to the unit. The large dark area rug that covered the hardwood floors was littered with bits of glass, most prominently beneath the blown-out windows. Not a single one remained, and a cold wind blew into the unit. The couches had been moved slightly, pushed outward from the large cocktail ottoman nearby—the obvious epicenter of the explosion. I didn't need to see the magical components sitting on top of the ottoman to know what had happened.

"Are you the resident, sir?" inquired an authoritative female voice at the door. The police officer's radio squawked. "I'm at the unit now," she answered. "Emergency services, stand by."

Sky glanced nervously at the components as I casually scooped them into one of the ottoman's compartments, shielding the police officer's view with my body. I cleared my throat, letting Josh know it was safe to let the officers inside, then rose and turned to meet them. There were two—they always came in pairs—and they weren't ours. An anxious-looking building manager followed them.

"Ma'am," the lead officer addressed Sky, glancing with concern at the cuts on her hands and arms, "do you require medical assistance?"

"I'm fine." She rose, gathering herself. "Just some minor cuts. I'll have my doctor take a look, but I'm fine." She added nervously, "It was just a gas leak."

I glared at Josh. This wasn't the first incident. Over the last few months, my brother had grown unusually reckless, pushing the envelope of his powers, and not just with Sky. There were safer places to test his magic—the retreat, for example. I was beginning to suspect that he wanted to draw attention to himself. Perhaps he was testing the limits of what he could get away with. As I watched him now, confronted by two police officers, the manager, and a host of unhappy neighbors, he appeared to be in his element, charming all of them to forget everything and walk away. Only not everyone was buying his story this time—not completely.

The scowling manager strode into the kitchen to check for more damage while the other officer, with both hands gripping his black belt, walked up to the broken windows—mindful of the glass he was stepping on—to look out.

I glanced at Sky, who looked miserable, as if she'd failed an important test, and felt my jaw clench. My anger stewed another fifteen minutes until Josh finally ushered everyone out of the unit, closed the door, and turned to me with a triumphant grin, his arms held out wide as if embracing our supposed awe. As usual, he wore faded jeans and a short-sleeved graphic t-shirt, drawing attention to the tattoos that covered both of his arms. His golden brown hair was a chaotic mess and the shadowy stubble of his beard never seemed to grow or fade. We were as far from each other in appearance as we were in temperament.

For the moment, I swallowed my anger to address Sky. "I'll take you home." I turned to my brother, glaring. "When I return, we are going to talk."

He rolled his bright blue eyes, letting his arms collapse until his palms smacked against his hips. He turned away, preferring to survey the damage to the condo than to face me.

"I'm fine," Sky insisted, remembering that I made her uncomfortable. She rose, avoiding my gaze. "I'll drive myself."

"Someone should be with you in case there is a residual effect from whatever magic you two were playing with."

"There won't be any 'residual effect,'" Josh snapped. He walked past me to take Sky's hands, clutching them together at his chest as he drew her gaze to his. "Check in with me later. Just to let me know you're okay."

"It's not like I'll be alone," she answered, somewhat exasperated. "Steven will probably be there."

My scowl deepened as I resisted the urge to shake my head. Sebastian had assigned Steven to keep watch on her, to keep her safe and connected to the pack while she took her time considering his offer to join us, but Steven had unilaterally taken the liberty of surpassing his mandate. He spent so much time at her home that he'd begun leaving his belongings, effectively moving in, which I found highly inappropriate.

Sky retrieved her keys, gave Josh an apologetic glance, then left.

After the door closed, he dropped onto the couch, his knees splayed and his hands in his lap. "Let me guess, this is going to be the big brother speech."

I fought back my irritation, glancing at the destroyed windows as I measured my words carefully. "Teaching her to use magic is an unnecessary risk."

"I admit," he said begrudgingly, "sometimes I push her too hard, but that's how witches are trained—testing boundaries. Ethan, I know this looks bad, but Sky is learning. A year ago she could barely raise a ward. Now she can move small objects. She still has to borrow my energy to do it, but she'll continue to improve. And her defensive wards are competent."

"Good," I snapped. "Then she's learned enough."

"She wants to learn," my brother insisted, his defiance rising. "And I'm going to continue to teach her."

I glared at him, which only served to harden his determination. "You confuse your endless pursuit of power with benevolence."

His face tightened into a scowl. "We agreed about the whole smothering thing."

"I've done my best not to interfere, but you're blatantly drawing attention to yourself. Josh, this isn't just about Skylar. Sebastian has noticed your behavior as well. You're not just exposing yourself; you're drawing attention to the pack. That's a problem. I know you don't want to hear that from me. Keep it up, if you want to. Eventually you're going to create a problem you can't talk your way out of." *Then I won't be able to help you,* I nearly added, but Josh would only have become more intractable.

He ran his hands through his hair, tousling it, as his cheeks turned pink, then red with frustration. "I'll be more careful," he conceded dismissively. I had the distinct impression that I was expected to leave. I glanced around the condo, calculating the cost of the damage. Josh could fix it, but too many people had witnessed the damage. If the windows were suddenly repaired an hour after the explosion, there would be questions. I had insurance to cover the damage, but this would be my third claim in a year to cover damage caused by my brother's experiments. My premiums were going to skyrocket.

"I'll help you clean up."

"I got it." From the couch, he began a series of gestures, drawing forth a gentle magical force that felt like a warm breeze as it blew through the room, sweeping the glass into a pile before the debris disappeared entirely. Then he cast a ward that enclosed the living room, shielding the broken windows from the cold wind outside. When finished, he turned to me expectantly, his gaze flicking toward the front door. "I'll open a gap for you so you can leave."

"Don't bother," I said, easily breaking the entire ward on my way out.

. . .

Leaving the building, I cursed myself for making such a gross display of breaking Josh's ward—reckless. After my mother's death, I'd inherited some of her magical abilities—Josh had gotten the rest. But were-animals weren't supposed to use magic. I wasn't just a were-animal, but that was my secret. Exposure would put my life and Josh's at risk. I'd hidden my abilities until last year, when I'd broken his magical field during a fight. Breaking a ward was possible, but a field was much stronger. I'd spent a good deal of time convincing him that breaking his field was a fluke, that my abilities were negligible. I'd just thrown that lie in his face.

I paused outside my Audi with the door open, then turned back to stare up at the blown-out windows of my unit. A pair of bicyclists stopped to chat with a group of gossipy tenants lingering by the curb, spreading the word of what had happened to anyone who would listen. I shook my head, resisting the urge to punch the Audi, then climbed into the driver's seat and drove away. I tried to drown my frustration with the radio, but after a few minutes of guitar-grinding rock, my knuckles remained white on the steering wheel. Disappointed, I turned the radio off.

Why is Sky so much more comfortable with my brother? The answer was immediate. *He dotes on her. He indulges her curiosity about magic. He puts her at risk to resolve his own curiosity and she doesn't see it, while I make the hard choices to protect her.* The realization didn't improve my mood.

Josh had always been a handful. I'd spent my entire life taking care of my brother: looking out for him, protecting him from others and himself—and he'd fought me every inch of the way. I squeezed the steering wheel with both hands, as hard as I could, wondering if I would ever figure out how to get through to him. My brother listened to few—none more than our godmother, Claudia.

According to the time on the dashboard clock, there was a good chance I would find her in her gallery nearby. I frowned, remembering it had been weeks since I'd last visited her, and turned onto Broadway. A few minutes later I parked outside a large brick building just off the main street. Inside, I strode past paintings and sculptures from Chicago's most sought-after artists without sparing a glance. Others came to Claudia's palatial gallery in awe, but I'd grown up here. Not that I wasn't interested in art, but Claudia was always my primary concern.

My heels clicked on the crackled, salmon-pink concrete floor. A handful of patrons were scattered throughout the gallery, some lingering on the strategically placed boutique sofas and benches, contemplating various pieces. I found Claudia with a young couple, discussing a painting of her own creation, though she had not signed it. Seeing her brought a smile to my face. She was an elegant, slender woman in her mid-fifties, with shoulder-length brown hair she always pulled into a bun. Always artfully dressed, she wore a cream-colored pantsuit with a pink camisole and long matching gloves—she was never without the long gloves that protected her while in public. A string of pearls hung gracefully around her neck.

I stopped a respectful distance away and waited patiently while my godmother gently informed the patrons that the painting wasn't for sale, a portrait of two boys she privately claimed represented myself and Josh. The smaller of the two, with short ruffled hair, lay on a bed in peaceful slumber, his expression angelic, while the other boy protectively knelt close by. His chestnut hair was flecked with gold and his deep blue eyes were somber and intense, displaying a wariness beyond his years as he watched over his sleeping brother, unaware of the looming shadow behind him. The painting was a gift for me—one I had yet to accept. While I admired Claudia's considerable talent, I found the imagery spoke more to her perception of my brother and me than to fact.

Curiously, Sky seemed to have become obsessed with the painting. According to Claudia, she visited the gallery frequently and never failed to leave without attempting to purchase the painting. Disappointed, she always left with another piece in her possession. *What did she see in it?* I had no idea. Claudia wouldn't have explained the painting to Sky. That wasn't her way.

"If you have any more questions, do let me know," she told the young couple, who wandered toward the far end of the gallery. My godmother's expression brightened as she approached me, smiling broadly and offering me her gloved hands, which I accepted. "Ethan."

I air-kissed over each of her cheeks, mindful not to touch her skin. "It's been too long," I said, grateful to see her.

"Whenever you have time is fine, dear," she said sincerely. "And the same is true for Josh."

I felt my jaw clench at his name. She noticed before I could relax, and I saw a knowing, eternally patient look come over her. "Why don't we retire to my office," she said politely, leading me there without waiting for an answer.

Her office was a private continuation of the gallery, complete with original artwork overlooking a pair of hand-carved wooden chairs next to a tea table, an elegant chaise couch, and an antique writing table with an old-fashioned pen and inkwell. I followed her lead as she sat at the table, sitting across from her as she poured our tea.

"Is Josh in trouble?" she asked casually—too casually.

I firmly regretted showing my frustration, but the door was open and I felt my exasperation pouring out. "He never listens to me."

She met my regard with a seemingly passive expression, but I recognized the slight crinkle in the corners of her eyes. She was protective of my brother. We both were, but in different ways. If she judged me, she said nothing, creating a void of silence. I knew the tactic well, having learned it from her. At times, even I couldn't resist filling that void. "My brother is determined to make his life as difficult as possible. He is an escape artist, and everything in his life—magic, relationships, even managing the club—exists purely to generate situations for him to escape from." *What's he done now?* I expected, but she only sipped her tea, waiting patiently for me to continue, and I obliged. Having started, I felt a need to clarify.

"He's obsessed with dark magic. He's using Sky to obtain it, and he doesn't even know why he wants it; it's just power to him. His quest has led to a number of highly visible disasters." To the rest of the world, magic and werewolves were the stuff of nightmares and legends. The pack thrived under that cloak of disbelief.

"Has anyone been hurt?" she asked.

"Not yet, but he's putting Sky at risk, and he's drawing attention to himself, and to the pack."

"I see." She sipped her tea thoughtfully. When she gently set her cup back onto its saucer, she remained silent, waiting with a neutral, motherly expression for me to continue.

"His ability to negotiate himself out of trouble is waning. If he doesn't get control of himself soon, he'll create a problem that he cannot escape. He'll shine a light in places that should remain dark."

She smiled. "I've often marveled at how different you two are. But it's not an accident that when it comes to control, Josh is your exact opposite."

My eyes widened at her rebuke. "You think I'm to blame for my brother's recklessness?"

My godmother laid a gloved hand over mine as she held my gaze. "Of course not. He's a grown man, Ethan."

"If he would just listen to me, just once, I could save him a lot of trouble."

"But you can't live his life for him. Look out for him, if you must—that's your way—but you can't make his decisions for him. Every time you try to steer him from trouble, Josh swerves toward it. You have the best of intentions, Ethan, but I don't see that your efforts are helping him. Quite the opposite, in fact."

I sat back in my chair, gaping at my godmother until I remembered to close my mouth. She lightly patted my hand before wrapping the fingers of both her hands around her teacup. After reassuring me with her warm smile, she glanced out the office window.

"It's been lovely to visit with you, dear. There are more patrons who require my attention."

"Of course," I said, rising. As a token of respect and affection, I offered her my hand. She took it gracefully, accepting my perfunctory assistance as she came to her feet.

"Are you available for brunch this Sunday?" she asked.

"I will rearrange my plans."

"Not necessary. Coordinate with Josh and we'll arrange another time. I'd love to have you two together."

"Of course," I said, hiding my irritation. If Josh had been available as well, would she have accepted my offer then?

"Invite Skylar, if you like. I am growing quite fond of her."

I nodded and opened the office door for her, following her out.

The drive to the pack's retreat seemed long as I pondered Claudia's advice. I couldn't accept allowing my brother to make mistakes that could be easily avoided with timely advice, but I wasn't in the habit of ignoring my godmother's insights. When I finally turned onto the hidden, private road that snaked through the woods toward the pack's retreat, my frustration was stronger than ever.

The retreat was a home away from home for pack

members, a three-story brick mansion hidden from view on three hundred acres of wooded land that afforded us total privacy. The boundaries of the property were fenced, deterring all but the most determined intruder—typically a hunter looking to poach our wealth of wild game. On those rare occasions, we made sure the intruder never came back. The land provided us with security, a safe place to hunt and exercise our animal nature without concern of being hunted. In more troubled times, Josh's magical field shielded the house from even our greatest enemies.

I parked the Audi in the garage.

Winter emerged from the house as I approached. Judging by her professional attire, she had dropped in directly from her job as an HR manager in an up-and-coming tech company based out of Chicago. Judging by her pace, she wasn't in a particular hurry. She was statuesque, with long straight black hair and flawless sun-kissed skin. Compared to most were-animals, she was small, but looks were deceiving. Most misjudged her, and Winter made them pay. She was our third, and one of the best fighters in the pack.

As we approached each other, I gestured to the faint yellow remains of a blackened left eye. "Sky?" I smiled. Winter had been Sebastian's choice to train her to fight, over my objection. When I'd first brought Sky to the retreat, she'd been targeted by Demetrius, the Master of the Northern Seethe. He'd intended to use her along with the Gem of Levage in a ritual that would have forever freed the vampires from the constraint of the sun. Some of the pack had seen her very existence as a threat—Winter and Gavin among them. Despite Sebastian's orders that Sky was to be unharmed, it would've been a simple task for Winter to arrange a training accident, something she couldn't be blamed for. As an instructor, she was ruthless, but Sky had proven herself up to the task.

"I let her give me a black eye," Winter confessed.

I grinned. "That was nice of you."

"I figured I'd beaten her butt enough, I should give her a reward. She was supposed to break my nose. Now that she knows she can do some damage, she's holding back."

Pack life was dangerous. We trained hard because we fought hard. If Sky was holding back now, she would instinctively hold back in an actual battle, which might get her killed.

"You'll have to piss her off," I suggested, drawing a mischievous grin from Winter.

"I think I can manage that. She can hold her own, Ethan. She needs to continue training, but she's not the helpless pup you initially brought to us."

"I must be talking to the wrong Winter, because that sounded like respect."

"Barely," she insisted, glancing at her nails. "She has a way of growing on you. Like a fungus. Admittedly, she has changed the minds of others. Her chances of being accidentally killed by a pack member are significantly down from this time last year."

I grunted. "Gavin?"

She scowled. "Once he's got a target in his sights, he completes the hunt. In his mind, he has the right to kill her since she's not a pack member. He blames you and Sebastian for getting in his way."

"I know what he blames me for."

"He might challenge you."

"He's welcome to try."

I strode into the retreat, leaving her behind. Just inside, I found Gavin leaning back against a wall, his arms folded over his chest, glowering at me with menacing gray eyes. He was slim and graceful, befitting his were-panther, with tawny skin and a hollow, stern look. In the pack hierarchy, he was after Winter and before Steven. He was a transfer from the East Coast Pack, a skilled hunter and one of our best fighters, but he came with a chip on his shoulder. When it came to me, that chip had become a mountain.

He jerked his head toward the office. "Sebastian wants you."

Gavin followed me into the office, closing the door behind us. Sebastian rose and came out from behind his desk. As a rule, he never discussed serious matters from behind his desk; for him, that was a gross, impotent attempt at expressing power. He didn't need a symbol, or a shield.

"How did it go with Josh?"

I tensed. "He understands the situation."

"He blew up his condo," Gavin said derisively, his Brooklyn accent prevalent.

Word travels fast. We had contacts in the vicinity of the club who called in anything unusual. I ignored him, keeping my attention focused on Sebastian. "He agreed to limit his training of Skylar."

"And the club?"

"We addressed the situation," I said tersely. "I will address it further, if necessary."

Sebastian gave a single nod, then changed the subject. "It's time for Skylar to make a decision."

"Good," Gavin said. I agreed with him but wasn't going to give him the satisfaction. His motives and mine were not the same. Once the offer was rejected, he assumed that Sebastian would lift Sky's protection, but he was wrong if he thought I wasn't going to stop him from harming her.

"You're giving her an ultimatum," I said. She'd had a year to make up her mind, which reflected unprecedented patience on Sebastian's part.

"Soon. We all know how Skylar reacts to being backed into a corner."

Gavin's sigh was almost blatant—just enough to avoid rebuke.

Sebastian continued. "Up to now, she has enjoyed the

friendship of the pack. I've instructed Winter and Steven to begin to pull back from her. We will give her a short amount of time to measure the absence of the benefits of pack membership before I require a decision from her."

"I don't get it." Gavin shook his head. "We're talking about our value to her, like she's a prize. What value can she possibly provide to the pack?"

My fists clenched as I fought back the urge to defend her to Gavin. I chose my words carefully. "She's had a year to consider her options. I think we have her answer."

Sebastian addressed Gavin's concerns first. "She has unique magical abilities. According to Josh, if her talents are properly trained, her value could be immeasurable."

He was right, of course, which was why I didn't want Josh to train her. The stronger she became, the more attention she would attract. "I don't think she's suited to pack life," I said. Sky wanted normalcy—something pack life could never provide.

"I think she's capable of deciding that for herself," Sebastian countered. "The reality is that someone with her abilities will always be vulnerable to someone or something that craves power. We can offer her protection, security, and family. Without the pack, she'll always be looking over her shoulder, and I'm not sure she understands that."

"That makes her a threat," Gavin insisted. "Why take the risk at all?"

"If she declines," Sebastian explained to me carefully, "we will be obliged to watch over her."

If she falls into the wrong hands and becomes a threat, we'll have to handle her as one, he meant. But she could live the life she wanted—I was convinced. I would make sure of that.

Sebastian straightened. "My decision is made," he informed Gavin with a dismissive look. The were-panther's scowl deepened as he looked to me, then left the office. Sebastian gestured for me to remain.

"Ethan, I know you want what's best for Skylar. There is some issue between you two that I suspect is giving her pause about joining us. If there is anything you can do to remove that barrier, you should try."

"Why does she need to join the pack when she's practically living with one of its members?" I blurted.

Sebastian smiled. "I take it you are referring to Steven. They seem to share a consanguineous relationship."

"His instructions were to keep an eye on her. Now half his apartment is strewn haphazardly about her home. He has a key and comes and goes as if he lives there. I find his behavior disrespectful. Don't you?"

"I'm fine with it." He shrugged, offering me an amused grin. "But you don't seem to be."

I scowled. Not much got past Sebastian, and I didn't like being assessed. My personal feelings aside, Steven's relationship with Sky was inappropriate. Josh's relationship with her was worse—he wasn't just flirting with her, he was putting her at risk. I realized that this discussion, while necessary, wasn't going to lead anywhere. I quietly left the office with my jaw firmly clenched.

CHAPTER 2

Three days later, I took the scheduled Skype call from home, my tablet propped onto the kitchen counter. I had met Soraia Queiroz once before, when I'd scheduled the one-on-one training session. She was a freelance language instructor who taught from wherever she happened to be in the world. At the moment, she was connecting from a small village on the coast of southern Spain. She spoke six languages fluently, but my only interest was her native tongue, Portuguese.

"*Boa tarde*," she said cheerfully, her bright smile broad and perfect. "Good afternoon, Mr. Charleston." Her skin was flawless, and she had rosy high cheekbones, a petite nose, and long black lashes that matched her dark eyes. Her long black curls gently flowed over her shoulders, framed in the background by a pair of almond trees.

"Ethan," I said.

"*Sim*. Yes. Okay. Well, shall we start?"

"I am ready."

"I will give you a phrase. Repeat it back to me, and I will correct you. So, we begin with something very useful: *Aonde e o quarto-de-banho.* 'Where is the bathroom?' Now it's your turn, Ethan."

I frowned and glanced at my watch, wondering if I had made a mistake.

"*Aonde e o quarto-de-banho?*" she repeated, meticulously pronouncing the syllables.

I repeated the phrase with little enthusiasm, which she noticed.

"Ethan, perhaps you would like to try a different phrase. You did not say that you were learning Portuguese for a specific reason, but sometimes a person wants to learn to speak to, or get closer to, another person. A woman, perhaps? If that's the case, I can teach you more specific phrases."

When Skylar was growing up, her adopted mother had insisted that she learn Portuguese, the language of her birth mother. She could be stubborn and difficult to communicate with. I had thought it might improve our communication if I could speak to her in her familial language, but I was having second thoughts.

Soraia took my discomfort as a confession. "Perhaps you would like to learn to say, *'Você é muito bonito?'* 'You are very beautiful.'" She beamed prettily. "Is there anything specific you would like to say to your girl?"

"Yes," I said, thinking. "'Are you injured?'"

Her smile froze in place awkwardly. "Are you sure there is not something else you would like to say?"

She's right. Get straight to the point. "'Where are you injured?'"

Before Soraia could react, my phone vibrated. A glance at the screen revealed the call was from Marko. He was the pack's sixth, after Steven. "My apologies, Ms. Queiroz. I must take this call. I understand that I am still on the clock. One moment, please." I muted our Skype call, cutting off her reply, and answered my phone.

"He's in," Marko said. "He showed up with a bottle of whiskey and lunch, so I'd say he's going to be here awhile."

I grunted. "What kind of whiskey?"

"He wears a Casio watch, so I'm guessing …" his voice trailed off.

He's probably settling in for the afternoon. I glanced at the clock on my phone. "I'm on my way." I killed the call and unmuted Soraia. "I have to leave. You may bill me for the entire session. I will contact you to reschedule."

I grabbed my keys and wallet from the island counter, stuffed an envelope from my desk into the inside pocket of my suit jacket, and then left, opting for my SUV.

A short time later, I parked on North Ashland Avenue, just outside a nondescript, tan brick commercial building. Between the laundromat and the dry cleaners was an unmarked door. Marko emerged from the laundromat to meet me. He was tall and lean and severe, with short brown hair and thick eyebrows that hid his intense brown eyes. Originally from Finland, Marko maintained his accent. This wasn't pack business. He'd come willingly, and I trusted him because he knew not to ask questions.

"Still upstairs," he said as I approached. "You should know, he carries a pistol in his left shoulder holster. He doesn't seem to do much business. I imagine he's up there drinking his sorrows." Marko had been tracking the detective for the past week—longer than necessary, but I preferred to be thorough.

I shook my head at Skylar's choice. She needed to be more careful.

Marko hooked a thumb over his shoulder toward the building. "You want me to—"

"Wait here," I said, and then entered the building. The door led to a dark, dirty, narrow stairway that smelled of mold. The next floor was a row of offices. From the looks of it, not much happened here in the daytime. Eventually, I found a door to my right, labeled "Dennis McDuffy, P.I." I opened the door without knocking, catching Dennis by obvious surprise. He looked up from a Styrofoam takeaway container of noodles. It took him just a moment to decide I wasn't a customer. His heart leapt in fear, then quickly slowed as he brought it under control. He leaned back in his chair, drawing his right hand to his belly—closer to his pistol bulging slightly under his jacket.

"Can I help you?" he asked, his voice friendly, but cautious.

I made a point to straighten my scowl. Knowing Dennis was nervous was useful, but I didn't want him on edge. Not yet. "I need a private investigator."

He relaxed, drawing his hand away from his weapon. "My apologies. You have an intimidating look about you," he said as he covered his lunch with a horse racing sheet, then pushed the two aside, trying to clear some space. "What can I do for you?"

He had been a decent detective at one time, until the gambling had caught up with him. I knew plenty about Dennis McDuffy, from the same source that had hacked Sky's phone for me—Stacy, a young paralegal at the law firm I worked for, who had a hidden talent for illicit research. I'd caught her siphoning data on our corporate clients and selling it to a Russian vampire Seethe in Ohio that specialized in cybercrimes and identity theft. They had threatened Stacy's family, and she was struggling to keep up with their demands. Having found out her story, I couldn't blame her for not going to the police. The regular world didn't know about vampires, werewolves, and witches beyond crappy television shows and over-the-top movies. I had no interest in traveling to Ohio, so I'd let Demetrius solve the vampire problem. He was old-school. He didn't recognize digital borders and didn't appreciate an intrusion on his turf. I got

Stacy off the hook and she did favors for me on the side, for cash.

"I need to find someone," I said.

Dennis winced. "I should just tell you up front," he said out of the side of his mouth, "I'm not that kind of detective." I scowled, and he continued. "Let's just assume you're asking about a missing relative." He nodded for the both of us. "Most of the time, people disappear because they want to. I don't really care about the reasons why, but I'm not dragging someone back to a life they've already given up on."

"But you do take missing person cases," I said. He did.

Dennis tipped his head back to look down his nose at me. He sniffed. "Depends."

I removed a small piece of paper from my pocket, opened it, then pushed it across the desk toward him. When he read the name, I heard his heart rate more than double. Once again, he quickly brought his fear under control—mostly. He folded the paper, holding it as he scrutinized me. After a moment of quiet contemplation, I removed the envelope of cash from inside my suit jacket and pushed that toward him.

The PI's forehead tightened as he contemplated the envelope before gingerly picking it up to examine the contents. His pupils dilated. He set the envelope down—closer to him than to me—and vigorously rubbed his chin with a palm, molding his lips into a scowl as he scrutinized me, for all the good it did him. His eyes flicked to the name on the piece of paper, then to me. "You already know Skylar Brooks is a client of mine."

"Not anymore."

Dennis grunted, amused. "Well, buddy, my noodles are getting cold." He tapped the envelope with a finger. "What are you buying, exactly?"

"I'm buying you. For six months. Exclusive retainer."

His scowl deepened. *Good.* "You want me to follow Miss

Brooks, find out what color panties she wears, who she dates, who she—"

"Your business with her is complete."

"Oh." He nodded, then winced as he shook his head. "I gotta tell ya, that's some intense jealousy on your part. You paying off her mailman as well? What about her dentist?"

I ignored the taunt. "What exactly does Skylar have you doing?"

"She's a nice kid. A little stubborn and a lot pushy, but nice. She's just looking for her family. Why don't you keep your money and leave the kid alone," he said, but left the envelope where it was.

"You think I want to hurt her?"

"No offense, pal, but you look like a guy that hurts a lot of people," Dennis said.

I smiled, showing my teeth. "She is safe, and I'm going to keep it that way. I want your file on what you found for Skylar. Tell her you found nothing, then resign from the case."

"That's it?"

"I might take advantage of your retainer. I might not. I'll let you know."

Dennis drummed his fingers on the table in front of the envelope as he chewed his lower lip, then snatched the envelope and quickly dropped it into a desk drawer, replacing it with a thin manila folder from the file cabinet behind him. "She doesn't know, yet."

I rose, took a card from my wallet, and placed it on his desk. "Whatever she paid you," I said, taking the folder, "refund it."

His lips pressed into a tight frown, but he nodded.

In the driver's seat of my SUV, I skimmed through the folder. After making sure I wasn't followed out of the building,

Marko joined me a moment later, standing next to my window. The file was thin, but Dennis had done his job. Sky's birth mother had four siblings: William, Caitlyn, Elizabeth, and Madalena. All of them had emigrated from Portugal and were living together in a small town in Northern Virginia, just outside of D.C. Several of Sky's cousins lived there as well. An unusual living arrangement, but why? Dennis hadn't bothered to ask. His job had been to find her family, and he'd done it.

Marko waited patiently while I thought my plan through carefully. "We're making a couple stops, and then we're flying to Virginia," I said, reaching back to drop the folder on the backseat.

His eyes widened slightly, but he nodded. "Commercial?"

"No." *I hate waiting.* I drove toward a small, private airport just outside of Chicago while he called Aidan O'Dowd, a charter pilot the pack kept on retainer.

After some conversation on the phone, Marko informed me, "He sends his apologies, but he's booked for the day."

I scowled. "Put him on speaker."

"Ethan," Aiden said cheerfully, putting his Irish charm on display. "My apologies. I've got a charter arriving in thirty minutes."

"Cancel it."

"If you say so," he said begrudgingly, "but I have to tell you, this one's going to be expensive."

I frowned. The pack retainer covered the charter and kept Aidan accessible, but it didn't pay him to sit around waiting for our call. He had wealthy clients who didn't appreciate being shuffled to the back of the line. Apologies were costly. Was it worth it? Until I could prove otherwise, I had to assume that Sky's family was a threat to her. If the private investigator defied my instructions and informed her of my interference, she would waste no time contacting them. I was pretty sure he understood his personal safety was at stake, as well as a generous retainer, but stupidity was always difficult to anticipate. If the family was a threat to Sky, I wanted it dealt with quickly.

"Bill it to me, not the pack."

"If you say so. My bird is ready to fly. What's your ETA?"

"One hour."

Four hours later, I drove the rental SUV onto the driveway of a large white cottage on the outskirts of a small, historic Virginia town. The parcel of land was several acres in a pastoral neighborhood. As I parked, an older man rose from a chair on the porch, eyeing us with suspicion, but that was hardly a surprise. I didn't like uninvited guests, either. I took my briefcase from the backseat. By the time Marko and I emerged from the SUV, the man was joined by a plain woman with amber eyes and a congenial smile. If they were family to Skylar, they didn't look it.

The man, if properly identified by Dennis, was Skylar's uncle, William. He had broad cheekbones and a friendly but practiced smile. The woman next to him was probably Aunt Madalena. A brown-haired woman emerged from the house to join them. She was more severe-looking, less congenial—Aunt Caitlyn, I assumed. She glared down from the porch with a hawkish gaze.

"Good afternoon," I said, offering my most professional smile. "My name is Ethan Charleston. I'm—"

"We're not interested in selling," Caitlyn said dismissively.

Her assumption caught me by surprise, but only for a moment. They were on choice land. "I'm not a real estate agent. I'm—"

"A lawyer, then," Caitlyn said heavily, as if the word were a weight dropping from her lips. "Real estate agents and lawyers—it's hard to tell the difference."

Uncle William intervened, showing more hospitality. "What can I do for you, Mr. Charleston?"

I noticed his eyes flicking toward Marko, who stood stoically a few feet behind me. At my gesture, he returned to the SUV. Intimidation, while easy, wasn't always the most practical tactic. For the moment, it wasn't necessary. "There's no easy way to tell you. I am here regarding the last will and testament of your sibling, Senna Nunes." I heard several hearts skip a beat, confirming the relation.

Caitlyn scowled. "My sister died over twenty years ago, unexpectedly. Even if there was a will, you're a bit late."

"The situation is complicated. Perhaps we can talk inside."

The siblings exchanged glances before the two women went inside. After them, William held the door open, wearing a polite smile as he gestured for me to follow them. From the moment I stepped inside, I scanned my surroundings, taking in as much detail about the family as possible. Small, magical talismans were quickly apparent, hung haphazardly throughout the cluttered cottage—not your typical, mundane good luck charms. I had seen the likes of these talismans before. These were wards against magic. *They might already know what I am.* That could be helpful, should it come to a threat.

I entered the kitchen just as a young brunette with a stern expression rose from a chair. She was slightly younger than Sky, but similar in appearance, with mahogany curls, green eyes, and an air of defiance. She swept a pair of old books from the table, but not before I noticed the kind of symbols that could be found throughout Josh's library. She regarded me with suspicion as she passed me on her way out of the kitchen, the books clutched protectively in her arms.

I took the seat at the table that was offered to me, though it put me at a tactical disadvantage, with my back to the living room. *Was that deliberate? A test?* A lawyer wouldn't have noticed such a thing, so I allowed them their game. The brunette returned to stare at me. She could've remained in the entryway behind me, observing, but she chose to stand where her arrogant glare would be most obvious to me. I gave her an appreciative half-smile and stared until Madalena introduced me.

"Senna, this is Ethan Charleston. He's an attorney, here to speak to us about your aunt's will." Senna drew a smartphone from her pocket as she gave me a distrusting scowl and began tapping the screen. "She is named after her aunt," Madalena informed me.

"You're a corporate attorney," Senna announced, looking up from her phone with a triumphant look. "You don't do wills."

"I'm helping a friend out," I lied without the slightest change in my heart rate or respiration, but Senna remained unconvinced.

William sat across from me. "You have a story to tell us." It was as much an accusation as it was an invitation.

"Your sister's will was in the possession of one Elena Brooks, who chose—for reasons unknown—not to reveal it. The will was rediscovered when Miss Brooks recently passed away."

"Our sister never mentioned an Elena Brooks," William said, cutting off a sharp retort by Caitlyn. "What was their relationship?"

If he lied, he gave no physiological sign. Neither did the others. Their breathing, their heart rates were constant, yet my gut warned me they were hiding something. I considered leaving without another word. A normal family, removed from the supernatural world, could be good for Skylar—but this was not a normal family. They knew of magic and who knew what else.

"Elena Brooks was the legal guardian of Senna's only daughter, Skylar," I said, reading their surprised and skeptical reactions.

"Senna's child is alive?" Madalena asked.

While pregnant with Sky, Senna, along with the baby's father, a were-animal, was attacked by a vampire. The father was killed outright, but the vampire attempted to turn Senna. While the mother was human, her baby was an inherent were-animal. Were-animals couldn't be turned by the vampiric curse. For her, the conversion process would mean certain death. Elena Brooks intervened in time to stop the vamp, but not before the damage was done. In order to save her child, Senna sacrificed her life, transferring Maya, a spirit shade, to her unborn daughter. Only Maya's presence kept Skylar alive, to be raised by Elena.

"Our sister was murdered while she was pregnant," Caitlyn insisted.

"Miss Brooks had a medical background. She happened upon the scene and successfully performed an emergency C-section. So you are aware of how your sister died, then?" I asked, fishing. *If Elena knew of the family, she wouldn't have raised Skylar herself. Unless she was asked to.*

"Our sister was estranged from us," William admitted. "We discovered her demise after the fact."

"Is her child still alive?" Senna demanded. "Where is she?" I met her gaze without answering, deliberately agitating her. She was visibly excited, with a curious sense of urgency. "What about Maya?" she asked Caitlyn, who was quick to shuffle the girl out of the room. "She might know where the *Aufero* is," the girl whispered excitedly—not softly enough to escape my enhanced hearing.

"Say no more while he is in our home," Caitlyn whispered.

I turned to William, scrutinizing him the way he scrutinized me.

"Perhaps our lost niece—Skylar Brooks—should join us for this conversation," he said. "Perhaps you should call her, or better yet give me her number. I'm sure she would appreciate knowing that she has family, after all." His lie was too perfect. He didn't blink at all for what should be an emotional moment.

"The will is very specific," I said blandly. "Senna Nunes left you a generous sum, but there are conditions."

The contract was a hasty affair, basically a template with some names filled in and a few conditions added. It didn't need to stand up to intense legal scrutiny. It was simply a deterrent. If the family violated the terms, it wasn't the court system that would meet out punishment. I withdrew the contract from my briefcase and unfolded it onto the table; I placed a pen next to it. Caitlyn returned just as I removed the cashier's check from the envelope in my pocket and placed it on top of the contract. I felt the sudden rise of tension suck the oxygen out of the room. The three of them remained perfectly still, calculating instead of surprised or curious. In that moment, I knew they were a threat.

Caitlyn took one step closer, enough to read the check from above. "Senna didn't have money," she said softly. "Not that kind of money."

"What conditions?" William asked.

"Skylar Brooks is to be left alone. Zero contact. If you reach out to her, even just an e-mail, there will be consequences," I said menacingly. "If she contacts you, ignore her. If she shows up at your door, don't open it. If you say so much as 'go away,' the repercussions will be severe."

"Is this the will talking?" Madalena asked. "Or you?"

I folded my hands in my lap, holding her gaze.

"In some worlds," she said carefully, "accepting payment is more than just a legal obligation."

"Then we understand one another."

Caitlyn stepped back from the table as if the check were poison. "Keep your money," she snapped.

William said, "I think I can speak for my sisters when I say we do not accept."

I folded the contract and returned it to my briefcase, followed by the pen, then the check. I rose, briefcase in hand. William and Madalena rose as well.

"Who are you, Mr. Charleston?" Caitlyn demanded.

I let my wolf rise to the surface, giving them a flash of gunmetal, canine eyes. Caitlyn stepped back, muttering a curse, but the other two remained cautiously still. "I represent the Midwest Pack," I said slowly, adding emphasis. They knew what that entailed—their fear finally showed itself, tinged with anger. "Skylar is nothing to you. Keep it that way. If I have to come back here, there will not be a conversation. I'll see myself out."

Certain that I had made my point, I left them in the kitchen and returned to the SUV.

Sensing my mood, Marko remained silent through the journey back to Chicago while my mind raced with questions. What was the Aufero Senna had mentioned, and how did it relate to Sky? What did they know about Maya? According to Sky, the spirit shade had gone dormant last year. To free Sky from the grip of the Gem of Levage, I'd been forced to kill her—in my nightmares, I still saw the moment of her death, my hands wrapped around her throat and tears streaming down her cheeks. I watched the fear and resignation in her eyes as she expelled her last breath. The few minutes it had taken Dr. Baker to bring her back to life had seemed an agonizing eternity, but he had succeeded. She'd spent the next four days in a coma, communing with Maya. According to Sky, Maya had revealed her life story to her before announcing that she was going dormant. Four days was a long time. Josh and I were both certain that Sky had left out some details—probably a lot.

I could've pressed the family for more answers, but they were artful; I doubted there was anything more I could learn from them that would be the truth, and I didn't want to give them any more information on Sky. They got my message, and understood the power behind it, but would need to be watched.

After landing at O'Hare, we picked up my SUV and made it out of the city before stopping for gas. Marko went into the store while I pumped, questions running on a loop through my mind. After a moment, I noticed a muscle-bound boy, human, barely twenty, wearing a tight t-shirt and a backward baseball cap, staring at me from the other island. A lit cigarette hung from his lips while he pumped gas into his daddy's Ford F-150. Our eyes met and he nodded once, a short quick jerk of his chin. His lips spread into a smirk as he stared at me, unblinking—a fool's challenge, daring me to call out his stupidity or submissively avert my gaze. I got that look occasionally from human men of all ages. He sensed the Alpha in me and instinctively wanted to prove himself, but he had no idea what I was. He wasn't a were-animal. A were-animal would know better. We weren't going to bump chests and dare each other to throw the first punch. I let the boy see the wolf in my eyes—just for a moment. He straightened, his own eyes widening in surprise, then looked away, pretending to casually observe the scenery, but his heart gave him away. It raced in rising panic as he tried to make sense of what he'd just witnessed. His fingers trembled as they pinched the cigarette from his lips.

His head flicked unexpectedly toward the store, drawing my attention to the large manlike creature that charged me from around the far corner. Its features were vague, but shifting in appearance. Its hands, I noted, were large fleshy mitts spiked with long, sharp claws—the kind that could eviscerate with one well-placed cut. At the sight of the creature, the boy dropped his cigarette and ran, abandoning his F-150.

Leaving the hose in the tank, I backed a few steps away from the SUV, buying just enough time to make certain I wasn't being ambushed from multiple directions. So far, the creature was alone. I took a defensive posture as it rounded the island and swung at me like an amateur. I dodged, then countered with a punch to the jaw, followed by a left-handed punch to the torso. My fist bounced off a dense mass of muscle, but the creature was forced back a half step. I followed with a flat-footed kick to its chest, tipping my toe at the end of the strike to drive the creature down, but it only stumbled back a few more inches, then came at me again, swinging wildly. I turned from one swing, ducked under another, then slipped behind the creature, leapt onto its back, and wrapped my arms around its massive neck. Whatever the thing was, it was unnaturally strong, resisting my full effort to snap its neck. I could barely turn its head. When it slammed me backward into the back of the SUV, I held on but let go when I saw the claws coming over its shoulder for my eyes. Releasing it, I kicked through the back of its knee, which should've cracked and buckled. Instead, my blow bounced back harmlessly. Even the creature's joints were heavily armored with muscle.

Swinging at me in quick succession, it drove me backward around the SUV until I tripped over the island between the pumps and landed sprawling onto my back on the concrete. Before I could rise, it was on me, mounting my chest. I raised my arms, hoping to deflect as much of the damage from those deadly claws as I could until the creature made a mistake or—

Marko crashed into the thing, knocking it off of me. The pair tumbled together toward the back of the SUV. He got to his feet first, kicking and punching with all his considerable might at the head of the creature that barely seemed to notice the blows. It rose, driving Marko back as he dodged a series of swipes until his back was pressed against the SUV. I rose to my feet, but too late. I heard the gory ripping as it slashed him four times in quick succession across the stomach. Each slash released a sideways spray of blood that streaked across the concrete.

I crashed into the creature's side, knocking it aside—enough to grab the collar of Marko's shirt as he slumped against the SUV and drag him several feet before laying him down.

The thing came lumbering after me. I led it away from Marko, drawing it around the island until I returned to the SUV, where I pulled the hose from the tank and sprayed the creature with gasoline until it got close enough to swipe at me. Dropping the hose, I backed up a step, then rolled onto and over the short hood of the SUV, landing on my feet on the other side, and ran to pick up the still burning cigarette from next to the front wheel of the F-150.

Without breaking stride, I led the creature away from the station. It was on my heels, too close for me to turn without taking damage. I was looking for something to put between myself and the creature when I felt the crackle of a familiar magic. Like fingerprints, each witch's magic had a distinct feel, and I instantly recognized my brother's.

The creature's heavy footfalls suddenly stopped. I turned to find it a foot away, trapped in a web of energy but steadily fighting its way free. Josh was near the SUV, arm extended, straining to keep the creature restrained. I showed him the cigarette as I backed away, hoping he'd get the idea, but I didn't have to wait. The creature clawed an arm free, tearing a hole in the energy mesh, and I tossed the cigarette inside. The creature instantly burst into flames, then disappeared. Josh waited a moment for the remaining gas fumes to quickly burn out before releasing the spell.

"Ethan!" he shouted, his tone urgent. Then a horrified look overcame him as he noticed Marko sprawled out on the concrete.

My sixth was still breathing, I noticed as I scooped him into my arms. Without Dr. Baker's help, he wouldn't last long. I turned to Josh, who understood instantly. A moment later, we appeared in the driveway of the retreat house. With Marko in my arms, I hurried past Sky's Honda Civic, noting the trail of blood that led from the passenger door toward the house. Gavin's dark blue sports car was parked beside it.

"Those creatures have attacked everyone," Josh said, stunned. "Skylar and Winter were attacked outside the gym." I hurried even faster toward the front door of the house. As I approached, I saw more blood trails. Inside was chaos.

CHAPTER 3

$\mathcal{T}$he scene inside the house hit me like a brutal defeat. I'd never seen our pack in such a state. The entryway was littered with bodies in various states of gore, bleeding red pools onto the hardwood floors. The air vibrated with the groans of the injured as Dr. Baker, assisted by the few unscathed survivors, moved among the wounded, tense with concentration as he instructed Kelly on who was to be treated, how, and in what order. He took one glance at Marko in my arms and quickly led me into the clinic, directing me to an unused table that was surrounded by the most grievously injured. The moment I slid him onto the table, Dr. Baker went to work.

Confident that Marko was in good hands, I turned to examine the rest of the wounded in the room and realized Winter was unconscious on the gurney behind me. I gasped at the sight of long stitched lines that closed slashing wounds that crisscrossed her chest and abdomen. The scarlet flesh around her wounds radiated heat, while the rest of her skin was ghostly pale. A thin sheen of sweat covered her entire body. The others in the room were in similar condition; their wounds had been sewn, but weren't healing. *Poison*, I thought, turning again to the intense inflammation of Winter's wounds. A glance to Marko revealed the same inflammation as Dr. Baker worked to stop the bleeding. Judging by his perplexed look, the doctor had no idea what poison we were dealing with.

Winter was with Sky!

Seeing she wasn't among the wounded in the clinic, I hurried to the next room down the hall, the entertainment room, and checked the injured there. Every room on the ground floor was littered with wounded. In the entryway of the house, I found Josh lingering, his expression lost as he slowly surveyed the carnage. She wasn't there, either, it seemed. Then I noticed three bodies covered by sheets, next to the far wall. Fear tightened in my chest as I strode toward them. As I approached, I saw her to my left, kneeling over an injured were-animal. Relief rushed through my body. Taking a moment to gather myself, I watched as she gently wiped blood from his lips with a towel, whispering comfort to him as he waited his turn for treatment.

She noticed me, obviously relieved, but turned her attention back to the were-animal.

"Those creatures have been attacking everyone," Josh said anxiously beside me. "Winter and Skylar were attacked outside the gym. She saved Winter."

My tactical mind took over as I took in the scope of the attack. Someone or something had expended a tremendous amount of resources to destroy us, and they damn near pulled it off. I doubted they would leave the job unfinished. So far, it appeared all of the attacks had taken place outside the retreat, which gave us the opportunity to regroup—unless the attacks were designed to bring us all to one place where we could be wiped out in a second wave of attacks.

"Is the field around the house secure?" I asked him. Josh nodded. "Sebastian?"

He entered from the entertainment room, his white

workout shirt doused in blood. Steven emerged behind him. My eyes met Sebastian's. Before either of us could speak, the front door of the house slammed open. Dr. Jimenez, the Southern Pack's physician, entered carrying a limp figure wrapped in a bloody white sheet. Taylor, a short blond were-cheetah, anxiously followed on his heels. *The Southern Pack has been hit as well.* My eyes were drawn to the figure's long red hair, sticky with blood that dripped from her head. *Joan.* Her face was pale, creating a stark contrast with the usually light freckles along her cheeks and nose. She was feverish and slick with sweat, and the thick stain of red on the sheet around her neck sickened me with worry.

Skylar gasped. Steven appeared frozen in shocked disbelief as Sebastian strode forward to gently take Joan into his arms and then calmly carried her toward the clinic. The rest of us followed, with Taylor almost directly on his heels.

"How many?" he asked without breaking stride.

"All but a handful. They were forced to scatter," Dr. Jimenez said, his voice choked with emotion. "Joan was like this when I got there."

"Taylor, stay here," Sebastian instructed as we passed through the entertainment room. She stopped midstep, surprised, as the rest of us left her behind. As we approached the clinic, I saw Skylar watching Steven closely, while his anxious gaze remained fixed on Joan. At the double doors to the clinic, Sebastian turned and backed his way in. "You have to stay out here," he commanded Steven. Still in a state of shock, he stared transfixed through the portals in the door as the two doctors worked to save the only family he had left. As a child, he had lost both his parents in an automobile accident. He'd been raised by his sister until, a few years later, she'd been murdered by a vampire. Joan, on the trail of the vampire, had found Steven and raised him as her own. It was Joan who had Steven transformed into a were-coyote so that he would have the protection of the pack. She was his family. That they weren't blood made no difference to him.

Skylar and I waited outside the doors with Steven as Sebastian laid Joan onto a gurney between Marko and Winter. Dr. Jimenez and Kelly waited for instructions while Dr. Baker cut the sheet with a scalpel, then tore the rest of it away from Joan, revealing raw, gaping slashes that covered her legs, abdomen, and chest, but the wound on her neck was the immediate target of his concern. It appeared Dr. Jimenez had largely staunched the bleeding there, which had probably saved her life.

Seeing the full extent of his mother's injuries, Steven rushed into the room before I could stop him. Sebastian corralled him, driving him back through the doors while he struggled, seemingly oblivious to anything other than his need to reach his mother.

"Steven, stay out of here, okay?" Sebastian urged.

Sky gaped at him, horrified. As cruel as it seemed, Dr. Baker needed to work quickly if there was a chance to save Joan's life. In the state he was in, Steven could only get in the way.

"Steven," Sebastian commanded, but the were-coyote seemed unable to comply. Recognizing Sebastian's patience was nearly exhausted, I stepped forward to intervene when Sky gently took Steven's elbow. He jerked free, nearly striking her. Sebastian pushed him back against a wall, pinning him there.

"Steven, look at me."

He stared wide-eyed at the clinic doors, as if he could see through them to his mother's broken body. Sebastian gripped Steven's chin, trying unsuccessfully to force his gaze to meet his.

"I have him," Sky said, lightly touching Steven's arm, which seemed to calm him. He stopped pushing, but his woeful attention remained fixed on the clinic doors. Sebastian released him, warily at first. After exchanging a look with Sky, he disappeared through the clinic doors. I followed him inside.

Together, we watched helplessly while Dr. Baker worked quickly, assisted by Kelly and Dr. Jimenez. Seeing Joan, Winter, and Marko ... We lived a dangerous life. Any one of us could face death at any moment, but to see the pack's strongest torn up at once was something I had never prepared for. Once the rest of Joan's bleeding was stopped, Dr. Baker began re-breaking and then setting bones. It was a gruesome sound. I glanced at the clinic doors, ready to stop Steven before Sebastian was forced to intervene, but he didn't appear. Perhaps Sky had managed to lead him away. I didn't pretend to understand their relationship, but Steven trusted her implicitly.

Sebastian and I watched until Dr. Baker began stitching Joan's wounds closed, but she wasn't likely to heal unless we solved the riddle of the poison. More than one of my comrades would likely die before the night was over. I glanced at Winter, and Marko, and pulled myself together, but I could see Sebastian remained fixated on Joan's injuries. Though I found her style of leadership to be far too deferential, she was as dangerous a were-animal as I had ever met—when she chose to be. Like Sebastian, she was a disciplined leader. I gave him a moment, until I couldn't wait any longer. Before I could speak, he directed me into the hall outside the clinic.

Skylar and Steven were gone.

"Who could take on the Southern Pack and us at the same time, and win?" I demanded. "Who has that kind of power?"

Amber sparked in Sebastian's eyes as his wolf rose to the surface, drawing mine as well. "Was Marko specifically targeted?" he asked.

"It was after me. He just got in the way. Winter?"

"I haven't had a chance to get the details," Sebastian said.

"There've been too many bodies. Have you asked Skylar about the attack?"

"No," I said, glancing aside.

Sebastian gave me a reproving look. "I know you don't approve of my invitation to her to join the pack, and frankly I don't care. We are under attack, so put your differences aside. The safety of our pack is your priority, and until this incident is resolved, our protection extends to her."

I held back a sharp retort. Sebastian didn't understand my concerns, but they hardly mattered now. At the moment, I wanted her in our protection as much as he did.

"Are we dealing with were-animals?" he asked, changing the subject.

If they were were-animals, they were something new. I had never known of a were-animal that could walk bipedal while in animal form. I preferred that they were something else. I didn't relish a war with my own kind, but I didn't like not knowing who our enemy was. Right now they were planning their next move, and I was helpless to stop them. "If they are, they're an entirely new species. They're like nothing I've encountered before. Primary weapons only—long claws on both hands, apparently poisoned, but we don't know with what. They're not skilled fighters, but they are powerful, difficult to kill by strength alone. The creature that attacked me seemed to change as we fought, as if it were slowly attempting to transform into my image."

"I've heard similar descriptions." Sebastian blew out a frustrated breath. "We need Josh. I'm going to call Cole and see if the East Coast Pack has been attacked as well." His anger swelled in the hall, suffocating me. "Ethan, find out what poison we're dealing with."

As Sebastian strode toward his office, I drew my phone and left a message for Artemis. Whatever poison was used, it was made or purchased in large quantities. Those kinds of deals were done in the dark. No one knew the dark better than Artemis. All I needed from her was a clue, a place to start.

I found Josh on his way to the clinic, still wearing his bloodied graphic t-shirt and jeans, and anxiously chewing his nails.

"Is she okay?" he pleaded.

I wasn't sure if he meant Winter, Joan, or both. "It's too soon to tell." His expression seemed to collapse, exposing just how lost he was. Once again chewing his nails, he began to pace the hall in front of me, temporarily blocking Kelly and Dr. Jimenez as they emerged from the clinic. She gave me a look as she jostled past Josh, who clearly hoped for news, but the pair ignored him on their way to assist the rest of the wounded. He almost followed them.

"Josh," I said, demanding his attention. "We need answers." He gave me a blank look, so I tried a softer approach. "Are they magical? The creatures."

"It's possible, but ..." His eyes were wide as he shook his head in disbelief. "The sheer scale of the attack. If those creatures were summoned, their master's power is far beyond mine."

Suddenly determined, he turned and started toward the double doors until I stepped in front of him.

"Perhaps you will think more clearly in the library," I suggested carefully, "with your books."

"I'm not leaving, Ethan!" he shouted, drawing anxious looks from the other were-animals that were lingering nearby, already on edge.

I carefully measured my brother's emotional state. "Josh, I know you're exhausted—"

"I've made mistakes before, Ethan," he whispered, stepping closer to me, "but never like this."

"What mistakes?"

He swallowed hard. "I didn't see it coming. I'm certain

there is magic involved, and I was oblivious. I failed the pack."

"You saved Winter and Marko. You saved me." He pulled away and shook his head, unwilling to listen, so I changed the subject. "Tell me about the attack on Winter and Sky."

"The creature overwhelmed Winter," he stammered. "I don't understand how. It ignored Skylar completely until she crashed Winter's SUV into it. She got Winter into the vehicle and escaped. Gavin and I met them on the road. I brought Winter here, and then I went looking for you." He returned to pacing, and I decided to leave him alone for the moment.

I left Josh to make a tour of the house, checking on the survivors and making my presence known. Wherever possible, I gathered accounts of individual attacks. The mood in the house was tense. Pack members were talking among themselves, drawing conclusions, and vowing revenge, but none of them knew yet what we were up against. I encouraged those I could and promised revenge to those who needed to hear it. We just needed an enemy to fight to pull the pack together.

I found Taylor crouched in a corner of the entertainment room, chewing on her nails the same way Josh did. Her expression was one of aimless fury, desperate for a target. There was nothing I could say to her now.

When I went to check on Steven, I found Sky sitting cross-legged in front of his door. She tensed at my approach, a reminder that my wolf remained close to the surface. With some effort, I suppressed it. The house was already on edge, and I didn't want my anger to draw others out of control. In response, I noticed Sky's heart rate slow slightly, but there remained a tension between us that had existed before the attack. "Can we talk?" I asked.

Reluctant, she peered into the room, checking on Steven.

"He'll be fine. Come with me." I started down the hall. Hearing no footsteps behind me, I turned and beckoned to her. Sky rose slowly, took one more peek into the room, then followed me to an empty bedroom down the hall—the room she'd been given when I'd first brought her to the retreat. Once inside, I saw the recognition in her eyes. I had hoped the familiarity would put her at ease, but it only seemed to make her tenser. *She had thought herself a prisoner,* I remembered. When I'd brought her to the retreat, it had been to save her life. She'd feared me then, and I saw the same fear in her eyes now. *What will it take to earn your trust? Do I want to?*

While I paced, calming myself, she turned out the chair of the mahogany desk and sat stiffly, watching. Eventually I realized I was as calm as could be expected, under the circumstances. I stood still, my hands scrubbing the tension from my face as I forced my jaw to relax. Instinctively, I stepped closer to her. She stiffened, turning her body toward the door as if anticipating the need to escape.

I sighed, exasperated, and took one step back. "Tell me about the thing that attacked Winter."

Gathering her thoughts, she rose and leaned against the far wall, beyond the foot of the king-sized bed—as far from me as possible. Her voice trembled as she said, "I've never seen anything like it before."

"What did it look like?"

"It stood upright," she remembered, "and had a massive body. Its arms were similar to a human's, but instead of fingers, it had claws, long sharp ones. That's what got Winter. And its face was short and scaly—"

"Like a snake?" I asked, surprised. Had the creature been attempting to transform into Winter?

Sky nodded.

"Was it a were-animal?"

She thought hard before finally shaking her head. "It wasn't a were-animal. If it were, something went terribly wrong with the change."

"Did it say anything?"

"I doubt it could. When I crashed into it, it groaned, but it was just a guttural sound."

I grunted. "Twelve different attacks with seven different descriptions of the creatures. I have no idea what these things are," I admitted. "The Southern Pack is virtually destroyed, and three of ours are dead. Three more may not make it."

I stopped, noticing for the first time that her jeans and shirt were stained with dried blood—Winter's blood. Her arms and hands were covered with bruises. *How could I not notice?* "Are you hurt?"

Sky shook her head at the bruises. "No, just the typical mementos from sparring with Winter."

I cautiously crossed the room, gesturing to her arms to make my intentions clear. Reluctantly, she allowed me to gently take her hands and examine the bruising there. My fingers lightly brushed against her cool, soft skin as I turned her wrists, remembering how long it had been since we'd touched. I released her and took a step back. "If you weren't there, I doubt she would have survived the attack."

Even before I caught Gavin's scent, I felt his hostility push into the room like an avalanche, filling it like a malevolent cloud. I turned to find him standing in the doorway, arms folded over his chest, wearing his naked disgust as he glanced between me and Sky.

Instinctively, I took a defensive stance between them. She had proven herself time and again—had just saved Winter—but to him, she remained a dangerous anomaly. Since the attack, he'd been on edge like the rest of the pack, spoiling for an excuse for violence. In his eyes, I was the only thing preventing him from killing his prey. It would be irresponsible for him to make a challenge now, but he was hardly in a rational state. Regardless, a challenge for my position meant a fight to the death. If that's what he wanted, I was more than happy to oblige.

As a pack member, Gavin was strong and efficient, but he had a problem with authority. The East Coast Pack had expelled him—only Sebastian knew why and he'd taken the were-panther on as a challenge.

"Why is it," Gavin said harshly, "that whenever she's around, someone gets hurt or dies? She's a thorn in our side —a poison without an antidote. Get rid of her."

"Gavin, leave," I commanded.

"No," he snapped. "She is no longer under the pack's protection—no longer our problem. Why is she still here?" He stepped closer, his imperial posture demanding an answer. But I didn't answer to Gavin.

"It wasn't a request," I said, drawing my wolf to the surface as I tensed, prepared for violence.

Gavin remained still, no doubt weighing whether this was his moment. When Sky took a step toward the door, hoping to slink out of the room, he sidestepped to block her path. I extended my arm between them. "You stay right there," I told her, my gaze boring into Gavin's. "He's going to leave." Killing him now would be a waste of a good soldier at a time of war, but the choice was his. We stood like that, glaring at each other for a long moment, before his venomous stare shifted to Sky. "I won't ask you again," I said.

His scowl deepened. "If Winter dies," he warned Sky, "so do you." He backed out of the door, bumping into Kelly, who was more annoyed than startled. If she sensed the violence in the air—how could she not—she ignored it. She knew how to survive in a house full of volatile were-animals, but there was an ignorance in her fearlessness. Though she spent a great deal of time among were-animals, we shielded her from the rest of the supernatural creatures—especially vampires. Over the years, she'd treated wounds they'd created and heard stories of their cruelty but had never actually met one. And never would.

"Hello, Gavin," she said dismissively as he pushed past

her, ignoring her. "Hello, Gavin!" she repeated, shouting after him. He grumbled a reply over his shoulder before disappearing down the stairs. She turned to me with an exasperated sigh. "He is quite … *intense.*" She hesitated, remembering why she had come. She said slowly, "Josh is—"

"In the way?"

Her lips curled into an empathetic smile. "I know he's trying to help, but—"

"I'll take care of it." I followed her a few strides, then turned back to Sky. "Stay away from Gavin," I warned. For once, she seemed more than willing to obey.

As I headed toward the stairs, Kelly stopped me, placing her hand on my arm. She gave Sky an apologetic smile, a quiet plea for privacy. After a quick peek into Steven's room, she disappeared down the stairs. Kelly whispered, "He's having a hard time."

"I'm aware."

"I think he feels as if he should've been able to save everyone." As I tried to slip past her, her grip on my arm tightened just enough to draw my attention. "I know sometimes he needs tough love," she whispered. "I just don't think this is one of those times. I can give you an update on Winter, if you like." She deftly diverted the conversation before I could respond. I nodded. "We're still trying to manage the fever. That's been the hardest part for most of the injured. Nothing we've tried has countered the poison. Dr. Baker and Dr. Jimenez are considering putting her into a medically induced coma to slow the poison and buy us some time."

"And Joan? Marko?"

Kelly sighed. "The same. We're not quite to the coma part, yet, but it's a distinct possibility."

"Thank you." I nodded, then continued past her down the stairs. I found Josh where I had left him, pacing just outside the clinic. He seemed more agitated, and had yet to change his bloodied t-shirt. Given the way he glanced at the door, as if it were a hostile barrier, I knew that he had been locked out. Not that he couldn't break in—only the Alamo doors, steel plates lined with iridium that slid out from the walls, could stop him. Josh knew better than to try. At the sight of me, his eyes darted to the side hall, as if he had just been talking to someone. He frowned at my approach. The few were-animals milling about scattered, anticipating violence. I couldn't blame them. My brother and I had a long history of battles, verbal and physical, as I tried to drill some sense through his hubris. At the moment, his usual arrogance was nowhere to be found.

I hated seeing him like that.

He stiffened at my approach, insisting, "I'm not leaving."

"Okay." I shrugged, taking a place next to him against the wall. He stared at me as if expecting a trick. Out of the corner of my eye, I saw a figure with long, curly hair peer around the corner at us, then quickly disappear. *Sky*, I realized, picking out her anxious heartbeat from all the rest. I resisted a smile. Keeping an eye on Steven wasn't enough. Sky had overheard Kelly and had to sneak down to protect my brother as well.

"Staying here isn't going to make things any better," I finally said, turning to Josh. I put my hand on the back of his neck and pressed my forehead against his, wishing I could take his pain from him. "You know that, right?"

He pulled out of my grip and returned to pacing. "What should I do, go home and wait for a phone call telling me she didn't make it?" he snapped. I let his misdirected anger wash over me. "You didn't see her," he said, shaking his head as his voice choked with emotion. "She didn't even look like herself —like a person."

"She'll be fine," I whispered, lying perfectly.

Josh stared at me, bewildered. "You don't believe that." What he lacked in supernatural senses, he made up for in pure intuition, or did he read some tell of mine I wasn't aware of?

I exhaled a long, ragged breath and quietly shook my head.

He sidled up to the double doors, firming his resolve. "I'm not leaving."

"Fine, we'll stay until we know something. Okay?"

He nodded, relieved.

After a long, quiet moment, I found my thoughts turning back to Sky's family. At first I brushed my questions for him aside, but then I realized he needed distraction. "Josh, have you heard of something called an Aufero?"

He turned to me in surprise. "It's one of the protected objects."

"Like the Gem of Levage?"

He nodded. "It had the power to absorb magic."

"Had?"

"About thirty years ago, Marcia found it in the possession of a witch who was using its power to steal magic from other witches—and I mean stealing *all* of their magic. Marcia destroyed it."

"You're sure she destroyed it?" I asked, surprised that she could deny herself such power.

"That's the story. I believe it. If she'd held on to it, she would've spend the rest of her life with an Aufero-shaped target on her back."

"But—"

"Ethan," Josh snapped, giving me an irritable, exhausted look, "this isn't the time. Why are you asking?"

I shrugged, glancing the other way, and remained quiet until he abandoned his curiosity and we settled in for a long wait. After an hour, he gave the locked double doors a forlorn look, finally accepting that the answers he needed were likely not coming soon. After repetitive assurances from me that I would let him know the moment something changed, he left to wander the house. He would be checking on the other wounded and brooding over his perceived failure, but at least he was out of the way. Eventually, I gave instructions to one of the other were-animals and left to make my own rounds.

I found Sky in the kitchen, gathering an armful of snacks from the cupboards—presumably for Steven. Before I could say anything, she acknowledged me with an apprehensive smile, and then left through the other door. A short time later I walked past Steven's room and heard her voice inside.

"*Attack of the Killer Tomatoes,*" she said, laughing when Steven did. "Really! My mom loved it, too. When I was in college, I lived at home. Friday nights were bad-movie night."

"*Krull,*" Steven said, his tone ominous.

"What is that?" she asked as if she didn't believe him.

"I've seen it three times, and all I can tell you is it's an eighties fantasy about a five-bladed boomerang."

"Seriously?"

"'Do not use it until you need it,'" Steven said, using a dramatic voice that elicited more laughter.

"I've got that beat." When he didn't respond, she said dramatically, "*Deathbed.* It's about a bed that eats people."

Hearing her laugh, I wanted to join her for a moment, but they were speaking a language I didn't understand, and I doubted I would be welcomed.

Embracing my melancholy, I traversed the living room, observing the wounded as Dr. Jimenez tended to them. He wasn't as skilled as Dr. Baker—no one was—but he was capable, dedicated, and eager to take his mind off the disaster that had befallen his pack. The wounded remained unconscious, in their own private battles with the poison, while those who were not injured hovered, watching and whispering to one another. I moved among them, answering questions without providing answers, and reassuring them that the enemy could not attack us while we remained in the house—an assumption I was not entirely confident of. "Eat. Rest. Prepare for the battle to come," I encouraged them.

I found Taylor where I'd left her hours ago, squatting on the floor of the entertainment room, next to a door, worrying the nails of her left hand and spurning any attempt at consolation. She was deep within herself, struggling with grief and rage in her own way. She looked up at me—a pleading look to leave her alone—and I saw the gold color of her animal rolling across her eyes. Honoring her need for solitude, for the moment, I approached Dr. Jimenez as he scrubbed his hands and arms at the kitchen sink, between patients.

"Joan was injured protecting Taylor," he explained solemnly. "She told me the story en route here. She just needs to hear that Joan will survive. So do I. After that, Taylor just needs to know who to kill."

I returned to the entertainment room to keep an eye on her and found Sky seated nearby, watching the young were-cheetah. Before I could say anything, a light knock struck the door. Tension filled the room as all eyes turned toward the sound. Taylor rose into an aggressive stance. I strode into the front room, drawing her and Sky after me. Gavin and Sebastian emerged from his office. Steven hurried down the stairs with a pair of were-animals as the door slowly opened and Chris strode into the entryway, observing the wounded with a look of casual concern. Her familiar, light floral scent was stronger than usual, a failed attempt to disguise the reek of Demetrius that emanated from her pores and choked my throat. I didn't bother to hide my disappointment.

Her eyes met mine, soberly measuring my reaction to her presence. At our last encounter a year ago, I'd issued her death warrant: a promise to kill her with my bare hands if she didn't leave the area by morning. Our relationship had always been tumultuous, but she'd overstepped herself. But that was then. With the Gem destroyed, I no longer held her to account, but she had the balls to come here, now, to find out.

At Demetrius's behest, I reminded myself.

Her attention returned to the wounded. "So the rumors are true. Your pack is under attack."

Before she could say more, Taylor crashed into her, sending her skidding several feet across the wooden floor before springing back onto her feet. She stopped Taylor's charge with a solid strike to the jaw. Chris had always been a clever fighter. As a human Hunter of the supernatural, she had to be. Thanks to Demetrius's blood, she was also fast—too fast for Taylor. Unable to match Chris in a standup fight, Taylor dropped and brought Chris down with a leg sweep. She rolled aside from the follow-up strike and was on her feet again, deflecting and countering a fury of blows as Taylor vented her pent-up fury. Chris knocked Taylor onto her heels with a kick, creating enough space to draw a Springfield XD-S pistol from her waist. Taylor stopped short, the barrel barely an inch from her skull, and growled.

"I know you're fast, cheetah, but I doubt you can dodge a bullet at this range." She raised her voice to Sebastian. "I've come here as a neutral representative for Demetrius's family, which has been compromised as well," she announced, her attention fixed on Taylor. "My intentions aren't to hurt anyone, but I will if forced to."

Taylor remained still, her gaze shifting between Chris and the barrel as she waited for her moment.

"Let her go," Sebastian ordered, striding toward them.

In our home, Chris had no choice and reluctantly obeyed. The moment she turned the pistol, Taylor knocked it out of her hand and had Chris by the throat. Without hesitation, she grabbed Taylor's arms and fell backward, pulling the were-cheetah down on top of her. Chris locked her legs into a perfect triangle choke around Taylor's neck, cutting off the flow of blood from her carotid arteries to her brain. Her arms pinned, the were-cheetah struggled uselessly to break free, her efforts quickly growing feeble as she began to lose consciousness. Sebastian chose to wait until the last moment, then intervened. Once again, Chris had no choice but to release Taylor.

Once free, Taylor stumbled back, but she wasn't as incapacitated as she'd led us to believe. She shook her head clear, then charged, but Sebastian hooked an arm around her waist and pulled her to him. She struggled wildly. Unable to break free, she turned in his arms and—lost in her animal rage—snarled at him. A direct challenge. Sebastian was within his right to punish her—many Alphas would do so without hesitation, but he was stronger than most; he could afford compassion. As she continued to struggle, he gripped her chin, forcing her eyes to meet his. His calm filled the room, but she was too far gone. She continued to struggle, and each time she caught a glimpse of Chris, her rage exploded anew.

Gripping her face between his palms, Sebastian did his best to bring her back. Tears streaked down her cheeks as she struggled against her animal nature to obey. Eventually, he pressed his forehead to hers and sighed. "I know," he whispered. Taylor could only grunt and growl in answer. She wanted to change, to surrender to her animal, but letting her loose was risky. The grounds weren't safe, and we couldn't let her run uncontrolled in the house. "Okay, Taylor," Sebastian conceded, releasing her as he backed away. Her clothing shredded as she dropped to her knees and shifted into her cheetah. As she ran toward the front door, Steven opened it just in time.

"Watch her," Sebastian instructed. Steven and a few other were-animals hurried out behind her. She was the fastest of us. They had their work cut out for them.

Chris retrieved her pistol, returning it to the waistband of her pants at the small of her back. After the front door had closed, she said, "Let's talk."

inter and Marko should be here, I thought, closing the door to Sebastian's office. Gavin stood glaring, while Steven uncharacteristically fidgeted. Sebastian frowned at Chris as she casually ran a finger along a bookshelf, then smugly admired the imaginary dust that she rubbed from her fingertips.

"Chris," he snapped.

She gave him a polite smile. "You all aren't the only ones who have been attacked."

I straightened, as did Sebastian. Gavin and Steven shared scowls, wondering why we should care, but it mattered. Was our enemy so confident of its power that it had attacked the most powerful vampire Seethe in the region as well?

Before she continued, Sebastian walked to the door and opened it, revealing a surprised Sky caught in a half crouch. Her eyes widened in anticipation of a rebuke, but he waved her inside. "You might as well join the conversation since you're going to listen anyway."

I gave Gavin a warning look, cutting off his objection. I wasn't about to let Gavin turn this meeting into a circus, but he wasn't wrong. As an outsider, Sky didn't have a role to play in our decisions. If this was a ploy to draw her closer to the pack, I didn't approve, but Sebastian had the right to include her.

"Continue," he instructed Chris.

She acknowledged Sky's presence with a small, surprised smile, then turned back to Sebastian. "Let's just say the attack went about as well for the Seethe as it did for you."

"Are the vamps poisoned, too?" I asked.

She nodded. "Do you know which poison?"

"I'm working on it."

"Not that Demetrius can't handle this threat, but it does seem we're all fighting the same war now. Why not fight together? A temporary arrangement, obviously. Once this situation is resolved, everyone can go back to killing one another, or dreaming about killing one another. Whichever."

"Let our enemies kill one another," Gavin said coldly. "We'll finish what's left."

Chris ignored him, her attention fixed on Sebastian.

"Does Demetrius know who we're up against?" I asked her.

"No. And now I know you all don't know, either. Whoever—whatever—is responsible, is powerful. If we go this alone, a lot more lives will be lost."

"Vampires aren't living," Gavin snapped.

Steven remained silent, but I could tell by his dark expression that he agreed with Gavin.

"Figure of speech," Chris said in feigned politeness. She turned to me. "You're going to lose more lives as well. Why not work together?"

"Did Demetrius send you?" Sebastian asked, suspicious.

"I wouldn't say 'sent,' exactly. This is my idea. 'You can't talk sense into a dog without a newspaper,' were his precise words, but I convinced him."

"The vamps will betray us at the first opportunity," Gavin snapped.

"You must miss Brooklyn," Chris said cloyingly. "Tell me, how are the Dodgers doing this year?"

Gavin's scowl deepened more than I'd thought was possible. "The Dodgers moved to Los Angeles in nineteen fifty-seven."

"Still hurts, doesn't it?" she answered with a sly smile.

"Enough," Sebastian snapped, glaring. "Are you negotiating on behalf of Demetrius, with his consent and knowledge?"

"I am, though it took some convincing. It seems ... well, you know. He doesn't trust you all, either."

Sebastian and I exchanged a long look. Such an alliance would be complicated and dangerous, but the pack was hardly in a position to turn down a potential ally. If Chris were telling the truth about a simultaneous attack on the Seethe, Demetrius needed us just as badly as we might need him.

"Where? And when?" I asked her.

"Call him. He's waiting."

"Any negotiation about an alliance must be conducted in person," Sebastian insisted.

"So we can look into your Master's eyes and see that he's lying," Gavin said.

I looked to Chris, expecting a violent response, but she demurred, showing a tremendous amount of self-control. But I knew her. She would make her feelings known to him, eventually.

She rolled her eyes. "We can do that. But then you'll need your people, so that you feel safe, and Demetrius will need his people to counter yours. And then there's the haggling over who gets to bring how much testosterone. That's a lot of hotheads in one room. It only takes one"—she threw a glance at Gavin—"to start a war neither party needs right now. Meanwhile, who knows what our mutual enemy is planning. Do you really have time for all that?" She gestured to the phone on Sebastian's desk. "He's waiting, but I'm not sure for how long. Demetrius may be over a hundred years old, but between you and me, at times he has the patience of a twelve-year-old."

Another silent exchange between Sebastian and me, but what choice did we have? Reluctantly, he picked up the phone and dialed the number by memory, then turned on the speakerphone. His jaw clenched tighter with each ring until Demetrius eventually answered.

"So you've decided to accept our assistance?" he asked.

"We will consider a temporary alliance of convenience, once you prove you can be trusted."

Demetrius's voice became shrill as he snapped, "The master needs to prove nothing to his dog!"

The insults descended from there until Sebastian got the last word by killing the call. He glared at Chris, while Gavin smirked.

"That went well," she said, disappointed. She drew her phone from her pocket and dialed. Demetrius answered immediately. "Perhaps we should try a face-to-face negotiation, after all. The home of the Seethe might—"

"It will take a week to remove the scent of dog from the curtains!" he shouted, loud enough for everyone in the room to hear.

She scowled, pulling the phone out from her ear as he carried on. She raised an eyebrow to Sebastian, suggesting the meeting be held in the retreat.

"Never," he vowed.

"Somewhere public, then." Demetrius uttered an audible, exaggerated sigh, then followed with something unintelligible. "Yes," she agreed, "it would reduce the chances of wholesale slaughter."

The negotiations continued, with the two leaders exchanging and rejecting several locations for a variety of security reasons. They traded insults, as well, obliging Chris to continue her role as peacemaker until they finally settled on a new restaurant that was popular with the vamps. I was familiar with the establishment. It wasn't on my list to try, but it was centrally located in a popular district, and we would meet at peak hour, making a surprise attack unlikely. Negotiating the parameters of the meeting, along with details of security, was even more exhaustive.

Once the arrangements were complete, Chris left. I followed Sky out of the office, but lost track of her as I checked my phone; no response from Artemis. Waiting left me with a frustrating sense of helplessness. I found Dr. Baker in the clinic, leaning against the counter with his eyes closed. He was exhausted. Winter, Marko, Joan, and several others remained unconscious, but their wounds were stitched up. The floor was freshly cleaned.

At my arrival, he jolted awake and muttered an apology.

"It's okay," I assured him.

"There is some good news," he sighed, adjusting his glasses. "Those with the lightest wounds seem unaffected by the poison. It seems the body requires a significant quantity of it to take effect."

That was great news, but didn't help Marko, Winter, or Joan.

"I should get back to work," Dr. Baker muttered.

"Jeremy," I said, getting his attention. "You did well."

He glanced down, shaking his head. "I didn't do enough."

"You've done everything asked of you, and more. I'm working to track down the poison, but I need a place to start. Is there anyone, any lab, that might be connected to it—no matter how unlikely?"

He considered for a moment. "I wish I had something for you. I can ask around, but if I present the wounds as evidence, my inquiry will raise too many questions."

I grimaced. "If you think of anything—anything at all—let me know."

"Of course."

"Get some rest," I suggested softly, squeezing his shoulder.

"I can't," he insisted. "There are too many wounded to attend to still. I can't just leave them to Dr. Jimenez and Kelly. They're exhausted."

"Okay. I'll have someone bring food for the three of you."

On my way to find Sky, Sebastian pulled me aside. "I sent her home," he said, reading my mind. "She's not a target, and she needed a break before the meeting tonight. I have requested she join us."

"There's no need to put her in danger," I objected, doing my best to repress my anger.

"Ethan—"

"Anything could go wrong at this meeting. This isn't her risk to take. Her presence gives us no advantage."

"Our people are on edge," he explained. "No doubt the vampires are as well. We will have a difficult time controlling tempers."

"All the more reason—"

"Skylar has an obvious soothing effect on some of our more volatile members. Steven, for example. And you."

I scowled. "I assure you, I am in complete control."

"Steven isn't. If there's trouble, we'll need him. But we don't need him triggering the violence."

"She has the opposite effect on Gavin," I reminded Sebastian.

"Then he will be focused on her, instead of starting a war with Demetrius. She's coming," he said, then walked away, leaving me clenching my fists. It was his decision, but I didn't have to like it.

I spent the next two hours making preparations for the security of the retreat in our absence. With our most powerful, surviving members attending the parlay, the security of the house would depend primarily on the strength of Josh's protective field. I gathered a handful of the least injured were-animals and rehearsed a backup plan. If the house was breeched, they would get the wounded into the clinic and activate the Alamo doors, then wait for reinforcements. As an added precaution, Josh would remain behind.

Once everything was prepared, I changed into a fresh button-down shirt and trousers, then waited, pondering all the ways this meeting could go wrong.

As the appointed hour approached, I picked up the keys to my Porsche Cabriolet and emerged from my room to find Sebastian in a tailored, pale sky blue shirt and silk-printed tie that contrasted with his dark skin. Was he waiting for me?

"We'll meet you at the restaurant," I said, on my way to the front door.

"I sent Steven," Sebastian said, stopping me in my tracks. I turned to meet his steady gaze. "He and Skylar will meet us at the restaurant. It's time."

Gavin, Taylor, and Hannah emerged from the front room to follow him out of the house. I hesitated, a venom building inside me as I wondered why he believed Sky was safer with Steven. When I finally strode outside, the others were waiting in a black SUV. I said nothing as I dropped into my vehicle and drove off faster thannecessary. I took the long route, venting my anger through speed and acid jazz played at full volume. By the time I pulled up to the valet behind Sebastian's SUV, my anger was at least manageable.

Steven and Sky were already waiting outside the door to the restaurant. I hesitated at the sight of her, taking in how beautiful she was in her violet single shoulder dress that extended to just above her knees and the slim three-inch heels that enhanced the curves of her legs. Her dark brown hair flowed in gorgeous waves around an olive-toned, oval face. My eyes lingered on her lips as I remembered our first and last kiss. Had it been a year? It had been primal and ravenous. I licked my lips as I imagined a longer, gentler exploration of hers.

A teenage boy in a valet's uniform appeared, distracting me. His wide-eyed gaze swept over the Porsche as he held out his hand. "Eight thousand twenty-seven and a quarter," I said, dangling the keys in front of him. "The number on the odometer." His excitement melted to respectful fear as he submissively averted his gaze. I gave him the key and joined the others.

Sky greeted me coolly, perhaps taken aback by my stare. She regarded Hannah cautiously before acknowledging Sebastian, then returned her attention to Steven. It was going to be a long evening.

The vamps were unsurprisingly late. Leave it to Demetrius to play his games to the last moment. They might not show up at all, but he did at least bother to make the reservation. Whether or not he showed up was the least of my concerns, but the demeanor of the staff put me somewhat at ease. They appeared calm, going about their business without any sense of danger. From the lobby, I kept my gaze on the parking lot. Hannah remained close to me, her demeanor calm, while Sebastian stood in the center of the room like an imposing statue. Steven paced anxiously between Sky and Gavin, who shifted baleful glares between Sky, myself, and the parking lot. As the wait continued, Steven's agitation grew worse until I thought he might leap to violence at just the sight of a vampire. I was going to escort him from the restaurant when Sky squeezed his hand affectionately, soothing him. He stopped pacing. Their fingers linked together. He gave her a knowing half-grin as he took a deep breath, then slowly exhaled.

I frowned as the pair shared a whispered exchange, amusing each other.

"Sebastian?" a hostess asked, her heart rate and respiration accelerating as he focused on her.

"Yes." He offered a forced, but polite smile.

"Demetrius said I would recognize you," she said with an apologetic smile. "He and his party will be late. Please allow me to escort you to your dining area."

Sebastian mastered his irritation before he acknowledged the hostess with a slight nod. At his lead, we followed her on a winding path through the restaurant, where the wait staff wore designer suits, appearing as pretentious as their customers. Sky seemed entranced by the luxurious decor—marble tiled-floors, contemporary oil paintings on the walls, leather chairs and booths—but the redolence that emerged from the kitchen relied too heavily on alder wood and an earthy spice blend that likely dominated the flavor of every dish.

The hostess led us to the far end of the restaurant, into a private room saturated with the scents of gardenia, jasmine, rose, and lavender, originating from a large, gaudy bouquet on the table. More gamesmanship. Sebastian frowned at the arrangement. "Please clear the table," he instructed the hostess, his tone tense. In less than a minute, the bouquet and accompanying wine were cleared and we took seats on one side of the table—except for Gavin, who preferred to stand lurking against the wall behind us. I gestured for Sky to join me next to Sebastian, where I could protect her, but she ignored me, choosing instead to sit as far from me as possible. Steven joined her, of course, then Taylor and Hannah.

We waited in silence.

Over the next fifteen minutes, the mood in the room declined toward a preference for violence. Though he restrained his anger, I knew Sebastian was offended—not for the simple embarrassment of being made to wait, but because he placed great stock in decorum. We arrived on time because that was our agreement. He didn't appreciate

61

the kind of games Demetrius was playing, and even Sebastian had his limits. The longer we waited, the greater the chance that this meeting—if it happened at all—would become violent. I worried for Sky. If trouble broke out, I would get her out first, though I might have to injure Gavin in the process as he hovered in her proximity like a predator stalking prey.

Just before the end of our patience, Chris arrived with Demetrius directly behind her. She strode gracefully into the room in a strapless peach satin dress that accented her toasted almond skin and clung to her curves. A glittering diamond necklace graced her cleavage. Our eyes met and her lips spread into an alluring smile. My attraction to her was automatic, as my body remembered every curve of her. I looked away, trying to break her spell. Chris had always been a distraction, and right then I needed every bit of concentration. As I gathered myself, I found Sky staring at me, offended—hurt, perhaps?—before she looked away.

My attention was drawn to Demetrius's hand resting possessively at the small of Chris's back, an unsubtle declaration of property that drew a reactive growl from me, which I quickly suppressed. He strode into the room in a finely tailored black suit and coral shirt, wearing the smug look of royalty gracing the unwashed. His hair was a wavy mess of black curls, contrasting with his pale skin and the red bands that ringed his onyx pupils.

Michaela, the Mistress of the Northern Seethe, surprisingly strolled in behind them, beaming on the arm of her pride and joy, Quella Perduta. If she resented playing second to Chris, she didn't show it, but that was what made Michaela so dangerous. Her legendary cruelty was capricious. She was shorter than Chris, thinner, with long, thick brown hair tied back, putting her cold beauty on display. Quell, I had met previously. Among the vamps he was known as the *Lost One*, the vampire with the faint heartbeat and peculiar, fluorescent green eyes—both puzzles I had yet to resolve. Whatever he was, he seemed to lack the cruelty that marked the rest of his kind. He didn't go out of his way to be a nuisance. As long as he stayed out of our way, I didn't particularly care what Michaela had done to create such an oddity.

Lastly came Chase and Gabriella, dressed in matching dark blue suits, her ample breasts barely contained within her suit jacket by a strategically placed clasp. The pair changed their style and appearance on a whim, but their infamy was persistent. Gone was the punk look of last year. Now Gabriella sported long blond hair with pink highlights that framed her heart-shaped face. Chase had exchanged his previous spiked hair for a buzz cut, exposing the tattoos that decorated his neck. A single metal ring pierced his left eyebrow. They were a lethal duo, devoted to each other.

I tensed as the pair recognized Sky with venomous looks. Last year, she'd staked Chase on the retreat grounds, forcing Gabriella to transport him to safety. No doubt they wanted a reckoning. Wounding one of the pair was like wounding them both. As he approached Sky, I slipped to the edge of my seat, leaning toward them on the balls of my feet, ready to spring into action. He planted an exaggerated, wet kiss on her cheek.

"Hey, wolfie," he whispered, his lips spreading into a cold smile.

She regarded him defiantly as her hand slipped into her purse. Her lips parted, no doubt to unleash a snarky comment, but Steven intervened, pushing Chase into a wall and holding a knife to his throat. The vampire's eyes drifted to the knife as if it were a harmless amusement.

I glanced between the other vamps, gauging their reaction, but they seemed pleased. Up to now, they had done everything they could to elicit a reaction, and Steven had obliged.

"Steven," Sebastian snapped. Steven glared at Chase, emphasizing his point, then reluctantly withdrew the knife and took his place next to Sky.

"If you can't control him, then I will," Sebastian warned Demetrius.

"Chase," he said casually.

"Sorry, I was just trying to greet my old friend. How does one greet the half-pups?" he asked, absorbing Sky's glower with a grin. "Gabriella, isn't she cute?" he added as the duo took seats directly across from Sky and Steven. "She's like a little poodle. All bark and no bite."

I gave them a warning look, but the vamps were exclusively focused on Sky. I considered forcibly changing seats with Steven, but that would show weakness. Despite his young age, he was an accomplished vampire killer, and I knew he would protect her at all costs, but that didn't change my anger at Sky for deliberately putting herself in a risky position, away from me. I gave Demetrius a warning glare, which only fueled his amusement.

Chris ignored the conflict entirely, eager to get down to business as she sat across from me, next to Demetrius. Surprisingly, Michaela allowed this breach of protocol without so much as an irritable glance, but I knew better. Even if she approved of using Chris to agitate me, Michaela would never accept one of Demetrius's lovers taking her place at his side.

Michaela sat next to Chris, gesturing for Quell to join her.

"Sorry about our tardiness," Demetrius said, provocatively resting his palm over Chris's thigh as he regarded me.

"I would expect nothing less," Sebastian answered. "It's shocking you didn't have your own score playing during your entrance."

I smiled, appreciating his sarcasm.

"Oh, the dog has a sense of humor. This evening should be quite entertaining."

"Call me a dog again and I'll show you just how humorous I can be," Sebastian said politely, in stark contrast to the warning amber flashing across his pupils.

"Gentlemen," Chris said soothingly, "I thought we were going to play nice. Please do so." She gave Sebastian a welcoming smile. "Thank you so much for agreeing to meet with Demetrius."

I noticed that Quell and Sky were staring at each other, both intensely curious in their own way. Michaela noticed as well. Neither of us were pleased.

Demetrius leaned back in his chair, releasing Chris. "Tell me, Sebastian, what you have done that has caused this unholy attack on our families?"

"I would be remiss if I didn't inquire the same thing of you. What careless, self-indulgent thing did you or your Seethe do"—he turned to Chase—"that has angered someone to this extent that they have misdirected their wrath?"

As the bickering and posturing continued, I realized that Sky and Michaela were engaged in a discussion regarding the Lost One, who endured his Mistress's attention with a practiced vacant expression, like an obedient dog called to heel.

"He is indeed one of my best creations," she boasted, appraising him appreciatively.

"Since the only thing you did was chomp on him until he was nearly dead and then give him a dab of blood afterward," Sky quipped, "shouldn't I render compliments to his parents?"

The table went quiet as all eyes turned to Michaela, who had committed unspeakable horrors for significantly less provocation. I pushed my chair back slightly and shifted my weight onto my toes. Steven tensed as well, prepared to defend Sky from Michaela. Chase and Gabriella, waiting for their Mistress's example, would be mine. The entire room teetered on the edge of violence until Michaela threw her head back and laughed—an honest, almost gentle sound that caught everyone by surprise.

"His eyes," Sky said, seemingly oblivious to the war she had nearly started. "They are … disconcerting. Why are they so green? In fact, why are they green at all?"

Demetrius chuckled. The other vamps joined him, breaking the remaining tension in the room.

"Go ahead, Quella Perduta," Michaela urged him, "tell her why your eyes are green."

He obediently nodded to her, then explained matter-of-factly to Sky, "Vampires do not necessarily need blood to survive, just the essence of life, which, in humans and animals, is blood. When we feed, our eyes reflect the source of life we choose, which is why it's deep red when we have recently fed but darkens after years of feeding, the result of aged blood in the body. We can survive on any life source: animals, humans, and, surprisingly enough, even plants."

Sky stared back at him as if anticipating a punchline, oblivious to the contempt exuded by the rest of us. As much as I despised the vamps, to not accept one's nature was a much greater crime. Was it his choice, I wondered, or was he simply serving Michaela's amusement in the interest of his own self-preservation?

"You feed from plants?" Sky asked, incredulous.

"I use one particular plant, *Hidacus*. It seems to be the only one that can sustain my existence."

"He has a greenhouse," Michaela chuckled in shocked disbelief. "He has these silly little plants flown in yearly and pays a gardener a ridiculous amount of money to tend to them. All this he endures when food is all around us."

Sky was fascinated. "You're a vampire that doesn't drink blood?"

Sebastian gestured toward the Lost One. "A creature of

the night that doesn't feed on humans. Is it possible that you have a civilized one among you? Perhaps there is hope for you all."

The amusement drained from Demetrius's smile. "You've never seen him in battle. Civility has no place in his heart. His adoration for torment and violence is absolutely exhilarating. If I weren't so proud of his abilities, I would be envious. Please don't underestimate him based on his unfortunate choice of sustenance. He is indeed one of us, and there is nothing civil about him."

Sky's fascination with him seemed to be mutual. In that moment, I knew that he was dangerous—not just for his capacity for violence, but because he was drawing her in. I recognized the look in her eyes that said, *Here is one who can be saved.*

"You are able to survive like this?" she persisted.

"Yes," Quell answered, enjoying the attention. "You should see it sometime—its stem looks like a human neck. Does that comfort you?" He smiled, his fangs on display in what should've been a warning to Sky, but she remained oblivious. As I shook my head at her, I caught a disgusted look from Gavin. He wanted to kill her now more than ever, and my silent warning did nothing to deter his desire.

"Is she finished interviewing Quell," Demetrius snapped, "or shall we continue to cater to her insipid curiosity?"

"No," Sebastian replied. "Let us continue our conversation. I am curious to find out what mess of yours I am left to clean up."

The bickering escalated from there. Normally, I wouldn't shrink from a good pissing contest, but I had Sky to worry about. And Gavin. And Michaela. And Steven. It wasn't long before Demetrius rose to his feet to shout down at Sebastian, who quickly rose to the challenge. In the blink of an eye, nearly every were-animal and vampire was on their feet, once more tensed and on the brink of murdering someone.

"Are you really going to make your enemy's job easier by killing one another?" Chris shouted, exasperated. "I don't suppose it's occurred to you this is exactly what your enemy wants."

Sebastian and Demetrius pulled back from each other in a measured move that was underappreciated for the improvised choreography required for neither of them to appear to back down first. Despite their differences, they understood each other as leaders. Following their example, the rest of the room relaxed and slowly returned to their seats—except for Sky. She made a disgusted sound and walked out, shaking her head.

A hell of a time to go to the bathroom. I started to rise when Demetrius shouted, "The world needs fewer dogs!" I turned on him, adding my anger to the roiling shouting match that traversed the length of the table. Once again, pack and Seethe were on the cusp of violence. Despite his obvious anger, Sebastian would never attack Demetrius first, though he might do everything in his power to entice the vamps to violate our truce.

"This is pointless!" Chris shouted.

Quell was gone, I realized. Had he followed Sky? Steven hadn't even noticed! My eyes darted between the dark corners of the room, but Quell wasn't there, either. I caught a smug, careless look from Gavin as he met my expression. As my fists tightened, I pushed them down into the table to control myself. He knew. He'd seen the Lost One follow Sky and said nothing!

Just then the unlikely pair returned together, surprised to find the entire room suddenly quiet, eyeing them with suspicion. Aware of the attention, Sky quickly returned to her chair while the Lost One returned to Michaela's side, acknowledging her chilly greeting with a submissive nod. The room remained quiet as Sebastian and Demetrius sized each other up, deciding whether there was any point of continuing.

"You two can put them back in your pants and quit the pissing contest," Chris said, annoyed. She leaned back in her chair. "I can assure you they are both quite impressive. You two don't like each other," she continued. "Some might be as bold as to say you hate each other. Your people are being slaughtered. We can stay here another two hours and be entertained by your witty insults and unsubstantiated blame and let more of them die, or you can put aside your differences and agree to work together. It's not a difficult decision."

Demetrius relaxed into his chair, his hand sliding onto Chris's thigh as his gaze met mine. His lips spread into an amused smirk as he watched my jaw clench. "I do believe we are being chastised for our unbecoming behavior." He turned his attention to Sebastian, who smiled casually.

"She's right," he said. "'Pissing contest'? I expected something with a little more subtlety from you."

"I couldn't think of anything clever that involved behaving like children, a time-out, and a sandbox fast enough," she quipped, "so I went with the obvious. It was crude. My apologies."

Sebastian considered Demetrius, making up his mind.

"Joan, how is she?" the vampire asked with surprising earnestness, which I warily appreciated, as did Sebastian.

"She will recover," he responded.

"Good. She has always been an asset to the Southern Pack and worthy of her position. It would be quite unfortunate for something to happen to her." Unlike most were-animals, Joan had earned a reputation for her poise and self-control. When aroused, she was as resolute and as deadly as Sebastian, but she was a natural diplomat. Her poise was her strength. Though she lacked Winter's ability to create a trance, Joan could disarm nearly anyone with her congenial manner. Her control over her animal, a jaguar, exceeded that of any were-animal I knew of, so much so that she could speak while in her animal form.

Sebastian asked reluctantly, "Have there been any attacks on the Southern Seethe?"

"No, they were left unharmed," Demetrius admitted.

"Good. Perhaps they can be used as a resource if necessary."

Michaela laughed. "I assure you that if we are in need of the Southern Seethe, then we are far worse off than I imagined," she said, drawing a polite smile from Demetrius.

The Southern Seethe were known to be careless, disorganized, and more interested in appeasing their appetites than exerting control—a surprise considering the Master of the Southern Seethe was Demetrius's prodigy. It was not an accident that Michaela drew our attention to his failure. Despite her seeming ease, she was unhappy at Chris's place next to him, a place that rightfully belonged to her. Did Chris know she was in danger?

Sebastian exhaled a slow breath. "Then it seems like we really need to work together to ensure we find out who's responsible. I am not willing to lose anyone else just because"—he grinned at Chris—"we're too busy seeing who's going to win the pissing contest."

"I couldn't agree more," replied Demetrius dryly.

The rest of the meeting involved calm, polite negotiation of the terms of our temporary alliance. At the end, Sebastian offered his hand, accompanied by a diplomatic smile. Demetrius reluctantly accepted the gesture, not-so-subtly wiping his hand with a napkin after the truce was sealed. Sebastian chose not to notice as he led us from the private room. At the doorway, I turned to see if Chris followed. Instead, she remained at Demetrius's side. He leaned into her, his hand on her thigh, laughing, and she allowed it. More than that, she smiled back, as if genuinely enjoying herself.

Was their arrangement more than business? Had she become that foolish? I was about to confront her when I felt a soft hand on the small of my back—Sky gently urging me toward the exit. I glanced back to Chris one more time, then sighed and followed Sky from the room.

We emerged from the restaurant, all but Gavin resigned to their disappointment. Gavin fumed.

"I'm taking you home," I informed Sky, dismissing Steven with a gesture. I didn't trust Michaela's interest in her—or Quell's.

We shared a stubborn, quiet tension on the drive to her home. I was too riled from the meeting, too angry from watching Demetrius fondle Chris as if he owned her. *How could she allow him to touch her?* The Chris I had known would have never given herself to him. I found myself in a rage that I couldn't vent.

While I was normally careful about taxing our arrangement with the local police in populated areas, I drove aggressively, speeding, darting around other cars, and riding the bumpers of those vehicles that got in my way. Sky said nothing, but I heard her heart racing. I was scaring her, and I didn't know how to stop. I gestured to the imaginary brake pedal beneath her, the one she had been instinctively jamming with her right foot. "It doesn't work," I said, trying to lighten the moment and calm myself, and failing miserably. Suddenly self-conscious, she prepared a snarky remark when we both saw the flashing red and blue lights riding up behind me.

I scowled as I pulled over and lowered my window. Sky nervously tapped her foot on the floor of the Porsche while we waited for the officer to approach. I recognized him instantly by his size and gait. He was a pack member, which made me wonder even more why he'd bothered to stop me.

He arrived at my window with a congenial smile. "Hello, Ethan."

"Tim," I answered.

He shone his light on Sky, beginning with her face and then slowly drifting down over her body, making her uneasy. She tensed further as he gave me a lurid, questioning look about her.

"I need to get her home," I answered with a wry smile. "It's past her bedtime."

Tim chuckled and brought the light back to her face. "One of ours?"

"No." I smirked for the show of it. She wasn't, but that didn't mean I appreciated his attention to her. She didn't, either. "Just a friend of the pack."

His curiosity became a disapproving scowl. Had he noticed the terait? Only the leading members of the pack knew of Sky's unusual trait. "She's different," he whispered, unable to place what made him uneasy. "Not your usual."

"How's your wife?" I asked, successfully diverting his attention.

Tim chuckled. "Still pregnant and getting more irritable by the day." Remembering his duty, he gave a subtle gesture toward his car. "I have a new partner. That's the reason I stopped you. You were going pretty fast, and he noticed."

I nodded. There were times when even I needed to go through the motions. I drew my wallet from my coat jacket and gave him my license, then reached over Skylar's left knee to retrieve my registration and insurance card from the glove compartment. I left my hand on her knee—silencing her nervous foot-tapping—as I transferred the documents to Tim. While he carried them back to his car, Sky shifted away from me toward the door, turning her knee so that my hand fell away. Tim returned a moment later, handing me a warning ticket.

"Be careful the next couple of exits," he cautioned. "We are out quite a bit, and they are not ours or pack friendly."

"You've heard what happened?" I asked.

He nodded, concerned. "How is Winter?"

The reminder sent a new wave of anger through my body —at whatever was responsible for her injury, and my inability so far to discover the poison that prevented her from healing. "She's not dead," I snapped. Tim tensed at my tone. Judging by Sky's scorn, I must've sounded callous.

He handed me back my documentation. "Have yourself a good night." He scowled at me and Sky both, then returned to his car. The moment he was behind the wheel, I started the engine and drove back into traffic, flagrantly accelerating.

"What's wrong with you?" she snapped as if I had wounded her. "Just stop it!"

"Stop what?" I snapped back, angry at my own lack of control.

"Being that way ... being like you ... cold, heartless." She shook her head as if she could no longer recognize me, which cut me to the quick. "I know you probably don't care whether Winter lives or dies, but can you at least act like it?"

Unable to meet the judgment in her gaze, I squeezed the steering wheel until my knuckles were white. *She doesn't understand.* My people were dying, waiting for me to save them, and so far my only hope for a lead seemed to have gone underground. The meeting with the vamps had brought my anger and frustration to a head and now my carefully constructed control over my impulses was disintegrating. We remained in uncomfortable silence until I finally conceded. "I care," I whispered, swallowing my pride. "I care very much whether she lives or dies." Every time I closed my eyes, I saw Winter's mangled body. And Marko's. And Joan's. I saw much of my pack, wounded, waiting for me to help them.

There was nothing more I could say, and Sky remained quiet for the rest of the drive. A few minutes later I parked in her driveway and made a point to open her door. She frowned at my offered hand, finally accepting my assistance as a courtesy. The cool feeling of her skin reminded me once more of that moment we had shared together. As I led her to the door, I scanned the bushes, the yard, and the neighborhood for signs of trouble, but it seemed a typical, quiet night. She hesitated at the door, presumably waiting for me to leave, but I wasn't going to go until she was safe inside Josh's ward that protected her home.

"Did you forget how to disarm the ward?" I asked.

"Would it matter if I did?" She frowned up at me. "Aren't you able to break them?"

A year ago she'd witnessed my dismantling of Josh's magical field. While I eventually convinced him to accept my excuse, she remained unrelenting in her pursuit for answers. I didn't feel like explaining myself then, and I wasn't going to explain myself now. Some secrets needed to remain so. I steadied my heart rate, my respiration, then gave her a diplomatic smile. "I suspect you could, too, if necessary. All wards can be broken or disarmed by someone, even the ones created by my brother. His magic is strong, but not indestructible."

She tried to pick out my lie, but I was far too practiced for her. Eventually she sighed, disarmed the ward, and opened the door. I walked in behind her, uninvited, and began checking the house, going from room to room, checking the closets and windows. To my annoyance, I discovered an assortment of Steven's clothes draped over the bed and floor of the spare bedroom. A stack of pens and some of his college textbooks rested on the desk. In the bathroom, I found his travel kit open, the contents splayed haphazardly around the sink. I scowled, shaking my head at the inappropriateness. When I returned to the living room I found her scrutinizing me. As I found my eyes roaming over the curves of her body beneath her dress, I couldn't help imagining my hands sliding around her hips and pulling her into me.

For the last year, I had kept my distance from her—for her good and for mine—but that caution seemed to belong to another lifetime. She grew suddenly self-conscious beneath my attention, running a hand over her dress as if smoothing a wrinkle, or hiding a nonexistent flaw. She really had no idea how attractive she was. I glanced at her purse on the table next to her and saw the protruding hilt of a knife and the butt of a wooden stake. Sky was a compelling contradiction. She began wringing her hands, glancing nervously about, but her heart betrayed her. She was as attracted to me as much as I was to her, but she was fighting it.

"You're a very pretty woman," I said.

She gave me a sideways look.

As if compelled to her, I slowly approached until our bodies were nearly touching, her eyes staring up into mine. Her lips parted as I leaned closer. *This is wrong,* I thought, unable to help myself. I was betraying everything I wanted for her, all the reasons I'd kept my distance for the last year. I was pulling her deeper into a world I knew she didn't want. Our lips nearly brushed when I barely managed to turn away. Until Sky, I'd never found a need to control my desires. With Chris, my desires made me vulnerable; with Sky, my desires made her life dangerous.

Like an anxious teenager, I focused my attention on the first distraction available—the artwork that decorated her wall. They were tasteful pieces, purchased from my godmother's gallery. Each piece represented a failed effort to purchase the one painting my godmother refused to part with.

Leave.

Instead, I shrugged off my jacket and laid it across the

sofa. "What do you have to drink?" She stared at me, confused. I tried again, careful to soften my tone. "Do you have anything to drink?"

She gave a short shake of her head before gathering herself and reluctantly walking into the kitchen to rummage the fridge. "Water, apple juice, orange juice … Wait … Steven finished that off…. Cranberry juice."

I scowled. My jaw clenched until I forced it to relax. "Do you have anything stronger?"

"Cabernet and this," she announced, holding up a bottle of that she found atop the fridge. "It was a gift for my birthday."

"Let me guess—Josh?" I chuckled. "My brother gave you a bottle of *his* favorite brand of Scotch on *your* birthday. That's my brother. I've received that same gift every year since he turned twenty-one."

Sky fetched two tumblers from a cabinet, dropped a pair of ice cubes into one, then filled the other completely before pouring the Scotch, barely covering the ice. Smiling, I took the bottle and filled the rest of her glass, which wasn't much more considering the amount of ice present.

I felt her discomfort as we stood beside each other at the nook, sipping Scotch. For once, I wasn't sure what to say. Finally, it was Sky who interrupted the silence. "Can Demetrius be trusted?"

"No," I said quickly. "He's an egotistical bastard and will cooperate with anyone that can help find the person responsible for the attacks. Right now, his arrogance is the only thing I trust and the only thing we can count on."

While she was prone to trusting creatures like Quell, who were far more dangerous than she realized, she at least had a healthy distrust for Demetrius. He had, after all, tried to murder her. She was learning, but not fast enough, I feared.

"Your help during this situation has been greatly appreciated and it will not be forgotten." I glanced down into my

76

empty glass, reminding myself that I should go home, but I didn't want to leave. When I looked up to meet her gaze, her resolve faltered. She took a nervous drink as I said, "You can walk away now." *From the pack. From me.* "No one will think any less of you if you do."

She choked on the Scotch. I did my best not to laugh as she fought to clear her throat. It was at least a minute before she could respond. "I would …" She coughed again. "I would think a lot less of myself if I walked away without doing what I could to help find out who did this to Winter."

"Skylar, consider this fair warning," I said, wanting her to understand. "If you keep getting involved with pack business, you'll find yourself so heavily entwined that becoming untangled will be impossible. The life you want, the normality you desire, will no longer be an option."

She slid her tumbler away from her onto the counter, glaring up at me with darkening green eyes. "Do you ever just give people friendly advice?" she snapped. "Does everything you say have to be a 'fire-and-brimstone' type warning with growls, snarls, and impending doom?"

I emptied my Scotch in one final gulp, slapped the tumbler onto the counter, then slipped my hand around her waist and pulled her firmly against me. I inhaled her scent as I brushed my lips against her ear, her soft curls brushing my forehead. "Here's your friendly advice," I whispered, my tone sharper than before—that was what it took to get through to her. She had to understand the stakes before she chose me, or the pack. "You were given a choice whether or not to join us, and you made it—and it was a wise one. If you stay involved when you have the chance to bow out gracefully, then you may no longer have that option—that is *not* wise. Go back to your so-carefully constructed normal life."

She pushed herself back out of my arms and I saw the wolf in her rising to the surface as if I'd threatened her. "I think you got your 'friendly advice' voice mixed up with your 'fire-and-brimstone' voice," she said coldly. "You should work on that."

I met her gaze evenly. "That *was* my friendly advice, Skylar." She was at a crossroads that could forever alter the path of her life. To be less than honest would be a disservice to her. She deserved better.

"I thank you for that. You won't be offended if I ignore it?"

"I wouldn't ignore it if I were you."

"Are we watching the same channel? I can't go back to normal. The moment you all came into my life, it was changed. Normal—faked or otherwise—is no longer an option for me!"

She glared at me, her stubbornness in full bloom while I tried to drill some sense into her skull through sheer will. We stayed like that, two forces of nature colliding, until she finally tried another tack. "Turning my back on this world is turning my back on Steven, Joan, and even Winter. I can't do that."

I glanced down for a moment, just long enough to steel myself to do what was necessary. Even though she wanted to, she would never walk away—not without being pushed. She was fiercely loyal, and I should've known that she would never willingly leave us. Had Sebastian known, when he instructed Winter and Steven to stay close to Sky? Had he been banking on her loyalty to draw her in the rest of the way? There was only one thing I could do for her now, and I dreaded it. I had to break that loyalty. I had to use her fierceness against her. When I met her eyes again, I was resolute. Steadily holding her gaze, I slowly backed her into the counter. "You seem to have a hard time turning your back on my brother and his magic as well. You're not just staying in this world. You're stomping around and making as much noise as possible while you're in it, and it is being noticed and drawing attention that you don't need."

"Attention from whom?"

When I didn't answer, she blew out an exasperated breath.

"You asked me not to join your pack and I didn't. What more do you want from me?"

She flinched when I touched her cheek—driving a stake into my heart—but it had to be so. Knowing this was the last time I would touch her, I slowly traced my finger along her jawline. "You asked for friendly advice. I gave it. Walk away from it all. There is nothing here for you."

I turned and walked to the couch, picked up my jacket, and left without turning back.

CHAPTER 5

The drive home seemed torturously long. No matter how many times I told myself it was for her own good, the memory of Sky flinching at my touch, of the anger—hatred, perhaps—darkening her green eyes remained like a fresh wound. I considered opening up the Porsche's six-cylinder twin-turbo boxer engine on the interstate, but I'd already pushed my luck. Once home, I changed into loose jeans and a black t-shirt, then poured myself a double Scotch and downed it in one gulp, relishing the sensation as the alcohol burned the back of my throat, then warmed my belly. I closed my eyes for a moment and saw Sky once more, flinching. I poured another double. The tumbler was an inch from my lips when I heard the rumble of an engine outside. Through the closed curtains, I saw sweeping headlights turn into my driveway before the vehicle came to a casual stop. The engine died, taking the lights with it. I glanced at my phone. It was 11:13 p.m., and no messages or calls. If someone had come looking for a fight, they were welcome, but this was hardly the sudden entrance of a surprise attack.

I heard the double-click of a car door open, followed after some hesitation by the creak of metal and the corresponding clunk of the door shutting. *Sky?* I half-smiled as I set the Scotch onto the counter. *Not likely.* Listening carefully, I heard the ambling tick of a single pair of boots climbing the porch.

Peering through the peephole of the door—the side of my boot braced against the bottom of the door as a precautionary measure—I found Chris on the porch, composing herself. I hesitated, as surprised by her presence as by her apparent discomfort. She knocked once and waited while I considered whether I wanted to hear what she had to say. As far as I was concerned, she'd made her choice when she'd walked out on me over a year ago. Our relationship had been passionate, but chaotic. I'd become so engulfed in my passion for her that my work for the pack had suffered. There was nothing left to talk about, but I couldn't resist the curiosity. I had already lived through one train wreck tonight; perhaps I needed another.

She knocked once more, frowning. Only when she appeared to give up, turning to leave, did I open the door, catching her by surprise. My eyes roved over her tight jeans and the light purple shirt that clung to the curves I knew intimately.

"What do you want?"

"We need to talk," she declared, less than thrilled as she tried to walk past me.

I shifted, blocking her. "We've said enough." *Go back to Demetrius.*

She stared at me a moment, head cocked in disbelief, then tried once more, as if I would simply bend to her will. I placed a palm over her stomach, gently stopping her. Her eyes narrowed accusingly at my hand, but I held it there until I was certain she wouldn't try again. *This is no longer a home to you.*

"We really should talk," she insisted.

I scowled, questioning my judgment for answering the

door. For a moment, I considered carrying on our conversation from the porch, but it was getting late. Begrudgingly, I stepped aside with a low grunt, allowing her to stroll into the living room as if she belonged there. Her lips thinned, hiding a frown as she failed to find anything recognizable. Since she had walked out on me, I'd changed everything. I crossed my arms, watching with smug satisfaction while her scrutinizing gaze roamed over the comfortable, cognac-colored Italian leather sofas that dominated the living room, along with a pair of deep mahogany tables. She frowned at the cream cocktail ottoman—either that or the rich Persian rug beneath it that protected the hardwood floor. The bronze lamps that dotted the room on small dark tables didn't seem to earn her approval, either. A glance into the kitchen proved that the wholesale changes extended beyond the living room.

Eventually, Chris turned to face me, her hands on her hips. Instead of getting on with it, she waited. Her lips parted and I found myself momentarily lost, remembering the softness of them pressed against mine in a mad desire as our bodies had melded into each other, as if we'd momentarily become one being. I shifted, drawing my attention to the present. That was the danger with Chris. She hadn't come to seduce me, but she wasn't above stirring some desire she could manipulate. I turned my attention to the wall behind her. "What exactly do we need to discuss?" I asked, taming the earlier edge in my voice. The sooner she had her say, the sooner she was gone.

"Are we going to have problems working together?"

The audacity! I gave her a wan smile as a litany of past grievances flooded my thoughts. "Will I have a problem working with my ex-lover who threatened to kill me and my brother? A woman who attempted to kidnap a person who was under my pack's protection, in order to help the vampires perform a ritual that would have left them invincible—a true threat to me and my pack. What do you think?"

Turning the tables, I stepped into her space with a single stride. My eyes were inches from hers as she looked up to me, but she held her ground, expertly disguising her discomfort behind a mischievous smile.

"I don't know. That's why I'm asking. We might as well lay all the cards on the table. Can I trust that you aren't still holding a grudge?"

"What's the matter? Is Chris having trouble determining who she can trust? Who will betray her, the vampire she's feeding and doing—well, let's just leave that up to the imagination—or the man she used to sleep with? What a dilemma she's gotten herself into."

"It's not a dilemma," she snapped, sidestepping to put some distance between us—a clever way to hide her retreat, but her respirations betrayed her fear. "Are you going to be petty, or are you going to get over it?"

"Me not 'getting over' you trying to kill my brother and me is far from petty—"

"If I'm not mistaken, you threatened to hunt me down like an animal and kill me. Rumor has it"—she choked off a rush of emotion—"that you were quite devoted to your search. I can't help but think that if you had found me, you would have carried out your threat."

You left me no choice.

"You are taking it personally," Chris insisted. "Don't. It was a job."

That's always your excuse, but there are limits. "Then hunting you like an *animal* was just an occupational hazard. You shouldn't take that personally."

"I need to know whether or not I can count on you when we are out in the field. I don't want to have to watch my back for fear you will have a personal vendetta to settle."

I didn't have a vendetta to settle, but I made a show of giving the question some considerable thought while I suppressed my anger. *Bygones*, I thought sardonically. "We're fine."

She nodded once, relieved. "Good. I already assured Demetrius of that, but I needed to hear it from you."

My eyes narrowed as I shook my head. *You just can't stop poking, can you?* I uttered a sound somewhere between a cynical chuckle and a grunt. "It's good to know that you two are able to talk about business between your extracurricular activities," I snapped, immediately regretting the outburst. I needed to let her go. I needed to not care. When we'd been together, we'd been a mess. I backed a few steps away from her, slipping my hands into my pockets in an effort to contain myself. I leaned against the wall, studying her.

Shaking her head at me, she started to pace, then stopped herself, but she couldn't hide the subtle twitch of her lower lip, the twisting of her wrist, or the shift of weight in her hips. While she was still making up her mind what to say next, I asked, casually, "Why did you leave me?"

She was the only woman who had.

Her eyebrows rose—I'd caught her by surprise. Two years since she had walked out and she still didn't have an answer. She struggled for a reply, leaving my gaze to roam her figure once more as my anger and frustration devolved into memories of our primal passion. She watched me, uncertain as I slowly closed the distance between us until I felt the heat of her body against mine. I gently touched the gemstone of the necklace that rested above her cleavage, then turned my wrist and lightly drew a single knuckle up along the slope of her neck, caressing her skin, until I found the smooth curve of her cheek. The softness of her skin brought back even more carnal memories that threatened to overwhelm me. Her eyes closed as she surrendered to my touch.

"Answer," I whispered, my lips nearly touching hers.

"Because it was time," she whispered back, a gentle, honest dagger into my heart.

"Have a good night," I whispered, slipping my hands around her waist and slowly pulling her to me as I lightly kissed her lips. *This is how you say good-bye.* I expected her to pull away. Instead, she pressed into me. Her kiss hardened, and I found myself falling into her, as I'd done so many times before. An old passion ignited. Our kisses became ravenous as our hands searched and kneaded each other in deliciously familiar patterns. Chris's left hand tugged at the waist of my jeans, then slipped up my shirt, sending electric ripples through my body as she caressed my skin until she pressed her fingers into my chest. With both hands, I tugged her shirt over her head, then laved my tongue over the swell of her breasts as I tried to unclasp her bra, until the tension became too much and I tore it from her body, eliciting a gasp, and tossed it aside. I stopped myself, pulling back just enough to take in the sight of her. I should've backed away, should've sent her home. Together we were trouble, but there was an inevitable finality to our relationship. I needed the distraction from Sky. Chris was here, now, and I wanted her. In her eyes I saw the same, urgent lust demanding satisfaction.

A deep growl escaped my lips as we tugged at each other's pants, pulling them off. Pressed together, we kissed and kneaded each other on our way to the ground, as if melding into a single, writhing body. My lips remembered every inch of her skin, brushing over her breasts and traveling down to her stomach, to—I stopped at the light scar on her abdomen that spread like a fading spiderweb. She met my inquiring look and pulled my face up to steal the questions from my lips. Her tongue licked at me and I forgot everything, lost once more in the heat of our primal sexual urges.

I held her gaze as I slowly slid into her, exhaling a ragged ecstatic breath. A deep moan escaped my lips as I moved rhythmically against her, kissing her and breathing in her moans until she surrendered beneath me. As her groans intensified, I moved deeper, commanding her pleasure until her body shuddered against mine repeatedly and I finally let go.

I awoke with a start, sitting bolt upright, to find Josh glaring at me from the entryway. Sky stood behind him, her mouth agape. Confused, I blinked at the sunlight filtering through the curtains. I was naked on my living room floor, I realized, with Chris sleeping naked next to me, barely covered by a blanket. Hastily discarded—in some cases torn—clothing surrounded us as if swept up and then abandoned by a tornado. The events of the previous evening came flooding back to me. I choked back a rush of regret as I watched my brother shaking his head at me, his face darkening in anger. I wasn't sure if Sky was angry or just shocked, but she was judging me as well.

I glared at Josh. *What is he doing here? I should've never given him a key.* He shouldn't have brought Sky. My jaw clenched, a rise of anger providing an anemic defense against their judgment. I turned back to Chris, cursing myself. *How did this happen?* But the answer was shamefully obvious. As it always happened with her, I had let my passions get the best of me.

She stirred next to me, her expression groggy as she squinted, taking in our predicament. She answered my brother's scowl with a mischievous grin as she sidled close to me, drawing the blanket to cover her breasts. As she brushed her lips against my shoulder, her attention shifted to Sky, who wrinkled her nose in disgust.

Leave it to Chris to make things worse. One night of indiscretion, and already she was a wrecking ball crashing through my life.

"Threatening and trying to kill each other is what ... foreplay?" Josh snapped.

She batted her eyelashes at him, relishing his revulsion as he shook his head. She kissed me on the shoulder—presumably for his benefit as well—then rose, drawing the blanket around her body. She made a casual show of gathering her clothing, gave Josh and Sky a pleasant smile, then went upstairs to my bedroom. I was much quicker about gathering my clothes, but he stopped me at the bottom stair.

"No!" he shouted, jabbing a finger at me. "You stay right there!"

I hesitated, surprised by the audacity of his tone. As brothers, we fought a great deal—he made mistakes and I tried to shout or beat some sense into him. I didn't appreciate the role reversal, no matter how deserved. I turned to him, waiting for more as I pulled on my underwear in plain sight of him and Sky. She remained angry and shocked, but surprisingly kept silent while my brother struggled to put his disappointment into words.

"I need to shower and dress."

"It can wait," he snapped.

I crossed my arms over my chest, scrutinizing my brother.

"What? Life isn't dangerous enough for you? You've decided to spice it up by sleeping with Demetrius's lover?"

"She's not Demetrius's," I insisted with a snarl.

"Really! I'm not sure he got the memo. Whether she accepts it or not, she is *his*. What do you think happens when they trade—they have tea and talk about the weather? You can't seem to have dinner with her without getting into her pants. You think he's any better? You just screwed Demetrius's lover! How do you think this is going to play out?"

I didn't appreciate my brother's tone, especially in front of Sky. "We are not going to have this discussion now," I commanded, glancing meaningfully between them.

"When should we have it?" He gestured broadly. "When Demetrius is trying to see what your insides look like as he rips you apart?"

Let him try. "I'll be fine."

"He will try to kill you over this out of principle because you dared to touch something of his—"

"She is *not* his," I barked, trying to shut him up. I already knew I'd made a mistake hooking up with Chris, but I didn't need my little brother's public admonishment. I sure as hell didn't care about Demetrius.

Josh shook his head, incredulous, while Sky turned away, seemingly unable to look at me.

"Drop it," I snapped. *I should've never given you a key.* "Why are you two here?"

He sighed, answering reluctantly, as if the reason for barging unannounced into my home no longer mattered. "Skylar thinks that Gloria's involved with the attacks. We're going to check it out."

Hardly a reason to barge into my home. I looked from Josh to Sky, expecting to hear more, but her expression twisted into a fresh grimace, as if my look alone somehow offered fresh insult. Confused, I turned back to Josh. "Give me ten minutes to shower and dress."

"Are you going to be able to *just* shower and dress," he scolded me, "or will you need a chaperone?"

"Screw you." I gave him a smirk, then climbed the stairs.

"It's not me I'm worried about you screwing," he called after me, but I ignored the jibe.

I entered my bedroom just as Chris emerged from the bathroom with a towel around her, her body glistening. "I'm going with you."

"Why?" I asked, pulling a fresh shirt from my closet.

"We have an agreement, remember?"

"The pack has an arrangement with Demetrius," I corrected her.

She gave me a half-smile, as if she felt sorry for me. "Did you think my business arrangement with Demetrius was going to end just because we had sex? It was nice, Ethan, but business is business. Clean up, and let's go to work." She slipped into a t-shirt from my dresser, then went downstairs.

I showered quickly, dressed, and was downstairs a few minutes later. Retrieving my phone, I noticed Josh had called me six times since last night, the last of the calls in quick succession. No wonder they'd come looking for me. My guilt deepened. Had I not been distracted by Chris, I would've heard the calls. I still didn't understand how Gloria's suspected involvement deserved such urgency. She was a Tre'ase, a trickster demon.

Is there something he didn't want to tell me in front of Chris?

I was about to ask him about the phone calls when I caught sight of Chris through the window, standing in front of the open trunk of her tan BMW. I watched her, entranced as she wiggled into a pair of jeans, then took off my shirt and replaced it with a button-down. She stuffed one knife each into her boot sheaths, then strapped another sheathed blade around her thigh. Next came a pair of shoulder holsters, followed by two pistols. A third pistol, already holstered, was strapped to her hip. I couldn't help my attraction to her. She was a distraction, but a sexy one. I realized my brother was staring as well. She noticed our attention, giving us a confident, knowing smile as she sauntered like a predator back into the house.

Josh gave an exasperated sigh. "This has disaster graffitied all over it."

"It's hard to stay away from her," I admitted, just softly enough so that Sky couldn't hear, but I needed to get a grip. Last night was just a last gasp of a dead relationship, and I had no intention of revisiting the past. We had work to do.

My brother frowned at me. "Maybe when Demetrius breaks your legs, it'll help."

A moment later we left the house. Chris got into her BMW, while Sky climbed into Josh's Jeep Wrangler. Judging by his glare and her scowl, I decided to ride with Chris. It wasn't my preference. The sooner we put some distance between us, the better.

"That was fun," she said with a mischievous smile as she drove.

I wasn't sure if she meant hooking up or being discovered by Sky and my brother. "That won't happen again."

Her smile became a grin, but we continued on in silence. I kept my eyes on the road, trying to distract myself from the memory of Sky's disgust. She didn't want me. She had no right to judge, but that didn't make me feel any better about my predicament. As much as I hated to admit it, Josh wasn't wrong about Demetrius. He clearly viewed Chris as his—whether she agreed with him or not. I could handle his wrath, but there was no guarantee he'd limit his revenge to just me. Putting the pack at risk because I couldn't control myself was unacceptable.

I gazed at Chris as she drove one-handed, her other elbow propped on the open window. I found it difficult to believe that she cared for him. Was she just playing him to get what she wanted? I hoped she knew what she was doing with him, but I doubted it. Our days as a couple were over, but I worried she was in over her head.

Once we reached the long, deserted road that led to Gloria's, a mischievous look came over Chris as she glanced into the rearview mirror. She hit the gas, quickly accelerating well past the speed limit. Glancing over my shoulder, I saw Josh angrily gesticulating as he sped to catch up.

"Slow down," I said, glancing at the speedometer.

Chris accelerated instead. It wasn't like her to be so reckless, but apparently I was along for the ride. I growled as I buckled my seatbelt. Glancing back at Josh once again, I couldn't help a small sense of satisfaction at watching his frustration. *Now you know what you put me through.*

A few minutes later, we parked in the driveway of Gloria's white and red striped house. The curtains were drawn, but I doubted she ever opened them. Fallen leaves littered the yard, and mail poked out of the stuffed mailbox next to the door. No one answered when Chris knocked at the door. Most likely, Gloria had left town a few days ago, which lent some credibility to Sky's theory. There was also the chance that we'd find her corpse inside. The supernatural world could be a violent place. Glancing around first to make sure the neighbors weren't watching, I stepped back to kick in the door, but Chris intervened. She knelt at the door as she drew out a small kit of tools. It took her less than a minute to pick the lock.

The door creaked open and I followed her inside, struck immediately by the obnoxious redolence of lemon and brimstone combined with ammonia and bleach. At first glance, the living room offered no hint of trouble. The floral-patterned couches and cherrywood end tables were undisturbed, and the hardwood floor was clear of debris. The entire room was immaculate, with seemingly nothing out of place. I signaled to the others to spread out through the house, then quietly stepped into the kitchen, which was just as tidy. Steel pots hung from the stove, and the countertops were clean and organized. The sink was empty, as was the dishwasher. I opened the fridge, not surprised to find only a few condiments—nothing perishable.

In the room next to the kitchen, an empty fruit bowl sat at the center of the dining table, and each chair was neatly tucked into place. Wherever Gloria had gone, she didn't plan to be back soon. I returned to the living room, converging there with the others.

"She's gone," Chris announced.

Josh looked around. "You think she was taken?"

"No, her things are too neatly placed," she frowned. "Just her necessities are gone. She's in hiding." She walked out the door, expecting us to follow. "We should visit her son. He may know something."

I scowled, surprised at the news. I didn't like surprises.

"Son?" Josh asked. He didn't like surprises, either.

Chris grinned. "It's a 'not-so-secret' secret."

"Where does this son live?" I asked in the BMW, once we were on the road.

"I'd rather show than tell," Chris answered.

I sighed openly as I drew out my phone and began tracking our movement and location via GPS.

"He prefers privacy."

"If he's not involved," I said, my attention fixed on my phone, "he has nothing to fear from me."

We found ourselves on an unpaved country road bordered by cornfields, driving farther and farther from civilization. Swiping ahead on my phone map, I saw that the road would soon come to an end. I saved the location, then retired my phone to my pocket. I expected a lonely farmhouse at the end of the road; instead, we came upon a dead end. Several trails led through a thick copse of maple trees, each blocked by traffic barriers. Gloria's son, it seemed, was serious about his privacy.

We parked the vehicles and gathered at the main trailhead. "He's not dangerous, but he spooks easily," Chris warned, gesturing for us to walk quietly as she led us onto the poorly maintained trail that was at times obscured by overgrown fauna. Fallen leaves and dry branches littered the path, frequently cracking beneath Sky's feet. The first few times, Chris gave Sky sharp, reproving looks at her clumsiness, but stealth didn't come naturally to her. The path wound its way into the increasingly bleak and desolate forest until it brought us to a small sienna brick house that appeared to be poorly maintained. The windows were closed and covered by drapes, yielding no opportunity to peer inside. I intended to circle the house to assess the situation, but Chris walked straight up to the door and entered without knocking. I hurried to follow her inside, with Josh and Sky following close behind me.

Crossing the threshold, I was immediately struck once more by the redolence of lemon and brimstone. The house was dark, and quiet. Unlike Gloria's home, this place was a mess. The furniture was old, mismatched, and carelessly placed. Unfolded laundry was piled on the couch, and an unwashed plate with silverware and crusts of food sat on the cluttered coffee table. I turned to investigate the hall and saw a shadow dart across, from one room to another. I tensed, prepared for a fight, but Chris seemed unconcerned.

"Thaddeus," she sighed impatiently. "I need to talk to you."

At first, he didn't answer. I took a quick look into the kitchen and saw a back door closed and bolted shut. Nothing would come from that direction without announcing itself. The only threat, then, was Thaddeus, and whatever else waited down that hall. Chris stared into the shadows, her hands on her hips, waiting. In the past, I would trust her lack of concern, but I wasn't so sure I could trust her judgment anymore. Since our breakup, she'd made a string of reckless choices, and I counted myself among them. Could I trust her now?

Something inhuman-looking eased itself out of the shadows, a broad-shouldered, grotesque figure with a goat like lower body. Its upper body was covered in coarse hair, permanently bent by a severe curve in its spine. Small horns protruded from its head, but the face was humanlike. *Thaddeus.* I had seen Gloria only once, a year ago during Sky's visit. She had appeared then as a typical old woman, but she did have the gift of morphism. Was this thing before me her true countenance?

Sky and Josh tried not to stare, but I shared no such compunction.

When Thaddeus spoke, his voice was surprisingly delicate. "What do you want?"

"Where is she?" Chris asked.

"Who?"

"This isn't the time for games. Where is your mother?"

"I wasn't aware she was missing."

Is he lying? I couldn't read the changes in his unique physiology. "If she's in trouble, we will help," I promised, taking a step closer.

Thaddeus shied with a fearful abhorrence at my approach, giving me pause.

"Do you hate your mother so much for bringing you into this world that you wouldn't help her if she's in need of it?" Chris asked.

"Make him leave," he pleaded, gesturing to me.

I wasn't entirely surprised by his reaction—Gloria had reacted to my presence as well. I was pretty sure why. Chris gave me an inquiring look, then nodded toward the front door. I wasn't doing any good here. Josh and Sky scrutinized me with baffled expressions as I slowly backed up until I stood just outside across the threshold.

"I know it's hard to live like this," Chris said, approaching Thaddeus cautiously, "unable to walk between the two worlds. It's unfortunate not to be gifted with the ability to change your form, destined to live in this way because of a mother who is too selfish to relinquish or even share her gifts." He tensed as she gently rested a hand on his shoulder. "I am sorry this is your life. But I will be even sorrier once I tell Demetrius and Sebastian that you were reluctant to offer assistance with finding the culprit responsible for attacking and slaughtering their people. I cannot imagine the downward spiral your life will take with them as your enemies."

Thaddeus hissed at her. "Are you threatening me?"

"No," she declared. She gave him a long moment to

respond, then shrugged, turned, and started toward the door, gesturing for the others to leave.

"I don't know where she is," Thaddeus said in an exasperated rush.

Chris posed for me with her hands on her hips and wearing a victorious smile, then turned back to him.

"She advised me to leave because people would soon start looking for me."

"Was she taken by force or did she leave willingly?" Chris asked.

"My mother is stronger than most people realize, but greedier than I care to ever admit or understand. I believe self-preservation is what drives her absence, and possibly a very good payoff."

"If she is in any way responsible for the attacks on the vampires and were-animals, then you will get the gifts you've desired."

Upon the death of a demon, as with witches, the eldest child inherited the parent's gifts. Thaddeus repressed a smile. "Contrary to what you may believe, I would rather have my mother safe at home than her gifts."

"If she isn't willingly involved, then you will get that wish, but if she is, then you will get your true desires," Chris stated, then turned toward me. I stepped aside as she emerged, with Josh and Sky in tow, then reached inside to grasp the door handle, giving Thaddeus a hard scowl before closing it.

Josh and Skylar walked a few feet behind us on the trail. With no need for stealth, we made good time toward the vehicles.

"This was pointless," I said softly. "His issues with his mother have nothing to do with the pack."

"She's on the run," Chris answered softly, confident. "If you trust the little wolf's sense of smell, there is a connection between the Tre'ase and the creatures. And if a Tre'ase is involved, it will be Gloria. At the least, she knows something she wants to keep hidden."

"Then you should've pressed your point with Thaddeus, instead of letting him off the hook."

She sighed. "He doesn't have his mother's power to change, which means she's alive. You saw how he looks. He's not going anywhere. If he knows anything, he knows how to contact me."

She hurried her step to get a few paces ahead of me. The rest of the walk was quiet. After a few minutes, the vehicles were in sight when I heard a sudden rustling in the bushes to my right. Chris stopped and turned, drawing her pistol as the tall, thick bushes began to shake and rattle. I crouched into a defensive stance, gesturing for Josh and Sky to get behind me as two misshapen humanoid creatures pushed through the thick foliage, groaning and hissing with the effort. They were similar to the creature that had attacked me at the gas station, with hooked claws at the end of thick, massive arms, but these had crooked fangs. Their features were twisted, incomplete as they seemed to slowly morph before our eyes.

Chris tossed me a knife from her thigh sheath as we backed away from the creatures that stumbled toward us, hooked claws raised. Without a word, we separated, drawing our creatures apart and away from the others. It had been a long time since we'd fought together, but all the right instincts came back to the surface. I dodged a clumsy swipe, slashing unsuccessfully at the creature's arm on the counter-attack. A shot rang out next to me. I risked a glance to find Chris backing away from her creature while seemingly staying just within reach of its claws, despite having her pistol drawn. A wild look came over her as she lowered the pistol from the creature's chest to its stomach and fired once more. The creature continued to advance on her, barely registering the shock of the bullet, driving her toward a thick cluster of bushes. Did she see the danger? It swiped at her.

She stepped back just enough to escape the creature's claws —she was taunting it, with no idea she was backing into a trap.

"Move!" I shouted at her, barely dodging another rake of claws from the creature before me. I sliced its arms twice in quick succession, then sidestepped, pulling it even farther from the others, and giving me an easier vantage of Chris's fight. Blood seeped from the wounds, but the creature didn't seem to notice.

Behind it, I saw Chris back into the bushes and stop. She smiled mischievously as the creature raised its claws to strike, this time in easy range. She raised the pistol to aim at the creature's face, then waited until the last possible moment before firing. The bullet struck the creature in the eye. Its head snapped back in a spray of blood as it stumbled back a step. Not a mortal wound, but it hesitated, its breathing ragged. Chris went for a knife.

I barely dodged an upward swing from my creature that would've slit my torso from pelvis to throat. A second blow followed. I ducked under the swipe to the creature's flank and stabbed several times in quick succession, searching for something vital. As it turned to stop me, I slipped around the creature's back and sliced the right Achilles tendon. The creature fell to one knee, collapsing with a groan. Grasping one of the horns, I yanked its head back, reached around with the knife to slice its neck, but the creature disappeared.

I turned to Chris to find her creature had disappeared as well.

"What was that?" she asked Josh. He appeared just as bewildered.

"That wasn't a demon," he answered. "They don't have powers like that. Most of them look scarier than they actually are, possessing minimal magical skill, defensive tricks that aren't strong enough to stop an inferior were-animal. And those gifted with the ability to change their appearance have mated so much with humans that their magic has been diluted to the point it is negligible. Whatever those were, they possess abilities greater than anything I have seen. When injured, most of us cannot travel." He glanced about the grass, presumably looking for some trace of the creatures, but they were entirely gone. Not even their blood remained.

"We should leave," I said.

Chris nodded, as did Sky.

"I need to go back to the house to do some research, Chris," Josh said as he climbed into his Jeep Wrangler. "Should I contact you or Demetrius if we find anything?"

"Call me," she answered, acknowledging a look from me. Demetrius coveted power. To him, Josh was just another witch, and I intended to keep it that way. The last thing I needed was for Demetrius to take a special interest in my brother's abilities.

I stopped her from getting into the BMW. "What part of me telling you to stay back didn't you understand?" I demanded.

"Just the *telling* part," she answered coolly. "The rest I ignored."

"Demetrius's blood doesn't make you invincible. What you did was reckless and amateurish. If you want to work with us, you won't do anything like that again. Do you understand me? You let yourself get cornered. If your shot had failed, you'd be dead right now. Is that what you want? Because if you have some kind of death wish …" I trailed off as she rolled her eyes, sliding into the BMW and then starting the engine. My fists clenched as she put the car into gear, then forced me to jump out of the way as she drove off without giving me a second look.

Fuming, I climbed into the backseat of the Wrangler.

"Did you two lovers have a quarrel?" Josh chided me,

ignoring my glower. "I can't believe it. You two usually get along so well."

"Just drive the damn car," I growled.

He put the Jeep into gear, muttering, "Maybe this time you two will learn it can't work and stay out of each other's beds."

CHAPTER 6

I spent the ride home fuming in the back of Josh's Wrangler. I had enough to worry about without worrying about Chris. After Josh and Sky dropped me off, I poured myself a Scotch, sat at the kitchen counter, then called my private detective.

"Dennis McDuffy," he answered optimistically.

"It's Ethan."

Silence, then he said begrudgingly, "Okay."

"Time to earn your retainer. I hope you're as good as you think you are." I gave him Chris's name, the description of her car, and a rough idea of where to start looking. "You're going to spend the next couple of days following her—from a *discreet* distance. Text me the address for everywhere she stops. She stops at a gas station, I want to know which one. She meets anyone, I want a description. Photos would be preferable."

"What exactly am I getting into?"

"Your job. I should warn you, she's not to be underestimated. If you do get caught, I suggest you give her my name before she beats it out of you."

"Okay," he said tightly, clearly wishing he'd never met me.

Was he smart enough to plant a GPS device on her BMW and track her from a distance? *Consider this a test.*

I gave him my number, then hung up and called Dr. Baker. When he didn't answer his cell, I called the line in the retreat clinic. He answered immediately, but I didn't like the news. Joan, Winter, and Marko remained in danger, as did the dozens of other pack members who had been severely injured during the attack. The poison continued to inhibit their natural healing abilities. Dr. Baker had exhausted his sources, and still the poison remained a mystery.

I hung up and checked my messages. Still no answer from Artemis, which was unusual. Not much happened among the local supernaturals without her catching some wind of it, either beforehand or after the fact. Not everything she learned was reliable, but that never stopped her from selling every bit of information she had, which was why her sudden absence bothered me. Word was out about the attack on the pack and the Seethe. For Artemis, that should've been a bonanza. I should be hearing from her hourly, trying to sell me every rumor she could scrounge up. *Did she know about the attack in advance?* More than likely she could've sold such a warning twice—to me and to Demetrius. She knew I paid well and would protect her as my source. Had she gone into hiding, or was her scarcity merely a coincidence? I didn't believe in coincidences.

I considered calling Josh and having him put out the word at the club, which she liked to frequent, but I would be betraying her confidence in doing so. If word got out that she was dealing with the Midwest Pack, some of her sources would clam up. I needed another way to find her.

Stacy, my paralegal at the law firm, answered her cell phone after a few rings. "Hey, I'm still researching the contract for the Quantis Corp account. I just need a few more—"

"I've got something else for you."

"Oh," she said, lowering her voice to a conspiratorial whisper. "Lay it on me."

"Artemis Hendricks. She sometimes uses the name Valerie Stein." *And probably other names.*

There was a long pause, both of us apparently waiting for the other.

"And?" she asked expectantly.

"What else do you need?"

"A birthdate would be amazing," she declared.

"I don't have that."

She sighed. "You want me to work another miracle, don't you? Well, if she's on social media, I can probably hack a profile, get her personal information, then access her credit report and branch out from there. You have a number?" I gave it to her. "An e-mail address or two would be even more amazing."

I gave her one. "Drop everything else. No breaks. If you need food, coffee, whatever, use my corporate card. Order in. If anyone hassles you, tell them to call me."

"What is she?" she asked, lowering her voice even further. "Is she a vamp? A werewolf?" She gasped. "Are werewolves real?" Stacy had no idea what I was. She just knew I was tapped into the supernatural world, and I paid in cash.

I ended the call without answering, finished my Scotch, picked up the keys to my SUV, and left. By design, I knew little about Artemis's personal life, but I had met her at Grant Park more than once, and she'd spoken of other parks and their gardens with an intimate knowledge. Most likely she plied her trade at nightspots, where people drank and lost track of their secrets, but night was hours away. The chances of happening on her in a park in the afternoon were slim, but until Stacy found me a lead, it was the only chance I had. After an afternoon of wandering Grant Park, Lincoln Park, and the other prominent parks of Chicago, I had nothing to show for my efforts but a fuming temper. Dinnertime came and went. I moved on from restaurants to bars, checking anyplace I even suspected was frequented by supernaturals. By nine, I was ready to start a fight in a biker bar, just to vent my frustrations, when Stacy finally called.

"Tell me," I answered.

"Hiya, chief. So, you wanted a miracle. Boy, did I come through this time. Hint. Hint."

"Stacy."

"This chick knows how to get off the grid. That other name you gave me led to other names that led to other names, but none of them have addresses or social media profiles, so I went back to the start, to Artemis Hendricks. You want to know how I found her?"

"Give me the address."

"She has a library account."

I sighed. "She would've used a fake address."

"Not if she wants to read the books she has delivered. Regularly. Apparently she has a thing for parks and gardens —coffee table shit."

"Tell me."

Fifteen minutes later I was in front of a small, rundown rambler in the suburbs. The drawn curtains appeared old and faded, and the interior was dark. I walked around the house, noting the disrepair. Siding was cracked and in some cases missing. The rain gutters were swollen with leaves. A kitchen curtain was partially drawn. Inside the kitchen seemed clean and orderly, but then I noticed a lack of countertop appliances. No dishes in the sink. No hand towels hanging from the stove or refrigerator doors. No magnets or taped notes on the refrigerator. Nothing at all to give the impression that somebody actually lived there. I walked back to the front and checked the mailbox. Empty. I scowled. Artemis used the house as a postal drop. Given enough time, I would find her here, but I didn't have the luxury.

I walked off the porch to my SUV, my eyes sweeping the

neighborhood. *For all I know she's right here on this block, and I'd never find her.* At first, I didn't even notice the wall of thick privacy shrubs across the street and three lots to my left. The shrubs, at least seven feet tall, seemed to visually blend into a dense copse of trees beyond the wall of greenery, providing a form of camouflage. A chimney rose directly behind the shrubs, indicating a house on the other side—a peculiar arrangement considering the rest of the open, well-manicured neighborhood. I crossed the street, glancing about once more to make sure I wasn't being watched. The privacy hedge formed a square around the house. The only gate was at the back, and tightly fitted into the shrub that grew over the top of it. I opened the gate slowly, wary of a telltale creak, but it opened smoothly. On the other side of the shrubbery appeared to be an intricate, well-groomed garden with a sandstone path that led to the back door and wound around both sides of the house. From inside, I could hear cheerful pop music.

I followed the path to the front door. The light, patterned curtains were drawn, but I could see a figure walking about. I paused and took a breath to calm myself. She was in hiding, which meant she knew something dangerous. What and why, I was going to discover one way or another, but I didn't think Artemis was likely to tell me the truth if she felt threatened. When I closed my eyes, I saw Marko and Winter and Joan slowly dying in the clinic at the retreat.

I knocked three times on the door with the bottom of my fist—solid, undeniable thumps. For a moment, nothing happened, then I heard footsteps crossing the front room and the music stopped. In the ensuing silence, I heard the rapid beat of a single, anxious heart. *She's alone. Good.* The footsteps grew softer as she crept to the door, then I saw a shadow pass over the peephole.

"Why are you here?" Artemis asked, her soft voice shaking slightly. She knew why. She was just buying time, but for what? "No one knows where my home is. How did you find me?"

"Open the door," I commanded gently. After a short silence, I added, "If you don't, I will break it."

A moment later, I heard the thump of a door bolt, followed by two more, then the door slowly opened to reveal Artemis. I had only met her in person once before, when I'd first made contact. Since then, she'd preferred we kept our distance in order not to taint her reputation. She was younger than I remembered—early twenties, I thought— most likely because the wariness in her cognac eyes spoke to a lifetime of hustling. Though she kept her history a closely held secret, I suspected she had spent time on the street from a young age. Her hair was brighter than I remembered, copper with symmetrical layers of loose waves that framed her fair, heart-shaped face. She held the door cautiously, her body turned in case she needed to dash toward the back of the house. Her right arm was hidden behind the door. I could see by the stiffness in her shoulder that she was holding something there.

I sighed and held out my hand. "Give me the weapon."

She scrutinized me, weighing the chances that I meant her harm. I didn't. Reluctantly, she stepped back from the door and handed me a baseball bat with a dozen or so nails partially hammered into the business end. After examining the bat, I returned it to her, catching her somewhat off guard.

"May I come in?"

Uncertain at first, she leaned the bat against the wall and backed farther into the entryway. I scraped my boots on the porch before entering and gently closed the door behind me. The house was small and cozy, and full of bookshelves filled with eclectic personal treasures. Each curiosity told a story, I suspected.

"How did you find me?" she asked again, worried.

"No matter how hard a person tries to hide, they can

never hide from their compulsions." I pointed to a stack of library books on her coffee table. "I suggest you purchase your books from here on. In person. Rotate which stores you use, and times of day you shop."

She hooked a thumb over her shoulder as if gesturing to something. "I just got your messages. I had lost my phone and just now got—"

I waved her excuses aside. She was an excellent liar, but not good enough to fool me. "Tell me what you know about the attack on my pack."

"I heard," she admitted sheepishly, taking a step back. "I am sorry for your losses. If I had anything at all to share with you about it, I would. As you know, I don't get involved in violence. I have a few rules, and that's the first one." She held up a finger like a ward. "The most important one."

Despite my growing impatience, I said nothing, preferring to draw her out with a steady, determined stare. Apparently she didn't like voids in conversation—most people didn't—because she rushed to fill the silence as she backed into the living room, slowly putting a couch between us. "That being said," she added cautiously, "from time to time, someone … misrepresents themselves, and I, being a purveyor of whispers and knowledge, sometimes sell my wares with the full but otherwise false expectation that no one will actually get hurt."

I felt my jaw clench and forced it to relax. "Explain," I insisted, slowly following her around the couch.

Sweat began to form on her forehead as her breath quickened. "Sometimes," she swallowed, "I just bring people together. People I don't know directly, for reasons I don't know. I'm at their mercy, really, in regards to intentions. Mostly there's just an asking for a need, followed by a fulfillment. Introductions are made, handshakes performed—"

"Payment issued."

She shook her head nervously, her curls bouncing. "I'm at the mercy of their projected integrity, really."

"Who?"

She sucked in her lips, glancing about the room as she took another step back.

I followed her, allowing no room for her to try and escape.

"Perhaps a brief negotiation?" she asked timidly.

"Too late, Artemis. Tell me everything." I squeezed my fists until my knuckles cracked loudly. "Tell me now."

She sighed as she brushed a wayward curl from her eyes. "A man wanted to know about antidotes—specifically about antidotes—and I … I knew another man—by reputation only—who could answer such questions."

In an effort to control my anger, I took in a deep exaggerated breath and slowly exhaled. "The creatures that attacked my pack used a poison that prevents my people from healing."

"I heard," she admitted sadly.

"And yet you said nothing," I snapped.

"I couldn't be sure it was my introduction," she explained, taken aback.

"That's never stopped you before."

"This attack … this monstrous attack—there's power behind this," she insisted, trembling. "Immense power. He found me once, Ethan, and not the way you did. I can't hide from him." This place, I realized, was her sanctuary; without its secrecy she was back on the street, always looking over her shoulder. "I'm sorry," she whispered sincerely.

I growled. "Artemis—"

"I brought two people together to make an antidote," she insisted, then swallowed hard before continuing. "But it seems those who make antidotes, also make … poisons."

"Who?" I demanded.

"A man," she said, swallowing fear. "That's all I remember.

That's all he'll let me remember. When I try to remember more, I-I fall apart."

I didn't understand, but I knew she wasn't lying. "Who made the poison?" I demanded, raising my voice.

"I-I can take you to him. If you're not with someone he recognizes, I don't think he'll talk to you. Which is to say, you need me alive and unharmed," she clarified.

"Artemis. If you lie to me now, if you mislead me, I will consider you an enemy of the pack. Do you understand?"

Her curls bounced as she nodded emphatically.

"Let's go."

"Yes," she fluttered about, grabbing a light coat and small purse. "I can't promise he'll be home."

"Let's hope he is. For both our sakes."

Artemis guided me by memory to Dr. Robert Yoshi's house, filling me in on what she knew about the man I suspected had created the poison that was killing my friends. There was nothing supernatural about Dr. Yoshi. According to Artemis, he was an immunologist who had quit a military biological warfare program for ethical reasons to teach chemistry at a local university. After leaving the military program, Dr. Yoshi had lived a seemingly simple, comfortable life until his wife was diagnosed with stage three liver cancer. The cost of treatment went well beyond what his insurance and salary would cover, leaving the doctor looking for sources of extra income. When the silver-haired witch found Artemis, Dr. Yoshi was the only name she had to offer.

"This witch showed up on your doorstep?" I asked, clarifying.

"Yes."

"And you can't remember anything about him?" I gave her a sideways look and saw the panic in her expression as she tried to remember, then shook her head. "How does that work?"

"Magic, I think. He did something." She bit at her nails as she turned within, her gaze growing dull.

"I know someone who can help you with that."

She appeared even more panicked than before. "Fudge no. Thank you. I don't need strangers poking around in my noodle."

I let the subject drop as she directed me to the entrance of a gated community. Josh would take a look at her whether she wanted him to or not, but there was no point in explaining that now. I needed to focus on this doctor. I pulled up to the guardhouse. A young man—probably in college—emerged to greet me with a clipboard.

"Name, sir?" he asked.

I drew my wallet out of my pocket, fished out a hundred-dollar bill, and flicked it up between two fingers. While he grappled with what I assumed was his first and probably last bribe, I stared ahead, waiting impatiently. He only needed a few seconds to take the money, then muttered a thanks and opened the gate.

"You're not going to kill anybody, are you?" he asked as an afterthought.

I drove through the gate without answering. Artemis pointed out the two-story brick house. Lights were on inside. The driveway was empty, so I assumed he didn't have guests.

"Kids?" I asked. A family would complicate matters significantly.

"No."

"The wife?"

"Didn't make it," she whispered.

I turned off the headlights and killed the engine just before coasting into the driveway.

"If you don't know, tell me. Does he live with anyone?"

"I don't think so, but I can't be sure."

As long as it's not kids.

She followed me to the front door. "Perhaps I should knock first. I can get him to let me in and then you can reveal yourself."

"No." I opened the screen and kicked in the front door with the flat of my boot. The house was a split-level, with the entryway between floors. I paused just long enough to locate a single heartbeat in the house. Following the sound, I reached the top of the stairs to find a short, wide-eyed Japanese American man with short graying hair emerging from the dining room with a red stain on his button-down shirt and a napkin in his hand. He saw Artemis behind me.

"Emily," he called her, "w-who is this? What are you doing in my—"

Without breaking stride, with one hand I lifted the doctor by the collar of his shirt and drove him into the wall behind him. He sank into the Sheetrock, and I held him there, watching the terror in his eyes as he saw the angry wolf in mine.

"Oh, crap," I heard Artemis mutter behind me.

"W-what's happening?" Dr. Yoshi stammered. "Take whatever you want. Take it all and go!"

"I want to know how you poisoned my friends."

"I don't know what you're talking about! Please!" he pleaded, but the look he gave Artemis told me he knew exactly what I was talking about. "You promised discretion!" he cried to her when he realized I wasn't buying his innocence.

She jabbed a finger toward him. "I brought you together to make antidotes, not kill wolves."

"I had no choice! When he told me what he wanted, I said no. I said no! But he did things to me. He used magic to make my life miserable until I gave him what he wanted."

"You're lying," I growled. He was too frightened for me to

distinguish if he was lying, but it didn't hurt to accuse him of one, make him uncomfortable to get to the truth. "I want the poison. And I want the antidote. Lots of it."

He hesitated, his will crumbling. "A-are you going to k-kill me?"

"Give me. What I want," I snarled.

"You should give him what he wants," Artemis suggested helpfully.

On the drive to his lab at the university, I told him, "I need enough antidote to treat thirty victims." I included the Seethe's injured, though I had to guess at their numbers. "How long will it take?"

"I have enough for forty already made," Dr. Yoshi declared from the seat next to me, but I didn't believe him. "The silver-haired man ordered the poison and the antidote, but when he picked up the order, he only took the poison. He didn't say why. I didn't know how it was to be used."

"You remember what he looked like?" Artemis asked, surprised.

"What's his name?" I demanded.

"He never gave me one."

I squeezed the steering wheel until I thought it might snap. "Describe him, then."

The doctor visibly struggled to remember, his eyelids blinking rapidly as he began to rock in his seat. "Bright violet eyes. That's all I remember—the eyes, staring at me."

"Magic," Artemis whispered from the seat behind me. "He's going through the same pain I go through when I try to remember. It's amazing he even remembers the hair and eye color."

The doctor led us into his laboratory, where he kept the antidote in a locked cabinet. He had a couple of vials of poison as well. I called Dr. Baker, who answered immediately. "I'm bringing the antidote," I declared. "Call our contacts in the highway patrol. Let them know I'm coming from the university. I'll be speeding."

"Hurry, Ethan."

Once the SUV was loaded, I put the doctor into the passenger seat and closed the door before Artemis could get in. "Go home," I said. If Josh could break the spell that blocked the doctor's memories, Yoshi would be able to tell us a lot more about the witch than Artemis could. I trusted her less now than before, but she remained a valuable resource. I preferred not to drag her into the light unless I had to.

"You're going to leave me here?" she said, eyes wide in disbelief.

"It's better you're not seen with me," I growled, glaring down at her. "If I call, you answer. If you don't, I will find you." Seeing that she understood, I climbed into the driver's seat and drove out of the parking lot, leaving her there.

"Am I going home?" the doctor asked softly, his voice wavering as he huddled against the door, staring out the window.

I locked his door and turned on the child safety mechanism so he couldn't unlock it. I didn't need him getting brave and killing himself trying to roll away on the highway. People did stupid things when they thought they were going to die. "You've got a lot to answer for, doctor." My jaw clenched as I concentrated on weaving through traffic. "Before you think about going home, I suggest you pray your antidote actually works."

His heart rate began pounding like a drum and his breathing became shallow and quick as he began to hyperventilate. He understood what was at stake.

"Take long breaths. Hey!" I shouted, getting his attention. "Long, slow breaths."

I made record time to the retreat, thanks to the appearance of a police car that changed into the lane in front of me and turned on its sirens and lights, clearing the way. After a while the car veered off and was replaced by an ambulance. We had pack members in all the emergency services, but we also held a lot of favors that could be called in. I pulled up to the front door of the retreat to find Josh, Sebastian, Dr. Baker, and several pack members anxiously waiting for us. From the dashboard, I opened the back hatch and Dr. Baker retrieved the box of antidote. When Sebastian opened Dr. Yoshi's door, he recoiled toward me.

"You're safe, for now," I told him. "If we decide to kill you, it will be much quicker and more merciful than what your poison has done to my people." At my urging, Dr. Yoshi stumbled out the door, immediately surrounded by angry, growling were-animals pressing in on him until Sebastian pushed them back. He roughly took the doctor by the arm and was guiding him toward the house when Steven emerged in a hot fury. He leapt onto the doctor, knocking him to the ground, and straddled his chest as he squeezed the man's throat with both hands. Yoshi's face turned bright red as he gasped and spat, struggling feebly to pry Steven's grip loose. By the time I emerged from the SUV, Sebastian had pulled Steven off, forcibly holding him back while I got the doctor to his feet, shielding him from the others. Every one of us had lost someone. Every one of us grieved for someone who was dying from Dr. Yoshi's poison. I needed to get him inside as quickly as possible.

"Steven!" Sebastian shouted, but Steven refused to stop pushing toward the doctor. "We need him! Stop! We need him to help your mother, Steven!" The mention of Joan gave him pause, but he was barely in control. "We need him to apply the antidote. We need him to show us what this poison is, and how he made it, so that this never happens again. When that's done, only when that's done, we will judge him. Understand?"

Tears welled in Steven's eyes as he struggled, until he finally forced himself to turn away. I hurried the doctor into the house, past more angry were-animals, and into the clinic where Kelly and Dr. Baker were already examining the vials from the box. Joan, Marko, and Winter were there, pale and slowly dying around us, as were several others. Two bodies, I saw, were now covered head to toe with white sheets. I squeezed my eyes shut for a moment, willing my own fury away.

Marko was my fault. He shouldn't have been with me in Virginia. That wasn't pack business.

"The most important thing you can do now," Dr. Baker instructed our guest in a calm, strained voice as he squeezed Dr. Yoshi's shoulder, "is help these people recover from this poison. I'll have a lot of questions for you later—questions you will be required to answer—but right now I need your help to calculate the dosage. If you have any hope of surviving this night, Dr. Yoshi, it starts with saving these lives behind you. Now. Let's begin."

Sebastian and I stood back against the double doors and watched as Dr. Baker and Dr. Yoshi conspired to calculate the doses, giving each one to Kelly to administer as it was prepared. After a moment, we stepped out of the room to find Josh leaning against the wall, while Steven anxiously fidgeted as he paced the hall. Hearing us, he stopped immediately, looking up for hopeful news.

"It will be some time before we start seeing an improvement," Sebastian said softly.

Steven's shoulders sank as he nodded, his gaze dropping to the floor as he returned to pacing.

"Ethan," Sebastian said, his voice suddenly tense as he turned to me.

I knew what he wanted. "He claims not to remember much about the man who hired him to create the poison, except that he was a witch with silver hair and purple eyes."

"That's pretty specific," Josh said, "but that doesn't match the description of any witch I know of. Probably from out of the area. He couldn't give you anything more?"

"Getting that much out of him caused him some kind of pain that seemed to cloud his memory," I explained. "Magic?"

"It's possible. If it's the same witch who sent those creatures to attack us, he's very powerful. I'm not sure if I can break his spell, but I have some ideas that might work."

"Once Dr. Baker is finished with our guest," Sebastian instructed Josh, "take him somewhere quiet and see what you can do."

Josh nodded.

"Was Dr. Yoshi a willing participant?" Sebastian asked me.

I shrugged. "He claims he was forced to create the poison. He was too frightened in general for me to tell if he was lying."

"We're lucky he left the antidote behind," Josh said.

Sebastian grunted.

I shared his doubts. "Or this witch is playing some kind of game," I explained to Josh. "He ordered the antidote made, but didn't take it."

"You think we were supposed to find it?" he asked, incredulous.

"More likely the antidote was to give the doctor a sense of deniability."

"Are we going to share this with Demetrius?"

Sebastian nodded. "After we verify that the antidote works."

Dr. Baker emerged through the double doors, wearing an exhausted, but relieved expression.

"It's working?" Steven asked, breathless with anticipation.

"Slowly," Dr. Baker smiled, "but yes. The poison is still inhibiting their ability to heal at their normal rate, but the healing process has begun in all of the patients."

I felt my shoulders drop, unaware until then of the tension I'd had been holding. Josh and Sebastian smiled, relieved, while Steven leaned against the wall for support. He started for the doors, then stopped when he met Sebastian's gaze. A silent exchange passed between them before Steven nodded slowly and disappeared through the doors.

"I'll get Dr. Yoshi out of there and check him over," Josh said before disappearing through the doors as well.

"Good work, Ethan," Sebastian said. "You look exhausted. Are you staying the night?"

"There's something else I need to take care of." I needed to check on Sky. Just because the creatures hadn't yet targeted her, didn't mean they wouldn't. For most people, a phone call would do, but not her. Not from me, anyway. With any luck, she wouldn't even know I was there. I just needed to know that she was home, safe within her ward, and then I could go back to the retreat and check on Marko and Winter.

"Go ahead. I'll let you know if anything changes here."

The drive to Sky's felt long. Now that the adrenaline from the evening had worn off, exhaustion was catching up to me. I turned on the stereo, relying on acid jazz to keep me awake. Several tracks later, I arrived at Sky's to find her Honda Civic in the driveway and lights on in the house. The front curtains were half closed. I parked across the street, giving myself a good view. I'd knock on the door if necessary, but it would be less problematic if I saw her from a distance. It wasn't long before I saw her, seemingly calm and safe, walk by the front window. I relaxed into my seat, relieved. I reached up to the dash to start the car, when I saw Quell follow her past the window. I blinked, shocked. He was inside the house! I reached for my door, intending to break the ward and barge into the house, when Sky's front door opened and she emerged with Quell behind her as they walked to her car. *Is he compelling her?*

She didn't have that blank look. She was actually smiling, excited.

My hands balled into fists and I felt blood rush to my face as I watched them climb into her car. *Where could she possibly be going with him?* The engine of the Civic came to life and I had to make a decision to confront them and further alienate Sky, or to let her leave with that vampire. I slammed the dash with my fist, then ducked beneath the window as she backed the Civic out of the driveway. As if the threat to the pack wasn't enough, I had to worry about Sky making friends with a killer who wouldn't hesitate to make a meal of her, or torture her. Even after a year, much of the supernatural world remained new to her, but she should have known enough to not trust a vampire. She saw them as individuals, rather than acknowledging their inherent lust for murder and mayhem.

I heard the Civic drive off and sat up, shaking my head at the taillights. Her desire to find the good in anyone was going to get her killed. I started the engine, but was already second-guessing myself. *I should've stopped them. She isn't safe.* But Sky would never accept my interference. The moment I was gone, she would go to Quell, and their bond—whatever it was—would grow stronger. Unless I killed him. But then I would lose her forever. There was the existing pact between the pack and the Seethe to consider as well. I cursed as I put the SUV in motion and followed Sky and her vampire from a comfortable distance. He would reveal his true nature to her, and I would be there to save her. Again.

Wherever she was headed to, it led her into increasingly rural areas, where traffic quickly became rare and I was more and more exposed following them. Eventually, I had no choice but to turn off or be noticed. Cursing my luck, I drew out my phone and found the app Stacy had installed for me when she'd hacked Sky's phone at my direction. But I hesitated. I'd told myself I wouldn't use it without an emergency.

At that moment, she was getting farther and farther from any hope of help, and she was with a vampire. I opened the app, which revealed a section of map with a blinking blue dot at the center. Slowly, the map shifted to accommodate the dot's movements. I consciously unclenched my jaw as I looked up to watch the headlights of the Civic fade into the distance, drowning between cornfields, and then disappear completely over a rise. I removed a phone cradle from the glove box, attached it to the dash, and adjusted the angle of the screen in the cradle. Satisfied, I pulled back onto the road, leaving my headlights off, and followed.

Why is she in a car with a vampire? What was she thinking?

My mind raced with the possibilities as I followed them farther and farther from civilization, the rural landscape giving way to vast fields. Whatever Quell's intentions, I doubted Demetrius was involved as the Seethe's home was some thirty miles behind us. No, Quell was on his own. He wanted Sky somewhere quiet and forgotten, where his plan could unfold over time. I wrapped my fingers around the steering wheel and squeezed, but I resisted the urge to accelerate. *Be patient,* I cautioned myself. Whatever his plan for her, I knew it wouldn't be quick. Had Quell intended to simply drain her blood and kill her, he could've done so in the quiet solitude of her home. I didn't want any harm to come to her, but she needed to see him for the threat he was.

I slowed as I saw the blue dot on my screen turn off the main road just ahead, then stop. A minute later I followed a curve in the road, alternating my gaze between the blue dot and the driver's side window of the SUV until I spotted a long, narrow driveway that led to an old farmhouse surrounded by cornfields. From what I'd seen, there wasn't another dwelling for at least a mile. While I stared, the SUV idling in the middle of the road, a light flicked on within the farmhouse.

I drove thirty feet farther—out of sight from the farmhouse—and parked on the side of the road. Careful to deactivate the interior light first, I got out of the SUV, gently closed the door, then walked up the driveway. Though I was confident I hadn't been spotted, I still maintained a watchful eye for an ambush; there was no telling who else was there. Approaching the house, I saw two cars in the driveway: Sky's Civic and another car, presumably Quell's. The house itself was rustic-looking and well maintained, but there was a lifelessness to it, as there was to all vampire homes. Around the back of the house I found a small greenhouse—reeking of lavender and a collage of flowers—a few feet from the back door. A glass vestibule connected the two.

Michaela said he feeds from plants. I shook my head as I realized why Sky had come here. *She thinks he is redeemable because he feeds from plants instead of humans,* I scoffed. *Why does she believe him?* Even if the story were true, Quell was a vampire; he could no more hide from his true nature than I could hide from my wolf. The lust to kill, the thirst for blood, was within him, driving its way free from whatever constraints he might put upon himself. Eventually, he would give in to his bloodlust. When he did, no one would be safe. Not even Sky.

I heard the back door open and ducked behind the side of the house. Using a windowsill for purchase, I leveraged myself to the roof and stealthily climbed up to the peak. When I peered over it, I found them standing below in the vestibule.

"You only feed in the evening?" she asked.

In answer, Quell reached to something on the wall that I couldn't see. Suddenly metal shudders extended from the top edges of the vestibule and greenhouse, enclosing the entire structure in metal plating. I instinctively ran down the roof, but stopped myself from jumping onto the vestibule, tearing off the shudders, and rescuing Sky. Would he attack her now? I could still hear their voices, but faintly. The noise of my run had apparently been disguised by the shudders closing. I could just make out the beat of her heart, if I pushed out all else. The metal was thin, I realized. Rather than enclose a security bunker, the purpose of the shield was to protect Quell from the light when he chose to feed. Should I need to intervene, it would take nothing for me to break inside.

"How did you find such a thing?" she asked.

"Many of us have known of its existence, few use it," he answered. "Blood, for many of us, is the preferred choice. Try it."

I scowled at the thought of her feeding from his plant. *She wouldn't.* I was certain, but a moment later I heard a low rumble from inside, like an inhuman moan, that made me nauseous.

"Do you find my diet so strange now?" he asked, amusement in his voice.

My nose wrinkled in disgust. *She has a terait. There is a part of her that is vampire,* I reminded myself. Sky experienced a mild form of bloodlust, but I had never known her to demonstrate any desire for living blood. My eyes narrowed as I considered that Quell's influence on her was an even greater threat than I'd thought.

Rather than answer, Sky changed the subject. "How long have you been a vampire?"

"Longer than you've been alive," he answered softly. "You are an inquisitive one, aren't you?"

"I find you interesting," she agreed.

"Are you flirting with me?"

"No … no … um, no," she stammered, taken aback. "I'm just curious." Her voice grew closer, as if she were backing away into the vestibule. I tensed, looking for the seams of the metal plates where I could get the best grip. She raised her voice to him. "You don't feed from humans because their immorality disgusts you, but you allow them to live—

unharmed, never forcing them to do penance for their crimes against humanity. By all logic, you should be society's greatest murderer, making them atone for their evil ways. Based on your beliefs, wouldn't it be just?"

What are you doing, Sky? Do you want him to kill you?

"You won't feed from humans because you find them deplorable and choose to have nothing to do with them," she continued, taunting him. "But you are a vampire. The people in your Seethe have done things just as, if not more, heinous."

In contrast to hers, Quell's voice grew softer. I had trouble making out his reply.

"Well, the whole pot and kettle thing does come to mind," she answered him. Once more, I couldn't make out his reply. "A human found a dying woman and tried to save her," she explained. "When she realized she couldn't help the woman, she saved the child and raised her as her own. And when she found out the child she had raised turned into a wolf once a month, she didn't abandon her. I've seen the best of humanity and that is what I choose to color my view. Despite all the bad that exists, there is still a lot that is really good.

"How long have you been like this?" she asked. "Your parents didn't give you the name Quella Perduta. What was it before?"

I shook my head. She wasn't going to give up. Sky never gave up on what she believed was right. It was her greatest trait and her deepest flaw. She was convinced that she could bring out his humanity, and nothing would deter her—not even Quell. When he eventually tried to kill her—and he would—she wouldn't see it coming. He had already admitted his loathing for humanity. What more did she need to know? *Listen to him, Sky. Not every being is redeemable.*

And he was equally as fascinated with her. Could I warn him off? Even if I could influence him, I couldn't stop her. More than likely I would have to eventually expose him for what he was, or kill him.

"Thank you for coming," Quell said stiffly. "I have enjoyed your company."

I made my way over the roof and onto the ground, running at a crouch to get to my SUV and drive, lights extinguished, down the road until I felt it was safe to turn back around. I followed her from a distance until the blue dot indicated that she was home. Knowing that she was safe did little to relieve the tension in my neck and jaw as I considered my options. None of them were good.

CHAPTER 7

*T*he drive back to the retreat was long enough to let my frustration get the best of me. I'd spent enough time worrying about Sky. *She can't naïvely stumble around in our world forever.* At some point I was going to have to let her face the consequences of her decisions, but trusting Quell was going to get her killed. I growled at the thought.

My phone vibrated. A text from Dennis. "She's in for the night. Alone. I'm going home."

He meant Chris. I answered, using voice-to-text. "She's an early riser."

"Your retainer doesn't buy overtime. Just how long am I following her?"

"Stay on her and send me a bill."

I turned off my alerts and returned the phone to my pocket. If Dennis replied, I didn't bother to notice.

The retreat was quiet. Much of the pack had gone to bed, which was where I wanted to be. Instead, I found Kelly in the clinic, quietly making her rounds. A book sat open and face-down on an unused table she was using as a desk. I assumed she would be there through the night. As I walked in, she greeted me with a tired, comforting smile. Marko, Winter, and Joan remained in their medically induced comas, connected to oxygen and several IV lines. Their skin was still pallid, but it appeared their fevers had broken, and their scars—once garish—had been reduced to long, rough lines. The antidote was working, albeit slowly. Joan appeared to be healing faster than the others, which was expected. She was a were-jaguar, felidae, one of the rarest and most powerful were-animals.

"It'll be a few more days," Kelly offered, "but the worst is over."

I nodded, relieved. *We'll need them soon.* Despite the lull, another attack was inevitable. I wondered if our enemy would show itself soon, or continue trying to cut us down one by one. We had an advantage, now, albeit a small one— we had the antidote, and we knew the enemy was coming.

"Dr. Yoshi?" I asked.

Her smile faded. "Josh took him to the library a few hours ago. I think they're still there."

The library was my brother's de facto office. When at the retreat, he spent most of his time there, among the well-stocked bookshelves that contained the pack's collected knowledge of the supernatural world—every experience, every bit of intelligence gathered over the years, no matter how trivial-seeming. Knowledge was power.

Dr. Yoshi and Josh sat across from each other at a table in the center of the library. Between them sat a clay bowl, a candle, and a few other objects I'd seen him use before, but I didn't know their exact purpose. Josh leaned over the table toward the doctor, with one arm fully extended, fingers splayed. His brow furrowed in concentration as he muttered an incantation. Dr. Yoshi slumped in the opposite chair, head tilted slightly, whimpering as his body spasmed under the power of my brother's magic. The air in the room was stifling. A witch's magic was unique, different from that of any other witch. Josh's magic often felt like a gentle breeze, but not now. The magic he was using felt heavy and oppressive, as if it sucked the air from the room—dark magic.

As I approached, I could see that the doctor had probably lost consciousness. "Josh." He didn't seem to hear, so I raised my voice, insisting.

He released the spell, collapsing back into his chair with his legs splayed, his mouth slightly agape as he stared at the doctor.

"I've never encountered anything like this," he insisted.

"Explain."

He gestured in frustration as the doctor's head drooped until his chin met his chest. "It's a simple spell. It should be simple," he corrected himself, "but there are layers to it. The more I start to peel those layers back, the more they seem to twist together." He didn't like the idea of there being someone out there more powerful than him. Neither did I.

I gently lifted the doctor's head to examine him. His eyes were closed and his face was slick with sweat. Patting his cheeks elicited a soft murmur, but nothing more. With a thumb, I raised one eyelid to find the doctor's pupil rolled up and quivering. I wasn't even sure he knew I was there. I gently lowered his head, then turned to Josh, frowning at his obvious indifference. Was he so caught up in his magic that he couldn't see the damage he was doing?

"How likely is it that Dr. Yoshi was forced to create the poison?" I asked.

"It's possible," Josh admitted reluctantly. "I've got one more idea to try."

"Get some sleep." I gently lifted the doctor from the chair, cradling him in my arms, and started out of the library.

"I'm not finished!" Josh snapped.

I turned, showing my brother the doctor's limp form. "He is. What did you do to him?"

Josh rose. "Have you forgotten what he's responsible for?"

"Dark magic, Josh?"

He sighed overtly, dismissively shaking his head, but he also looked away. "I'm doing what's necessary for the pack. You of all people should appreciate that."

"Are you? You're sure you're not using this man as a test subject for your magical experiments?"

Josh rose and kicked a chair across the room, then ran a hand through his ruffled hair. I didn't bother to stick around for the rest of his theatrics.

On rare occasions, we found ourselves the temporary hosts of reluctant guests, typically were-animals who became impermanently lost in their animal nature. For their protection, three of the rooms were simple cells, with a cot and toilet and steel-reinforced walls. The fourth room was more comfortable; a bedroom like any other in the retreat, except for the closed-circuit camera and the steel-reinforced door that bolted from the outside. As prisons went, it was comfortable. I doubted the doctor would sleep well tonight, but we couldn't risk a sedative in case one of the patients took an unexpected turn.

I laid the doctor on the queen-sized bed, confiscated his wallet and cell phone from his pockets, then covered him. After verifying the refrigerator was well stocked with water, I locked him inside and pocketed the key—the only key. There were plenty of were-animals in this house who would be tempted to take their revenge for wounded and lost friends, but the doctor would be safe—for now, at least. In the morning I would have him check his voice mail and change the outgoing message to indicate that he was out of town to deal with an unexpected emergency. Even in the best-case scenario, he was going to be with us for several days; we didn't need a missing person report complicating the matter.

Once the doctor was safely locked in, I started typing a

text to Tim, then stopped myself. *I must be tired.* As a police officer, he was well-positioned to alert us should Dr. Yoshi's disappearance become a public matter, but I'd be a fool to inform him directly by a text to his personal phone. I yawned. In the morning I would send him a coded message, telling him to call me using a burner phone. We had contingencies for everything. For now, the best thing I could do would be to go to bed.

Once I got there, my mind refused to rest. Preferring to distract myself from thoughts of Sky and her vampire, I turned to analyzing the purpose of the attacks on the pack, a winding path I'd followed a dozen times already. *We should've received a demand by now.* Were the attacks about power? Was there some new force attempting to establish its superiority in the region? The Midwest Pack was the most powerful pack in the country, which put a target on our back, but our enemy wasn't just taking us on, it was taking on the Seethe as well, driving traditional enemies to work together. The smart play would be to pit pack against Seethe. It wouldn't take much manipulation to trick us into destroying one another, clearing the path for a new force to move in. Driving us together was either hubris or deliberate. *Has to be deliberate. This enemy is too well organized and too powerful to be otherwise. But to what end?* Who was our enemy? The question never stopped rattling in my head. *Who?*

The changelings were strong, but clumsy and not particularly bright. *Soldiers.* Unlike were-animals, they seemed able to transform into any shape, though never completely, from what I'd seen, which suggested their power to transform was poorly developed or was being used in a way the creatures weren't accustomed to. So far, we hadn't found any references to creatures with such power—not living, anyway. Only the *genums* had a similar transformational power, but they were small creatures, limited by their mass. They were also extinct, and had been for some time.

Could our enemy have found a way to mutate a were-animal's ability to change? For now, it was the only possibility that made sense, but it still brought me no closer to answering, *Who?*

At some point I fell asleep for what felt like minutes before I instinctively woke up at dawn, then pushed the fog from my brain with a few sets of one-handed push-ups. After a quick breakfast, I brought a plate of steak and eggs to Dr. Yoshi's room and found Steven lingering outside the locked door.

"No one bothered him," he reported, subdued. He frowned at the door, as if trying to make up his mind. "Josh said you think he was compelled to create the poison. If that's true …" Steven shook his head. "I can't forgive him for what he's done, but I don't want to see an innocent man punished, either."

"We'll find out," I promised. "Nothing will happen to the doctor until we know for sure. At that point, we'll decide his fate."

He nodded. Something else was on his mind. He hesitated, but decided to walk away, taking his thoughts with him.

Only after he disappeared around a corner did I unlock the door to find the doctor huddled on his bed, his back against the wall, hugging his knees to his chest. My arrival was greeted with a panicked expression before his attention drifted hungrily to the plate of food I placed on the desk.

"Dr. Baker will come for you. Or his nurse, Kelly. You'll be taken to the clinic where you'll continue to instruct Dr. Baker in the creation of your poison, and the antidote. You'll be treated well, as long as you follow their instructions." I watched his eyes dart about the room, then settle on the door behind me. He was an animal in a cage, looking for a way out. "I think it was clear last night that you're not a popular man in this house. There are only two places here where you are safe—this room, and the clinic. Anywhere else in this house, you'll likely be killed on sight." Did he understand me? "Don't. Run." After he nodded acknowledgment, I left him to eat, locking the door behind me.

A few minutes later I heard Chris and Josh in the library. I was on the verge of joining them when I saw Sky inside as well and felt a sudden, intense anger confused by frustration. I wanted to talk some sense into her about Quell, convince her that vamps couldn't be saved, but I knew she wouldn't listen, and I'd probably start shouting. For once, I wrestled my temper under control and took my frustrations to the gym instead.

I found Sebastian alone, running on a treadmill. With a slight nod, he invited me to join him. I took the next machine over, programmed it to the most challenging setting, then started running. I had just worked up a sweat when he finally spoke.

"You and Chris are back together." His flat tone spoke volumes.

Josh. I scowled. He had no business sharing mine, but I understood Sebastian's concern. "It was a one-time thing," I said dismissively.

"I understand that you and Chris have a long and complicated history together."

"She won't be a problem," I said, suppressing my irritation. I'd already gotten the tenth degree from my brother. I didn't need it from Sebastian, too.

"We need everyone focused on the challenge in front of us," he continued. "We need *you* focused."

"It was a mistake," I snapped angrily, my temper rushing to the surface. Sebastian didn't take the bait. As we quietly ran beside each other over for a while, the pressure built up in me to explain further. "I was worked up from the parlay with the vamps. She showed up at my door asking if we were going to be able to work together and ended up staying the night. I don't know how it happened, but it did." I sighed, recognizing my irritation was aimed primarily at myself. I added, choosing my words carefully, "I'm aware that in the past I let my situation with her get in the way of my responsibilities to the pack. I've informed her that what happened last night will not be repeated. She's changed. Since she started working for Demetrius, there's a desperation about her. She's taking risks."

"Is that your only concern for her working with Demetrius?" he asked stoically.

"I'm concerned for her safety."

"You can't save her from her choices, Ethan."

"I can try," I said.

"Okay." Sebastian remained silent for a long moment before changing the subject. "You should know that Sky was attacked the other night."

I gaped at him, slowing almost to a standstill on the machine. "When? How?" I demanded.

"After you dropped her off from the restaurant, she decided to return on her own to the parking lot where Winter was attacked."

I scowled, stunned. Had she lost her mind entirely?

He continued, "She was attempting to investigate a smell she remembered from their initial encounter."

"Lemon and brimstone," I said. That was how Sky and Josh had ended up at my house. *That's why Josh had been calling me all night, while I was with ...* I swallowed, my mouth suddenly dry. "She should've told me." If I hadn't tried to drive her away, she would have. Every muscle in my body vibrated with anger I could only direct at myself. At least she had gotten away unharmed. She was safe, now.

"She obviously escaped unharmed," I said, soothing my guilt. The creatures weren't particularly fast or cunning. She could've easily outrun them.

"It slashed her across the abdomen," he corrected, his tone heavy and precise in his judgment, like a scalpel.

I stopped running entirely and turned to face him. She had shown no sign of injury at my house, at Gloria's, or walking in the woods to Thaddeus's house. "The poison—"

"The explanation Dr. Baker gave her was that her injuries weren't severe enough to receive a sufficient dose of the poison, which might be the case. The wound was borderline, but she healed much faster than expected. Josh suspects Maya might have played a role."

"She's supposed to be dormant," I said absently, distracted by the recriminations ricocheting inside my brain.

"Yes," he said grimly. "Unfortunately, we have no way of knowing for certain."

My fault. I stepped off the machine and began pacing with a rising intensity. For the last year, I'd held my desire for Sky in check. After the restaurant, I finally let it get the best of me. Instead of trusting me to protect her, she'd gone out on her own and nearly gotten herself killed. I imagined her wounded, bleeding out alone in an empty parking lot while I was with Chris. I'd messed up, and Sky had nearly paid the price.

"Was it Josh who brought her here?" I asked absently.

Sebastian stepped off his machine and retrieved his towel from a nearby rack. "The odd vampire, Quell, saved her," he said, then walked out of the gym, leaving me alone.

For a moment, I stood as still as a statue, allowing the fury to build. When it threatened to overwhelm me, I carried a pair of twenty-pound dumbbells into the next room, where we retired the older equipment, and proceeded to demolish everything there. When there was nothing left to break, I tore apart the walls. By the time I came to my senses, I was standing in a field of broken, twisted metal, staring at Swiss cheese walls. My fury not yet spent, I left the house and ran hard through the woods that surrounded the retreat house.

Eventually, I exhausted everything but my disappointment. When I returned to the house, the other were-animals steered clear of me as I glowered, radiating anger on my way to my room. After a shower and a change of clothes, I checked my phone. I found a text message from Dennis, a street address along with a picture of a house I recognized. Gideon's. Chris's BMW was in the driveway. "I swear to God," Dennis added, "there's a storm brewing just over this house."

"Get out of there," I texted back. Who knew what else he was going to see if he stuck around. "I'll tell you when you're needed."

"Yeah. Happy to."

Within minutes, I was on the highway in my SUV. Why Chris took it upon herself to visit an elemental elf without backup, I couldn't explain. I didn't trust magic. I trusted elves even less. If the elves were involved in the plot against us, she could be walking into a trap.

Despite Gideon's self-imposed exile, I doubted that he'd fully removed himself from elven politics. The son of a legendary leader, he'd been expected to eventually take his father's place. But Gideon had gotten used to a carefree lifestyle. When the time came, he'd turned down the nomination. Whether he'd acted out of defiance or insecurity was anyone's guess, but he remained a popular figure. Soon there would be a new election. There was a good chance Gideon would be nominated once again.

Chris's BMW was still in the driveway, blocking it, when I arrived and parked across the street. A quick glance around the neighborhood failed to locate Dennis's Cutlass. *Good.* As I approached the front door of the house, a shadow passed over me, accompanied by a rumble in the sky that stirred the hair on my neck. As I looked up into the gathering purple cloud just—and only—above me, a bolt of lightning jabbed downward, accompanied by a loud roar. The flash was blinding. The electricity crackling in the air raised every hair on my body. My arrival had not gone unnoticed.

Before I reached the door, Chris emerged from the house with a scowl, the door slamming shut behind her as if by its own volition. "What are you doing here?" she demanded, walking past me toward her BMW.

"Josh was concerned about you," I lied, following her.

"Oh, how sweet. Now I have two of you worrying about me unnecessarily."

"Did you learn anything from Gideon?"

"Yes, but let's discuss it back at your place."

She was rounding the back of her BMW when I heard a growl. I turned to find one of the creatures a few feet away, charging Chris. She barely managed to draw a pistol from her shoulder holster when the creature swept her aside with its arm. She fell back against the car, her pistol falling to the paved driveway and bouncing under the car. Despite her vulnerable position, the creature ignored her, charging me instead. I barely dodged a swing of its knifelike claws, then unleashed a barrage of punches to its stomach, then its chest. It should've collapsed. Instead, it only stumbled back a step, stunned. Drawing a knife from my ankle sheath, I stabbed the creature once in the side. Before I could stab it again, it disappeared.

Chris grunted as she rose to her feet, pistol in hand, scanning our surroundings in anticipation of a second attack. It appeared the creature had been alone. Judging by the way she guarded her right arm, keeping it stiffly pressed against her body, I assumed her shoulder was dislocated.

"How's the arm?" I asked.

"It's fine," she snapped, grimacing.

"Are you going to let Dr. Baker look at that shoulder, or are you going to pretend it's not hurt?"

"Do you think he will?"

They had been close, once. When Chris had walked out

on me, she had severed all ties with the pack. Dr. Baker had taken it the hardest. "For you," I smiled, "of course he will. Give me your keys."

She scowled at the steering wheel of her BMW, debating, then fished out her keys from a pocket and tossed them to me. "What about your SUV?"

"I'll send someone to pick it up," I said as I crammed in behind the wheel, then lowered the seat and pushed it back. Chris looked uncomfortable in the passenger seat, and not just from her shoulder. "You've got control issues." I smiled. "On the way, you can tell me what you learned from Gideon."

"He told me the genums are missing," she said as we drove off.

"Genums are extinct."

"Apparently not. Gideon claims he'd seen them until recently."

"Even if he told you the truth, the creature that just attacked us was too large to be a genum. They're also harmless."

She shook her head. "Not according to Gideon."

When she didn't say more, I asked, "Is that it?"

"Until you showed up and pissed him off."

We drove the rest of the way to the retreat in silence.

Dr. Baker seemed more than happy to help Chris, guiding her into an out-of-the-way exam room that kept her away from Dr. Yoshi. She knew nothing about our guest, and I intended to keep it that way. Earlier that morning Dr. Baker had informed his counterpart at the Seethe that he had identified the poison and created an antidote, which we promptly delivered. The origin of the poison was our secret. I didn't need Demetrius banging on our door demanding Dr. Yoshi's blood. More importantly, I didn't need Demetrius getting his hands on a scientist who could design custom poisons that affected were-animals.

I waited in the entryway while he treated her, which wouldn't take long. I knew she would try to slip out quietly, and I wasn't disappointed. "Chris," I called to her just as she reached the front door.

"Yes," she answered with a resigned sigh.

"I want you to stay here, or at the very least, at my place."

"Why?"

"Because you're injured."

"This?" She gestured to her shoulder. "I've had worse."

"I know. It's quite unfortunate, but I need to make sure you're protected while you are injured." She was already at a disadvantage against the creatures. If she were attacked again, her chances of survival were low. I preferred that she stay at the retreat instead of my place—for both our sakes.

"I won't heal any faster here or at your place than I would at my home."

"You're right," I acknowledged. "At least I will make sure you won't get any more injuries." *And I can keep you away from Demetrius. Maybe I can talk some sense into you.* I wasn't taking no for an answer.

"Ethan," she said soothingly as she approached and kissed me on the lips, gently at first, but then our old passion for each other took over, drawing us together. She pulled away before I could. Smiling, she held my cheek in her palm. "I am not staying here nor am I staying with you. I'm going home *alone*."

She had the wrong idea.

"We aren't going to fight about this," she said, cutting off my retort.

I glanced at the injured arm she held tightly to her side. "As if you are in any condition to fight with anyone."

She backed toward the door, giving me a sad smile. "I'll see you later."

Disappointed, I texted Dennis, "Time to get back to work. She's on her way home."

Two hours later I was in my room, researching some new investments, when I received a new message from Dennis. "She's at her home, and she's got company. Looks like an underwear model. I swear he just appeared out of thin air at the door. Seemed like they had a dustup, but quiet now. He must've left, but no idea how he got past me. Maybe he just disappeared. I hate this job."

Demetrius. My fists clenched into fists.

CHAPTER 8

The next morning in Sebastian's office, we were joined by Gavin, Josh, and Steven. Steven had a lightness about him now—a look of relief, as if he'd been thrown the worst and couldn't imagine a greater challenge. Dr. Baker planned to bring Joan out of her coma in a day or two. She would be the first, followed by Winter and Marko a few days later, depending on their progress. Now that the crisis was over and we were close to full strength, decisions needed to be made.

"According to Chris, the vampires are in the dark, just as we are," I said.

Gavin snorted. "So far, our alliance with the vampires has been a waste of time." He had opposed sharing the antidote with the Seethe, but in that he'd stood alone. Like it or not, we were in an alliance until the conditions of the alliance were met, the vamps betrayed us, or Sebastian brought it to a formal end.

"Despite the current lull in attacks, this will end in a fight, eventually," I said. "We will need every advantage. Either this enemy wants to destroy us, or it intends to leverage its power for some concession. Either way, the attacks will continue. And they will get stronger."

Gavin leaned back against the wall, crossing his arms. "So we just wait?"

"For now," Sebastian said. "The first step to launching an offensive is identifying our enemy." If he had any ideas, he kept them to himself. He preferred to gather every opinion he could before giving his own.

"Somehow," Josh said, "he's enabling the genums to shapeshift into creatures so massive and powerful that they can easily kill a were-animal or vampire. And he's capable of powering several of them at once."

"He's a witch," Gavin said, stating the obvious. "That means Marcia's involved somehow."

"I've made some inquiries," Josh answered. "I have some connections to the Creed that Marcia is unaware of."

"It wouldn't be the first time witches were responsible for the mass killing of were-animals."

"That was a century ago," Josh conceded with a slight nod. "Things have changed."

Gavin scoffed. "They've never stopped hating us."

"Marcia is as baffled by the attacks as we are. She believes the witch is from outside the area, and will probably come after her next."

Gavin wasn't convinced.

"Fae?" Steven suggested. "Could they be manipulating the genums?"

"Not their kind of magic," Josh answered. "They could compel someone to injure another, but that would require constant physical contact."

"The elves are unlikely as well," I added. Elves, like Gideon, were annoyingly mischievous, but not particularly ambitious. They were dangerous when cornered but rarely went out of their way to pick a fight.

"I wouldn't rule them out entirely," Josh cautioned.

"Mason seems to be developing a taste for power. According to my sources, he is pursuing an alliance with the witches."

"So we pay Mason a visit," Gavin suggested, eager for a fight.

"It would take a significant show of force to get him to talk," I warned. "That still wouldn't guarantee his cooperation."

Sebastian was silent in thought for a moment. "If Mason needs an enemy to consolidate power, he wouldn't target the pack and the Seethe together."

"He might know who would."

"He wouldn't tell us," I said, earning a derisive look from Gavin. "Our witch has left the elves alone, for now. Mason wouldn't risk drawing attention."

The room was quiet for a moment.

"So that leaves us where we started," Gavin complained, "waiting for our enemy to show himself."

"Or make a mistake," I added.

The next day, I investigated the farmhouses closest to Quell's until I found one that had long been shuttered. The fields around the house were well maintained but it seemed the family had moved to a more modern house on the other side of the farm. After parking the SUV out of sight from the road, I hid the keys under a nearby rock. From the glove compartment, I retrieved a small tracking device attached to a gold necklace that I draped around my neck. I checked once more to make certain I wasn't observed, then removed my clothes and transformed into my wolf, welcoming the cool comfort as my body quickly elongated. By the time I landed on all fours, the transformation was complete. I shook out my dark gray mane, feeling the necklace shift around my neck.

Winding my way through the cornfields was time-consuming, but it was still daylight. The chances of being seen by a random observer were small, but a large wolf prowling farm fields would draw a lot of attention. An hour before dusk, I finally arrived at the edge of the cornfield just outside Quell's house. The curtains were closed. I couldn't be sure he was alone, but only his car sat in the driveway.

Hidden from view on the far side of the car, I transformed from my animal, removed the tracking device from the chain, and attached it magnetically to the underside of the car. After a quick look around, I shifted back into my wolf and trotted back into the cornfield, taking a circuitous route to the greenhouse in Quell's backyard.

Neither the pack library nor the Internet had offered any mention of the Hidacus, but I knew the plant existed; he'd made Sky feed from it. I repressed a growl at the memory. Most likely it was the tall plant that towered over the rest. The stalk was treelike, sprouting numerous thick stems that ended with a single wide leaf. Only when I got a closer look from the other side of the greenhouse did I notice the dark veins that ran along the stems from stalk to leaf, disrupted by wide nodes that pulsed like a heartbeat. I could just make out the tiny ripples of the veins as fluid was pumped to the small buds at the tips of the leaves. *Blood?* I'd never seen anything like it.

I trotted back into the cornfield, just far enough to hide while maintaining a view of the greenhouse, then lay down to wait. When dusk arrived, Quell wasted no time emerging from the house and walking through the glass vestibule to the greenhouse. After examining and rejecting two long stems of the plant, he raised another stem to his lips and bit, sucking greedily as if he hadn't fed for some time.

Witnessing him feeding from the plant did nothing to quench my distrust. Was the plant merely an alternate food source, for convenience, or a means to maintain an image that pleased Michaela? Did he feed exclusively from the plant? Even so, his nature would eventually draw him toward blood. Human blood. It was only a matter of time, and I was going to catch him in the process. Only then would Sky believe me that Quell, like any vampire, was a murderer.

Once his thirst was slaked, he walked back into the house. A moment later he went out to his car and drove off toward the city. I ran back to my SUV, less concerned about being spotted this time. I changed quickly, dressed, retrieved my key, and started the vehicle. While the engine ran, I accessed the tracking app on my phone. By default, it was keyed into Sky's phone. She was home. I switched to tracking Quell's car. He appeared to be heading straight toward her.

My jaw clenched as I sped to catch up to him. Instead of Sky's, he stopped in a park near her house. *Perfect hunting ground.* By the time I arrived, he'd left his car. I presumed he was on the trail, looking to make a meal of a lone jogger. The park was largely empty, but too many people had trod the paths during the day for me to pick out the vampire's scent. After a short walk into the park, I found a secluded area, then changed into my wolf. With my animal's more refined sense of smell, I picked out Quell's scent immediately. He wasn't far, but I needed to keep out of sight, and not just from him. There was still the occasional jogger or hiker taking advantage of the quiet. I stayed off the paths, mindful to keep myself downwind from him whenever possible.

After a few minutes, I spotted him on the trail, taking what seemed a casual stroll. A young woman wearing bicycle shorts and a light top, listening via earbuds to music from the cell phone strapped to her upper arm, approached him at a lumbering jog. She looked exhausted, at the end of an intense run. No one else was within sight. She was a perfect target—an easy kill. I crouched forward onto my front paws, ready to leap to the woman's defense the moment Quell revealed his intentions. I would be within my rights to kill him, without violating the truce.

But nothing happened. The woman jogged past Quell, who gave no indication that he even noticed her. He seemed distracted, glancing about as if expecting someone to appear. Had he seen me, caught my scent? Suspicious, I continued to follow him, at times circling around his position to avoid being upwind from him. He spent hours wandering—first the park, then through the nearest neighborhoods. At times, he circled the same areas multiple times. His gaze seemed to drift toward nearby bushes and anywhere from which something or someone might be lurking. Was he paranoid, or hunting? On several occasions, he was given the perfect opportunity to kill a lone passing human, to feed when he thought no one would ever know, but he actually seemed to veer away from them—almost unconsciously. If he wasn't hunting humans, what was he hunting?

This went on for hours before I realized that Quell had taken a circuitous route into Sky's neighborhood. I tensed as he approached her home from the copse of trees behind her house. He stopped there, just outside the property, staring at the lights inside the windows. He spent an hour there, staring. When Sky appeared, passing by a window, his shoulders rose slightly, then fell, as if with a sigh. I suppressed a growl. Was he enamored of her? Had this vampire wrapped himself around her finger? I understood how he'd happened to find her when she'd had been injured by the creature two nights ago—he'd been stalking her. If so, he was more dangerous to her than ever. What was this power Sky had that made men so obsessed with her?

Eventually, Quell returned to his wandering hunt until he found himself back at his car shortly before dawn. For a moment, I thought he hesitated, noting my SUV as the only other vehicle in the parking lot, then he got into his car and drove.

After making sure he didn't circle back, I returned to where I had stashed my clothes, transformed, then dressed.

From the SUV, I tracked Quell's movements until I saw he'd returned to his farmhouse. Exhausted, I returned to the retreat at dawn. Rather than surrender to the laziness of sleep, I found a couple of sparring partners and went down to the gym to work out my frustrations. The door to the side room had been shut, and someone had taped a sign on the door that read, "No longer in service."

The next two nights were much the same. Confident that Quell was only feeding on his plant while at home, I waited to pick up his trail until he came into the suburbs. The locations changed, but his mysterious hunt continued. Plenty of opportunities presented themselves for him to feed on human blood, to exercise the vampiric lust for cruelty. Each time he seemed oblivious, focused entirely on his fruitless quest. At the end of each night he waited outside Sky's house, watching, before going home.

By the third morning, I was exhausted. After a quick shower, I was headed to the kitchen for breakfast when I glanced into the treatment room. Joan was awake, sitting on the edge of her bed, hugging an emotional Steven. Taylor stood nearby, next to Dr. Jimenez. Both appeared teary-eyed. Sebastian stood with Dr. Baker, arms folded across his chest and wearing a relieved smile. I wanted to join them, to share my relief, but Steven didn't need a bigger audience. Such a moment should be private, though I couldn't blame the others for wanting to be there—Taylor, in particular. She had blamed herself for Joan's injuries and had suffered tremendously during the long wait for her recovery.

After breakfast, I was summoned to Sebastian's office. Dr. Jimenez, Steven, and Joan were already there. She'd shed the hospital gown and dressed like any other day, but she remained pale and weak on her feet. I embraced her warmly, something I rarely did. She seemed surprised at first, then returned the embrace, but I kept it brief, respectful.

"Welcome back," I said.

She nodded, smiling.

"I hear a lot has occurred since the attack," she said.

Sebastian and I filled in the details of the events since she'd arrived at the retreat.

"The Southern Pack?" she asked, anxious for the answer, but she knew the answer intuitively. She'd seen enough before her defeat that she was prepared to hear the worst.

"Most of the Southern Pack were killed," Dr. Jimenez explained in a gentle, but direct voice, the kind Dr. Baker frequently used.

Steven watched her intently as Joan's chin fell, hiding her expression. She accepted the news with a forced deep breath, released in a single, resolute exhale, then looked up with a wounded but determined expression. "But not all."

"There's Taylor and myself," the doctor said. "I've been in touch with a few others. They've scattered. Gone into hiding to protect themselves."

"I have to go back."

"No," Steven said, shaking his head.

Joan rested a hand on his shoulder as she explained to Sebastian, "I have to restore the Southern Pack, before it's lost altogether."

"It's not safe," Steven insisted.

She offered him a gentle, understanding smile. "I have to. We will need everyone for the fight to come. I'll be careful, Steven."

"You won't!" he shouted, exponentially raising the level of tension in the room. "None of us are safe! And you won't have a pack to protect you."

"Steven," Sebastian said, his patience wearing thin.

"No! She can't leave. She isn't ready."

"Steven," Joan said soothingly.

"Sebastian, you can't let her do this! She's not ready," he continued, desperate and angry.

I'd gotten so used to relying on Steven's usual steadiness that I'd forgotten he was still a teenager.

"Calm down," Sebastian insisted.

"She's barely healed and you are going to just let her leave?" He postured defiantly. "There is no fucking way I am going to let that happen!"

"Steven!" Joan and Sebastian snapped almost simultaneously.

"What?" he challenged them. "I'm the only one who seems to be thinking here. You are so preoccupied babysitting Demetrius and his Seethe. We don't need to babysit them, nor do we have anything to prove. Screw them!" He turned to Joan. "And having your ass handed to you again or worse isn't going to prove anything except that you have poor judgment and allowed your pride to compromise it. Who the hell wants an Alpha like that?"

Sebastian tensed, and so did I. Steven hadn't just crossed the line—he'd leapt over it.

"You're not leaving," he commanded. "No damn way!"

"Leave," Sebastian finally ordered.

Steven hesitated out of defiance or because the command stung him; either way, Sebastian's patience had been exhausted. In a single stride he gripped Steven by the neck and opened the office door. Joan gasped as Sebastian pushed him to the hardwood floor just outside.

"I've been more than tolerant of your little tirade," Sebastian said, standing over him. "She's your mother and you're upset—I understand that. But you will not speak to either of us that way, do you understand? Don't push my patience. I guarantee you will not be happy with the results of that." While Steven gawked, Sebastian strode back into the office, slamming the door behind him.

"You aren't leaving," he informed Joan, his tone noticeably calmer but still firm.

"Sebastian."

"You have a mess to clean up when you go back. Putting yourself in harm's way will not make it any easier. You are the Alpha now; you'll need to demonstrate it. You will be challenged more times than I can even prepare you for."

"The longer I stay away, the more credibility I lose. It'll look like I ran. They need a presence there—my presence. The longer I stay, the weaker I look."

Sebastian considered for a moment. I agreed with Joan, but she was in no shape for a fight. I wasn't even sure she'd be able to help us.

"I will make it known that you had no choice," he decided. "If anyone has a problem with that, they can take it up with me."

"Oh great, the Elite came to my rescue. I assure you that will work well in my favor," she snapped derisively.

"The South is destroyed. If you want them to trust you, follow you, and reduce the number of challenges you have, then return with the person responsible for killing your pack found and the situation handled. Then no one will doubt your ability to lead. You will return with more than a 'presence.'"

I could see the sparks of gold feline rage in her pupils as she glared at Sebastian.

"This conversation is over," he said, softening his tone, but the command was unequivocal. "You can let yourself out."

Joan angrily strode to the door and opened it, but hesitated to leave. I hoped she knew better than to challenge him further. After a moment's pause, she gathered herself and left, gently closing the door behind her.

I waited respectfully until Sebastian asked for a report on the current defensive posture of the retreat. I made the presentation as brief as possible, for his benefit and for mine. Sometime earlier, I'd told Josh to meet me in the library. Normally I would expect to find him fuming at the delay, but I suspected that he and the rest of the pack had overheard the argument in the office.

On my way to the library, I noticed Sky in one of the recovery rooms, sitting next to Winter. Dr. Baker had moved her out of the clinic yesterday. Like Marko, she remained in a coma, for a few more days, at least. I hesitated, watching Sky's concern as she brushed a tangle of hair from Winter's eyes. A rush of emotions came over me in a confusing wash, guilt and admiration swimming in compassion and anger— mostly anger. I tore myself away before she could notice.

I found Josh slouched with his legs crossed in a leather club chair in the far corner of the library. At my arrival, he looked up from the large tome in his lap. "How are Joan and Steven?" he asked, concerned, as I leaned against the corner of a bookshelf and crossed my arms.

"They'll live."

He frowned at me, debating a snide remark, then shook his head as he closed the book.

"Any luck?" I asked.

"None. Given the limitations you'd dictated," he snapped. After his first attempt to remove the spell that blocked Dr. Yoshi's memory, he had nearly driven the doctor to cardiac arrest. I'd forbidden my brother from using potentially dangerous magic on the man. "If we're going to have any chance to identify our nemesis, you'll have to let me take the gloves off."

"The doctor is no good to us dead."

"You don't trust me." Josh buried his rising temper with a haughty chuckle. "How many times do I have to prove myself?"

"If you were certain how to break the spell, I'd accept the risk."

"Right now, he's the only chance we have to identify who this witch is," he pressed.

"We already know the witch has silver hair and purple eyes, and still we can't identify him. How much more detail can the doctor give us?"

"A name?"

"Probably false."

"Ethan, I know you've decided Yoshi was manipulated into creating the poison. That may be, but we don't know for sure. We can't know until we break that spell."

"Find a way that doesn't put his life at risk. We don't pass sentence before the trial." I watched as he ran a hand through his hair, then nodded. "Whatever game this witch is playing," I said, "he'll have to reveal himself."

"You'd think. None of this makes any sense, Ethan. Why the reprieve? Nothing has happened. Three days and there hasn't been any movement from these things, not a single attack."

Before I could answer, Sky tentatively stepped into the library, glancing between Josh and me as if waiting for a formal invitation. Josh brightened, offering her a warm smile. He was as caught in Sky's web as Quell was, I realized.

"Did you need something, Sky?" I asked dismissively, my tone sharper than intended.

She shook her head, but stubbornly held her ground, waiting for Josh to continue. I sighed. There wasn't any point in trying to dismiss her further.

"I just spoke with Chris," he continued, "and there hasn't been any activity with the vampires, either." His brow tensed as he laid an arm vertically over his chest and nibbled thoughtfully at one of his fingernails.

I was tired of not having answers. My hands turned slowly over each other as I paced the corner of the library.

After a moment, it occurred to me that the only possible source of information left to us, as unlikely as it seemed, was the Tre'ase Gloria. That she'd left town suggested that she knew something. Even if she hadn't returned, a more thorough search of her home might yield some clue. I turned to Josh in time to see him lean forward, as if he had an idea of his own. "You think we should—"

Josh nodded.

"Are you going to Gloria's?" Sky asked, surprising us both.

I didn't answer as I followed him out of the library, but I noticed her falling in behind us. Before I could deny her, he asked Sky, "Are you sure?"

She nodded.

I scoffed. *Once again, he just gives in to her, without any regard for the risk.* Like the rest of us, she seemed glad to have anything to do, but we had no idea what we would find at Gloria's. This time, we might well find a trap. I stopped, gripping Josh's arm to get his attention.

"That's not a good idea."

He shrugged his arm free, giving me a sideways look in the process. "It'll be fine. An extra person can't hurt."

I sighed, exasperated. Did she always get her way with everyone? "I assure you that around her finger is not a place you want to be," I snapped as I strode past them both.

"Perhaps you'll remember that advice when you find yourself twisted around Chris's!" she shouted after me.

I stopped short, entirely taken by surprise. Against my better judgment, I was taking Sky into a potentially dangerous situation simply because she wanted to go. My objection had hardly been unequivocal. I wasn't wrapped around Chris's finger, but perhaps when it came to Sky I wasn't any different than Josh or Quell. No matter how angry or how determined I was to keep Sky safe, inevitably I always gave in to what she wanted. And she didn't have a clue. It wasn't something she did—just something about her I couldn't put into words. I nearly laughed, but didn't want to give her the satisfaction. I turned, giving her a sharp glare, then continued on in silence.

Unlike our previous visit, Gloria's home was now protected by a powerful magical ward. I felt the vibration of it as I emerged from my SUV in the driveway. Was she home? The curtains remained drawn and the lawn appeared just as unkempt as it had at our last visit, but the mail had been collected. While I stopped at the edge of the ward, assessing its force, Josh obliviously passed through it—the advantage of being wholly human, though I was surprised he didn't sense the magic. Apparently Sky didn't sense the ward either, because she walked right into it, triggering a spray of gold and black embers as she was shoved back. She caught her balance, surprised and indignant.

Preferring not to draw her wrath, I kept my smirk to myself.

Josh hurried back from the house as she approached the ward once more, seemingly determined to force her way through sheer will. Black and gold embers appeared once more to warn her approach, this time accompanied by a shrill alarm-like sound. Josh intercepted her in time, gently encouraging her back a step.

He felt the boundaries of the translucent wall, then held his hands just against it and began an incantation. Glowing sparks flickered angrily against his hands, but he ignored them. After a moment, the ward began to moan as faint undulations spread through it, with Josh's hands as the epicenter. He continued until gold sparks began spreading like cracks through the invisible barrier. The incantation ceased, but Josh held his hands in place while he nodded for Sky to proceed.

It was hubris on his part. I could sense that the ward's

power was reduced, but far from broken. She leaned into the ward to push through, triggering a horrendous wail that could be heard throughout the neighborhood.

Josh frowned and doubled his efforts, but the wailing continued. At any moment the neighbors were going to investigate, and he showed no signs of resolving the ward soon. I strolled around the back of the house until I was out of sight, then touched my hand to the ward and broke it into a shower of purple sparks. The wailing ceased. Just as casually, I strolled back to the driveway, feigning surprise, then proceeded to the front door, giving Josh no chance to query me.

Even through the door, I could sense the intense power emanating from the house, the same power that had erected the ward. I glanced back to make sure Sky was behind Josh, then tested the door—surprisingly, it was unlocked. *Odd.* Gloria went through a lot of trouble putting the ward into place just to leave the front door unlocked for any human to waltz through. I tensed, prepared for anything as I pushed the door slowly open—and was immediately struck by the putrid stench of death that shocked my enhanced senses. Had I not developed an intimate relationship with that smell, it would've left me reeling. Behind me, Josh blanched, raising the collar of his t-shirt over his nose, while Sky pinched her nose shut.

Dark magic, I realized as I stepped inside. Josh seemed oblivious to it, for the moment. Following the stench, I found Gloria's corpse on the dining room floor. "She's dead," I announced, scrutinizing the room.

"Was she murdered?" Sky called after me from the doorway, worried.

I smelled the sweet scent of lemon and tea before I noticed the two cups on the dining room table: one empty, the other a quarter full.

"If so, it wasn't violent," I answered.

"It wouldn't have to be," Josh said as he slowly walked through the house with his arms away from his body, his hands splayed. "There is some really strong magic in here, powerful."

Gloria's death proved one thing—she was involved somehow, which meant she knew the silver-haired witch; she had also given him reason to kill her. After years of living in this house, her magic permeated every part of it. The ward wasn't her creation, and the magic Josh and I felt wasn't hers, either. Most likely the silver-haired witch came here to kill her, or to convince her of something; either way, it hadn't gone well for Gloria. Her death had been quick. From the position of her body, I guessed she'd gotten up to fetch something from the kitchen and been killed instantly. The witch had erected the ward on his way out to hide the killing. A human would've locked the door as well, but this witch didn't seem to think much about humans. Now we knew our witch was … something else.

CHAPTER 9

The next morning, I stopped at Beverly's Diner for breakfast on my way to the retreat. From the poorly maintained exterior and the no-frills interior that was more bar than restaurant, the diner gave the impression of a classic greasy spoon, but the locals knew better. Disillusioned with the misogyny that came with being one of the city's first female executive chefs, Beverly had left her culinary pretensions behind and opened a place closer to her heart—the kind of place a food snob would never notice. For her it wasn't about a creative menu. She just did the basics— really well. I'd probably driven by the diner a hundred times without batting an eye before Artemis had clued me in.

After a hearty breakfast of steak, house-made sausage, eggs, and a stack of pancakes, I checked the time. Claudia should have just opened her gallery. I considered visiting her in person, but I had a busy day ahead of me. Alone in my booth in the back of the restaurant, I called her. She answered almost immediately.

"Ethan," she said. I imagined her smile and smiled back. "Lovely to hear from you."

"Claudia, how are you?"

"I'm enjoying a delightful morning on my patio. I've decided to close the gallery for the day and take a stroll through the gardens at Grant Park. Why don't you join me?"

"Another time, unfortunately."

"Of course." I did my best not to burden her with my troubles, and she did her best not to ask. "What can I do for you?"

I glanced around me to make sure no one was within hearing. "I need to ask you about the Mouras," I said softly. "Can you talk?"

Her slight hesitation spoke volumes. "Yes. I'm alone." A Moura herself, my godmother protected a powerful mystical object known as the *Vitae*. Though she had never declared the subject off-limits, Josh and I knew not to ask of it, or of her responsibilities. The best-kept secrets were the ones forgotten. I'd only ever seen it once, at a time of great need.

I hated to ask, but I needed to understand the connection to Sky. "Can you give me the names of the other Mouras?"

"I'm afraid that's a complicated subject," she said dryly.

"My specific concern relates to the Aufero," I explained.

"That's been destroyed, dear."

"Yes, but it's come up in another matter." She didn't want to know more than necessary.

"You would like the name of the Moura who lost the Aufero?"

"Yes." I swallowed. "And the names of the others. The Gem was lost, and the Aufero. I'd like to verify that the other objects are safe as well. After the troubles last year, I don't want to run into any more surprises."

"This information is important to you?"

"Yes."

She considered for a long moment, but I waited. I had no intention of pressing the matter. "If I give you what you ask, you cannot contact these people in any form, Ethan. Do you understand? You cannot disrupt their responsibilities in any way, even for the protection of your pack."

"I understand."

There was another long pause before she finally gave me the names, which I memorized. "Thank you, Claudia."

"Yes. I'll talk to you another time, Ethan. Please call again when you don't need something from me."

She disconnected the call. I stared at my phone for a moment, feeling her disappointment, then called Stacy and put her on the names. Afterward, I paid my bill and left.

I began organizing my day as I strolled through the parking lot toward my SUV. I had my hand on the open door and my foot on the runner when I heard heavy feet pounding toward me from behind. A glance over my shoulder revealed one of the creatures, as tall as I was, just a few feet away, its long claws extended to strike. With only a sharp intake of breath to react, I pivoted on the runner, jumping back onto the front seat just before the creature slammed into the open door. I kicked the side of the creature's head with the heel of my boot. Unfazed, it climbed into the driver's seat after me as I scooted backward across the seat, reached behind me to push open the passenger door, then rolled backward out of the SUV and onto the concrete. The creature lunged across the seat, slicing air with its poisoned claws as I drew a knife from my boot sheath. As it came at me, I slashed at the hands and arms, drawing blood. The creature disappeared in an instant.

So it's back on. I knew the lull wouldn't last. *How many others are being attacked right now?* My thoughts immediately turned to Sky, until I heard more feet rushing up from my left. The knife still in my hand, I pivoted on my right foot, but this time my reaction wasn't fast enough. I felt the claws driving into my side as the creature slammed both of us into the open passenger door. Even though I felt the pressure of the claws stabbing into my flesh, my adrenaline blocked the pain, but that wasn't going to last. The creature snapped its claws free, then struck again. This time I dropped beneath the swipe, straight down to the concrete, and rolled under the door to the other side. By the time I was on my feet again, the creature rounded the door, driving me backward toward the busy street as it repeatedly threw its claws at me in wild, sweeping arcs. Realizing I'd lost the knife—probably when I'd struck the door—I glanced over my shoulder to gauge the street. Traffic was fast and heavy. The creature backed me all the way to the edge of the curb before I ducked under a swipe of its claws, just missing the backswing as I got behind it. When the creature turned to face me, I landed a flat-footed kick to its chest, knocking it stumbling back into the street—into the path of a loaded dump truck. The creature disappeared on impact.

I turned my back to the traffic, wary of another attack. When none came, I examined my wound. Blood soaked my shirt. Probing gingerly with my fingers, I knew the wound was bad. The poison was already inhibiting my body's healing ability. The blood wasn't clotting. I needed help. Fast.

The distant wail of an approaching siren started me stumbling toward the SUV while clutching the wound in an attempt to staunch the bleeding. I put my foot on the runner. When I put my weight on it to lift myself into the front seat, the pain came on in a rush. I made it groaning into the front seat and doubled over the steering wheel, growling and grimacing until I was able to shake off the pain. There wasn't time to waste. I needed to get to Dr. Baker at the retreat, where I'd soon be needed if there were more attacks. *Call Josh*, I thought, but quickly changed my mind. He could transport to me in an instant, but then he'd be vulnerable, and I wouldn't be able to help him if another creature appeared. Gritting my teeth against the pain, I started the engine, then pulled out into traffic.

. . .

A short time later I turned onto the private road that led to the retreat, not quite remembering the journey. *Blacking out. Not good.* I pushed the SUV as fast as I dared—too fast, the back of the vehicle drifting as I made my way along the narrow winding road. Finally reaching the house, I drove across the driveway and onto the lawn, braking to a sudden hard stop directly outside the front porch. The momentum bounced me off the steering wheel, sending a fresh jab of pain through my side. I gritted my teeth, bearing the pain for a moment before I could move. With my hand still over my wound, I could feel the flesh there was now burning hot. The poison was doing its work. I glanced down, tipping my hand from the wound, to see my palm quickly fill with blood.

I practically fell out of the SUV and stumbled inside. My brother appeared from nowhere, the color fading from his expression as he gaped at my condition. I straightened, trying to smooth my gait, but I wasn't fooling anyone. Rushing to my side, Josh draped my arm around his neck and helped me toward the clinic. My entire awareness became focused on completing each individual step without collapsing. Without Josh, I never would've made it.

As we approached the clinic, he tried to pull my hand from the wound, but I brushed his hand aside.

"Let me see it," he insisted.

"Of course I'll show you." I tried to smile, but the pain was too much. "As soon as you show me a medical degree."

He guided turned me into a treatment room where Kelly, in bright pink scrubs, was gathering antidote and other supplies. She seemed in a hurry until she saw me and helped him get me onto a table. The effort sent an unexpected stab of excruciating pain through my side.

"I'll get Dr. Baker," Josh said, turning away, but Kelly stopped him.

"He and Dr. Jimenez are working on the wounded. Help me slide him over."

Somehow I managed to center myself on the table. "How many?" I asked through gritted teeth as she cut the shirt from my wound.

"Six," she said, calmly professional as she examined the wound, wiping away the blood that should've clotted by then. *Fucking poison.* "Two died. I think we got to the other four in time."

Josh waited, wide-eyed and breathing rapidly while she quickly prepared a dose of the antidote. She pulled my shirt sleeve up and injected it into my shoulder. "The wound is fresh, so the antidote should take effect pretty quickly." Once finished, she tossed the empty syringe into a hazardous waste container, then retrieved and opened a packet of white powder directly into my wound to staunch the bleeding.

"What about—" Josh started until she politely but firmly guided him out of the room. "He'll be fine," I heard her say. She returned a moment later with a damp cool washcloth to dab the sweat from my face and forehead while I struggled with the pain.

"Do you want something?" she asked.

Yes. "No." I needed to stay alert. *If there's an attack on the retreat, I'll need to be involved.*

After a while, the pain began to subside. A sudden wave of exhaustion accompanied my relief. *Stay awake in case you're needed. Just focus on ... focus...*

I woke up a few hours later to find Josh hovering over me like a mother hen.

"How are you feeling?" he asked.

I wasn't one hundred percent, but I was close. "Fine. The others?"

"They'll make it. The vamps got hit as well."

He stepped aside as I eased up into a sitting position—not

without some discomfort, but it was tolerable. The wound was freshly bandaged.

"Chris got a sample of the creatures' blood," he announced. "Don't ask me how."

I wasn't surprised. She was a resourceful Hunter. "Did you source it?"

He scowled, frustration clouding his expression. "I took it to London. She said it's *unsourced.*"

"That's not possible."

"It takes very strong magic to hide the source of blood. Best guess, a Tre'ase might be strong enough. If not, I don't know what is."

"Gloria is dead." The only other Tre'ase in the area who could've disguised the blood was—

"Thaddeus," Josh said, finishing my thought.

I slid off the bed and started for the door. As he followed me, I stopped in the doorway, leaning against the frame as I glanced over my shoulder at him. "Stay here."

"I'm going with you," he insisted, tensing for an argument.

"Is Sky here?" I asked. He nodded. "Stay close to her in case there's an attack."

"The creatures have never attacked the retreat," he insisted, his tone tired, as if we'd had the argument a dozen times already. Or was he just tired of arguing with me in general? *Try listening for a change.*

"This could be the endgame," I warned him. "No telling what will happen. Josh, stay close to Sky. I'm trusting you to keep her safe. I'll call you if I need you."

"Like you did before?" he snapped.

Fair enough. "I will," I promised, then walked out to find my keys and get a change of clothes.

Someone had cleaned the blood from my SUV and parked it in the garage.

Finding Thaddeus's home was easy. Chris had done her best to keep the location secret, but I'd recorded our journey using the map application on my phone. Retracing our previous steps, I found the dead end easily. From there, finding his house was a matter of following the trail. It seemed the farther I walked, the quieter the forest became. When I came within sight of the house, I understood why.

The stench of death surrounded the small house. The front door was open, drifting slightly in the breeze. I hesitated just outside the door, listening for several minutes for any sound of movement or breath. The house was eerily quiet. Stepping inside, I knew what I was going to find, but I wasn't prepared for the severity of it. Were it not for Thaddeus's unusual features, I might not have recognized his grotesquely mutilated body on the floor of the kitchen. I had rarely seen a death so gruesome. His killer either hated him with a raw passion, or just plain loved killing.

Beneath the smell of death, I barely caught two other scents in the room. Chris. And Demetrius.

My phone vibrated. A text from Dennis. "She's at the underwear model's house."

I growled, striding out of the house in a fury. From what I'd gathered in my previous visit, Thaddeus was a gentle, shy creature that kept to himself. He'd trusted her. The Chris I once knew would've never allowed such pointless brutality. Did she need Demetrius's blood so badly that she'd stand by and watch Thaddeus be brutally murdered?

When I pulled into the driveway, her car was missing and Dennis's Cutlass was nowhere in sight. She hadn't yet returned, which irritated me further. After half an hour of angrily pacing in her yard, I remembered that I once had the keys to her house on my chain. Had she remembered to take them back? I fished my chain out of my pocket. There they were. If I had to wait, I was damn well going to wait inside. Perhaps a search might yield some insight into her relationship with Demetrius. Did he have something over her, or was it just the blood? How far was she willing to go? If she felt she needed his blood to do her job, then it was probably time for her to quit.

The key didn't work. *She changed the locks. Of course she did.* I sighed, resigned to wait outside. Presumably the key to the back door no longer worked, either. I didn't bother to find out.

Another text from Dennis. "She left. Really pissed off, too. Probably another dustup."

I waited for her in my SUV, running our impending argument through the various possible outcomes. The odds of talking some sense into her weren't good, but I was going to make a loud, argumentative effort. She needed to break Demetrius's hold on her and save something of her old self, before it was too late.

After a short wait, she parked her BMW next to me, glowering at me from the driver's seat with something like loathing. She emerged from her car, ignoring me as I stepped out of the SUV and followed her toward the door of the house. I was doing my best to hold my tongue until we were inside, but she came to a sudden stop before we reached the porch. Her shoulders rose and fell in an exaggerated sigh before she reluctantly turned to face me.

"You already know that Thaddeus is dead. Demetrius didn't have anything to do with it, and that is all I know," she stated with a tone of finality. When I followed her to the porch, she gave me a dour look, demanding, "Why are you here?"

I tossed her the pair of keys from my chain. "You changed the locks."

"Did you think I wouldn't?"

She didn't appreciate my concern. I accepted that, but she was going out of her way to be dismissive. "Bad day at the office?" I quipped. That's when I noticed the bloodstain on her shirt, the slight swelling of her lip, and the bruising around her throat that resembled the print of a hand. My jaw clenched along with my fists, and I felt the hot rise of anger flushing my cheeks.

"Demetrius and I had a *misunderstanding*," she explained, glancing aside as she made a half-hearted attempt to cover the marks on her throat with her hand before giving up. She opened the door with a resigned sigh and walked inside, leaving it for me to close behind me. She walked into a hall, heading toward her bedroom, but I wasn't letting her off so easily.

"Did you stake and behead him?" I asked expectantly, already knowing the answer would be disappointing. The blood belonged to Demetrius—she had no obvious wound—but it wasn't enough to suggest she'd finished the job. Most likely she'd given him a warning, which was far better than he deserved for laying a hand on her.

"No," she grumbled, then pivoted sharply on her heels. Her dark brown eyes narrowed into slits as she jabbed a finger at my face. "He better stay that way. Don't touch him." She glared for a moment, then walked into the bedroom and slammed the door behind her. A moment later, I heard her shower running.

In the years Chris and I had been together, our relationship had never evolved past the fighting. It was the one thing about us that I could always count on—that and the passion. That's what made being with her so easy and so frustrating. We fought and we screwed and we avoided actual intimacy like the plague. For a time, that had worked. Had she changed, or had I? Was that how I was with Sky? *No. Maybe.* Sky was different. We fought because she didn't know our world; she didn't know to trust me. Or maybe I fought with her to keep her at bay. I glanced down at the floor as I massaged the strain from my forehead.

Demetrius had laid his hands on Chris, and she'd let him live.

I gently turned the door handle and walked into her bedroom to find a trail of bloodstained clothes leading to the closed bathroom door. As much as I hated the thought, I couldn't rule out that her relationship with Demetrius was something more intimate than a simple blood trade. In that light, was her fight with him much different than her fights with me?

I never tried to kill her.

If she were accepting gifts from him, I would have my answer. I glanced about the bedroom, but I found nothing obvious. A quick search of her dresser drawers revealed nothing, either. I was so intent that I didn't hear the shower stop. I'd turned to lift her mattress—finding a pair of knives there—when I heard the click of the bathroom door.

Instinctively, I dropped the mattress and jumped onto the bed, posing supine with my arms folded behind my head and my ankles crossed. She emerged from the steamy bathroom wearing a towel wrapped around her curves. Finding me on her bed, she hesitated in the doorway and gave me a suspicious look. As I smiled back, I noticed a bra on the floor beside the dresser that hadn't been there prior to my search. Her gaze began to follow mine.

"There was a time," I blurted, drawing her attention, "when if you had a *misunderstanding* with a vampire, he wouldn't be around long enough for there to be another." I held her attention as I swung my legs over the side of the bed and stood.

"Those vampires weren't Demetrius," she snapped. "His status as the Master of the most ruthless Seethe in the country affords him more consideration."

"Are you sleeping with him?"

"Does it matter?" she asked, suddenly suspicious as she noticed something out of place but couldn't find it.

"If we are going to be together, then yes," I said, provoking her as I took one step closer to her, placing my foot on the bra.

She laughed, "Is there a *we*? And when has monogamy been important to you? You have always had a rather distant acquaintance with it."

"With you, I was always faithful—"

"Until you weren't." She dropped her towel as she stared at me, daring me to turn away. My gaze drifted unbidden over her glistening, almond skin. Images from our last night together assaulted my senses. My old passion for her stirred, threatening to overwhelm me until I noticed the web like scar on her abdomen—until she covered it by self-consciously pulling on a t-shirt from a dresser drawer. But she couldn't hide the bruises on her neck.

"Should we talk about the two bimbos?"

The accusation struck me like a slap. I held her gaze, surrendering nothing as I crossed my arms over my chest. *How did she find out? Was that the real reason she left me?* "It had been three weeks since you took that job. I asked you not to because it was too dangerous. For all I knew, you were dead." *I thought you were. Either that, or you just weren't coming back.*

"You have a strange way of grieving."

"And you overreacted, as usual."

A flash of irritation slowly melted into a broad, mischievous smile. "You pay that much for a car, you wouldn't think a little splash of brake fluid would ruin a custom paint job or a few licks with a tire iron would damage the body so much. And I thought the negative effects of sugar in the gas tank was simply a myth." White-hot anger raised the hairs on my skin as I glared down at her. Only ninety-nine of the '03 Aston Martin DB7 Vantage Zagatos had ever been built. I'd spent years obtaining one. I'd thought it was destroyed by a random act of vandalism—just punk kids making an incoherent statement. She'd even encouraged the idea! She'd destroyed the one thing I'd loved more than her and lied to me about it.

Attempting to distract me, she asked, "Have the witches contacted Josh?"

I held my ground for a moment, my jaw clenched so tightly I thought my teeth would fuse together. I unclenched my fists and flexed my fingers. When that wasn't enough, I forcibly swallowed my anger. *What's done is done,* I told myself. *No need to give her the satisfaction, now.* I couldn't let her get me off-balance.

"Why would they?" I demanded, wary that she was fishing for information. *Always scheming.*

"I have no idea what deal you have with them to keep Josh as an ally. But I assure you, as strong as Josh is, they are always aware of what is going on with him and your pack. If they aren't concerned, perhaps they are involved in the attacks."

I silently waited for her to offer more, but she held her tongue.

"Demetrius thinks of you as his," I said, changing the subject. *Sauce for the gander.* "You're his possession."

"Hmm, then you two aren't as different as I thought."

I gave her a wan smile. "The differences between the two of us are not by any means subtle. Don't ever compare me to that thing." Whatever faults she had, naïveté had never been among them. She was too far down the rabbit hole to make a clear assessment of her working relationship with Demetrius. I needed to get her away from him—give her time to come to her senses. "Quit. Come work for us."

"Switch teams in the middle of the game?" she scoffed. "Quite admirable of you to make such a request. I have ethics. Whether you approve of them or even understand them doesn't mean I don't have them. Go home."

The stray bra still trapped under my boot, I stepped closer, discreetly pushing the bra under the dresser. "Most

Hunters retire after five years because by the sixth year they have more enemies than allies, and by year seven, if they haven't retired, someone retires them for good. You've done this for nine years. Ryan, by all accounts, was exceptional," I admitted, anticipating her argument. "Seventeen years as a Hunter, before he came along, was unheard of." Despite all those extra years, he'd died the way all Hunters did, unless they got out. I admired her, but the warning signs were screaming; she'd reached her peak as a Hunter and was on the decline. "It's your time, Chris. Trading with Demetrius isn't helping you. You have more enemies than you have allies."

"What exactly do you propose I do?" she snapped. "The real world is just a little too vanilla for me. It won't let me capture the naughty, shoot or stab the deserving, and be an overall badass without a badge. Isn't there a distressed damsel somewhere waiting for your help, Ethan? Because I don't need it."

I scowled and walked out of the bedroom, pausing in the doorway. "I think you should retire and get a hobby," I said over my shoulder. "And for the record, being obstinate and bitchy isn't considered one." I left without looking back.

CHAPTER 10

*B*y the time I returned to the retreat, I realized I hadn't seen Dennis's Cutlass outside Chris's house. So far he had evaded her notice, which meant he was discreet, but he still had to keep her within his line of sight. I texted him for an update, then spent the next few hours working out my frustrations in the retreat's gym. Eventually, I was forced to concede that nothing was going to improve my mood. After a shower and a quick meal, I went to the library looking for Josh.

He wasn't alone. Sky was there as well. And Chris, which surprised me. *She's looking for information,* I realized. Nothing that happened between us was going to get in the way of her doing her job—an admirable quality, once. Now it was going to get her killed. Or worse. I frowned. *There's no shame in a tactical retreat.*

They continued their conversation, oblivious to my presence in the doorway.

"Witches detect one another's magic," Josh explained to Sky. "Like a fingerprint, it leaves a distinct mark. It is so strong that I can sometimes determine the witch that performed it."

"You were around the creatures for such a short time," Chris pointed out, "not nearly close enough to sense anything. How can you be so sure?"

"It doesn't matter, because Ethan was exposed—" Josh's mouth clamped shut as he saw me scowling in the doorway. Realizing he had said too much, he quickly turned his attention to his hands. "I just know," he insisted.

Following his previous gaze, the women spotted me in the doorway. Sky seemed intensely curious, while Chris's eyes narrowed in suspicion.

"Why does Ethan being around it have anything to do with it?" Chris asked, her eyes locked on mine. "Were-animals can't perform or detect magic."

I walked into the room. "He knows the witches are not involved. That is all the information you need." Before she could inquire further, I added, "That's all the information you will get. No more questions."

"No," she said, coldly insistent. "That's not enough. I need more."

"That's quite unfortunate for you."

She rose, sauntering toward me. "You will not shut me out. Tell me what you know."

She thought she could back me into a corner, the way she had trapped Josh. I grinned. "I'd like to see you make me."

We remained like that, posturing, until Chris finally rolled her eyes, made a dismissive sound, then walked past me out of the library. After making sure she wasn't lurking in the hall, I closed the door.

"Stop sleeping with her," Josh snapped, rising to meet me.

I scowled down at him. "This again? Are we advising each other on who we should or should *not* pursue now?" I glanced meaningfully toward Sky, but he was too riled up to notice.

"She's your Achilles' heel," he continued, "your weakness, and you don't seem to realize it."

"We aren't so inept that we would allow our other activities to compromise our ability to do our jobs. I do what is necessary and best for my pack—even if it called for eliminating her, and you know that."

"Those were just words," he stated, disappointed. "If anyone else would have threatened to kill us, betrayed the pack, and adamantly worked against us, like she did last year, what would you have done? You definitely wouldn't have warned them and given them a heads-up before dealing with them. But with her, you extended such courtesies."

I folded my arms over my chest, grimacing as I endured my brother's continuing tirade. If he hadn't slipped up in the first place, we wouldn't be having this conversation.

"The very reasons you find yourself drawn to her are the very things that will become *our* problem. She is smart, resourceful, and inquisitive." He lowered his voice, suddenly remembering Sky's presence, but he couldn't stop himself. "The flimsy excuses you have given me about your peculiar abilities won't be as easily explained away to her. Your secrets won't be your own anymore. When she knows, so will Demetrius. Once again, leave her alone."

I scowled. I didn't need my dirty laundry aired in public. Not in front of Sky. "I guess if I am too preoccupied with her to do what is necessary, then finally, you will have to. That will be quite interesting to see." I turned and left before he could reply.

I fumed as I patrolled the grounds, furious at my brother—but he wasn't wrong. My attraction to Chris was a weakness. Now that her curiosity about my abilities was piqued, she would be relentless in her pursuit of answers. Had it not been for his outburst, she would've remained clueless—a point he conveniently left out during his little tirade. *Not entirely clueless,* I corrected myself. In our time together, I'd given her a number of reasons to suspect my abilities. I'd gotten too close. I'd trusted her too much and let my desire for her blind me to the danger she represented. Last year, she'd endangered the pack by working with the Seethe to capture Sky. Chris had threatened to kill my brother, and I'd let her live. I should've killed her. If she'd been anyone else, I would have. Instead, I'd let her live. Eventually she was going to discover the truth about my abilities. No doubt, she would put that knowledge to use against me. She was going to put the pack in danger, once again, and any risk to the pack was a risk to Josh and Sky. At what point, I wondered, had my devotion to the protection of my family and my pack taken second seat to my desires?

I clenched my fists, gritted my teeth, and growled, straining every muscle in my upper body until I ran out of breath. I couldn't just erase my feelings for Chris. I still cared about her. We didn't belong together, but I couldn't just watch her become Demetrius's toy, either. She was on a path of self-destruction. The sooner I put some distance between us, the better, but that couldn't happen until we solved the mystery of these attacks—unless I convinced her to retire, first. *Unlikely.*

There was Quell to worry about as well. I accepted that he fed on his plant instead of humans, but I'd hardly call that admirable. He was a vampire. No matter how hard he worked to hide from that, one day his plant would fail him and his true nature would come rampaging to the surface. I'd seen too often the bloody mess left behind by a were-animal that had finally succumbed to its animal nature after years of resistance. Quell would be no different. If the only way to save Sky was to show her his true nature, I would need to expedite the inevitable.

Upon my return to the house, I was called into Sebastian's

office, where Josh and Gavin were already waiting. My brother's eyes were darkly intense as he nervously chewed on his nails.

"Josh has a plan," Sebastian said as I closed the door.

"We need a meeting with the vampires," Josh explained. "Not like last time. Just their best hunters."

"A public meeting would be dangerous for civilians," I said. Given the intensity of the latest attacks, we had to assume that any large gathering of our kind might draw a significant attack—the kind we didn't want to occur in public. "And we're not going to the Seethe." Regardless of the alliance, we would be walking into a trap Demetrius couldn't resist springing.

"I have a plan for that, too," Josh answered, straightening. "We're going to invite them here."

The vampires had never been invited into the retreat for a reason. Once invited, they could enter at will. The retreat would become vulnerable. The idea was preposterous. I turned to Sebastian and saw the resignation in his expression. The argument had already been made, I realized. I turned to Gavin. For once, I shared his anger.

"I can revoke their invitation after the meeting," Josh explained in a rush. "But it's a complicated spell. I recommend waiting until the crisis is over."

I growled, shaking my head. "This is an unnecessary risk."

"We need the vampires, Ethan. I think I can get us some answers, but I need one of those creatures, the sooner the better. Whatever else they are, the vampires are experienced hunters. It would be irresponsible not to take advantage of their skills."

"Chris gave you the creatures' blood. You weren't able to source it."

"It's not the blood I need," he said, his eyes brightening with excitement. "I'm going to source the creature itself."

There was no use in arguing. Judging by Sebastian's

resigned expression, he didn't like inviting the vampires into our home any more than I did, but he'd made his decision.

"They'll be here at dusk," Sebastian said.

"I hope you thought this through," I warned my brother. "If this goes wrong, it's on you." I strode out of the room. As I made my rounds through the house, I felt the walls closing in as every possible stress exerted itself.

At the end of my rounds, I caught the strong scent of peppermint drifting from Winter's recovery room, just across from the clinic. Kelly and Dr. Baker had done their best to create the appearance of a bedroom, even going so far as to paint the customary white walls with an earthy tone. Nature-themed pictures dotted the walls except for the far one, which was dominated by a large TV. Next to a cherrywood nightstand, Winter's large hospital bed was draped with a floral duvet. Despite their best efforts to make the room comfortable, it was still filled with various medical equipment, and several IVs connected to her arms.

Sky sat next to Winter, braiding her hair while Kelly changed the television channel to some melodrama. When she saw Sky's surprise, Kelly touched a finger to her lips and whispered, "It's her guilty pleasure. Let's just keep it between us girls."

I shook my head and walked away.

Seeing the vampires stroll smugly and freely through the halls of the retreat made me ill with anger. That Josh could revoke their invitation as soon as our alliance was at an end didn't matter. Their presence here was a violation.

We gathered in the conference room, where the table and chairs had been cleared away—no need to make the vamps comfortable; they would be out of the house as quickly as possible. Chris stood next to Demetrius on the far side of the room, going out of her way to ignore me. Sebastian had allowed Sky's presence, over my objection. A year ago, she had played a front and center role in spoiling Demetrius's scheme. It was possible he might still hold a grudge against her. I didn't see the point in offering him such a stark reminder of his failure, but Sebastian had decided otherwise. He was hoping that including her would bring her closer to accepting his invitation to join the pack.

She lingered at the back of the room, leaning against the wall and trying not to be noticed as the vamps settled in on the far side of the room. Unlike the previous meeting at the restaurant, where our alliance was formed, only eight vamps were here. Their presence at the restaurant had been a show of force. This was a business meeting.

I tensed as I noticed Michaela's attention fixed on Sky, peering through the crowded room of vampires and were-animals to single her out with a cold, predatory stare. Sky tried to ignore Michaela, but her discomfort was obvious in the way she shifted, her eyes darting about but repeatedly returning to the vampire that had briefly captured her a year ago. Only Josh's intervention had saved her from Michaela's notorious lust for torture and brutality.

I was about to put the Mistress in her place when Michaela turned and gave me her most innocent smile. I folded my arms over my chest and glowered.

Josh frowned as he glanced about for Gavin, who wasn't present. Given his propensity for causing trouble, I didn't mind. The room was tense enough without throwing in a lit stick of dynamite. Sebastian, just as irritated as Josh, shrugged and nodded.

He strode to the center of the room and waited as the vamps and were-animals slowly quieted to hear what he had to say. He cut an odd figure; one of the most powerful witches in the country commanding attention while wearing baggy jeans and a bright blue t-shirt with the Sesame Street characters posed on the front, displaying in black writing: I WAS RAISED ON THE STREET. Demetrius sneered in revulsion at Josh, while the rest of the vamps appeared amused and unimpressed.

"Nice shirt." Chase grinned as he leaned against the wall.

Just as Josh was about to speak, Gavin decided to make a grand entrance. His cold glare passed over the vamps like a rude warning as he sauntered to the back of the room. For their part, the vamps barely regarded his arrival, except for Sable, a young vampire with parchment-like skin, who followed his every move with a childlike wonder. Possibly sensing her attention, he turned to meet her gaze. Instead of receiving the warning his look intended, she rushed toward him like a child going for a cookie jar. Had Quell not reached out and pulled her to him, Gavin would've killed her without hesitation.

Before Chase had turned her at the age of nineteen, Sable had already earned her reputation as a callous, ruthless killer. Her parents and sister had been murdered in a home invasion, leaving her an orphan. Despite her youth, she'd showed an unusual dedication, taking two years to track down the murderers, who had eluded the police. Rather than kill them outright, she'd made them watch as she'd assembled, tortured, then murdered their friends, family, children, and anyone they cared about. Then she'd let them grieve and suffer until she'd finally killed them. Her lack of remorse during the very public trial that had followed was notorious.

It wasn't surprising that she'd drawn the attention of Gabriella and Chase, who staged her death in order to rescue her from prison to become their psychopathic protégé.

"Sable." Quell tried to soothe her, but she remained mesmerized by the were-panther. He repeated her name, finally drawing her attention. She smiled, as if his presence were a welcome surprise.

"Quell." She rose up on her toes to kiss him on the lips—a hungry, lurid kiss that apparently passed for platonic among vampires. The were-animals in the room shifted uncomfortably. None of us wanted to endure the vampires' perversions. "It's a were-panther," she exclaimed, breathless. "I've never had one of them before. Look at him. He's so beautiful." She absently laid her head against Quell's chest while her attention remained fixed on Gavin. "I want him."

Gavin made no effort to discourage her interest. Sable presented him with an opportunity to throw our alliance into chaos. All he needed was for her to attack. Despite her reputation for violence and cruelty, which had only grown since she'd become a vampire, she was no match for him. He would kill her easily. And he would enjoy it. If she initiated the attack, he would be well within his rights to do so, but the alliance would likely come to an end—possibly in violence.

"Yes, he is quite intriguing," Quell acknowledged. "Do you remember the mean wolf that you despise?" Her genteel face puckered as she nodded. I wasn't sure who he meant. "The panther will be a hard one to feed from. Compared to him, the mean one is as gentle as a pup."

Her bottom lip extended into a pout, but she allowed him to guide her to the other side of the room. He sat on the floor near Michaela and drew Sable next to him. She lay with her legs propped on him, regarding Gavin as Quell kneaded her legs.

"I have her," he informed Chase.

As I leaned against the wall, arms folded over my chest, I noticed Kelly trying to blend into the corner of the room. She watched what transpired with a delighted, secretive smile. I bit back a curse. This was no place for her. Until now, she'd never even seen a vampire. She had no idea how dangerous it could be to attract their attention. Her fearlessness among were-animals made her an asset, but it also made her vulnerable. Judging by the tension in Sebastian's shoulders, he'd noticed her as well, but was trying not to draw attention to her.

Demetrius, on the other hand, made no attempt to disguise his curiosity. Under his dark gaze, her heart rate quickened, drawing the attention of the rest of the vamps. He listened intently, closing his eyes as he slowly tilted his head back as if he were being lulled into ecstasy. After a moment, he opened his eyes, his piercing stare intently focused on Kelly. He inhaled, drawing in her scent, and smiled—an easy, innocent smile, the kind I imagined he used to put his prey at ease just before he killed them. It was working. She seemed mesmerized, unblinking as she returned his stare. I tensed, as did Sebastian and every were-animal in the room. Before either of us responded, Demetrius violently ripped his gaze from hers. His body was rigid, straining, as he cast his eyes to the floor in an attempt to stave off his bloodlust.

Kelly's gaze, however, remained transfixed as she chewed on the left side of her lip. Her breathing became ragged. Caught in a panic she seemed unable to escape, she started forward—not toward him, but toward a young, unfamiliar vamp next to him.

"Stop it. Now!" Josh shouted at the vamp, who ignored him.

Sebastian charged, but Demetrius reached the grinning vampire first, taking him by the throat and driving him back against the wall. I saw the stake in Demetrius's hand just before he drove it into the surprised vampire's heart. In his rage, he drew a knife and finished the job, brutally decapitating the vamp, who collapsed to the floor in a pile of dust.

Josh intercepted Kelly, anxiously gazing into her eyes as he held her face between his palms, then leaned close and whispered an incantation to break the charm. Freed from the vamp's grip, she began to tremble, tears filling her eyes as she tried to make sense of what had happened to her. Steven gently escorted her from the room. On her way out, she glanced back at the vamps with revulsion.

Sebastian remained like a tense statue in the middle of the room, glaring at Demetrius as he stood over the ashes. Sebastian's fists were clenched. The muscles of his neck were rigid. Only his principles kept him from violating the truce and killing Demetrius.

"We are not here for games or to indulge our desires," he announced. "Our Seethe is being hunted like animals and I won't tolerate anything but compliance until the person responsible is found and punished. If you don't behave, there will be consequences."

His speech did little to ease the tension in the room. If anything, we'd just been reminded how precarious our alliance with the vampires was. They were slaves to their bloodlust. Even Demetrius, with his power and experience, could barely stop himself from preying upon Kelly. I glanced at Sky, wondering if I should escort her from the room, but I didn't want to draw attention to her. And she wouldn't go willingly. I glanced at Quell. Hopefully she'd learned something.

Demetrius ignored Sebastian as he flippantly gestured to Josh. "You have our attention. Get on with it."

"I have a task for you all," Josh said, glad to move on. "I need one of the creatures. But I need it alive and unharmed." The disappointment in the room was palpable as he continued, "Those of you who have killed or injured one realize that they disappear when injured. That is why I need it alive."

"For what?" Demetrius inquired.

"To source the creature. To track it back to its creator."

"And you can do this?" he asked, his brow rising with interest. When Josh nodded, Demetrius told Sebastian, "He's more gifted than I imagined."

I frowned at the vamp's newfound interest in my brother, but I knew when Josh had asked to arrange the meeting that we wouldn't be able to hide him from Demetrius's attention any longer. Up to now, he'd known Josh was a witch, but to Demetrius witches were a dime a dozen. Now Josh had done worse than display his talents—he'd impressed the Master of the Northern Seethe.

"Yes, he is an asset, one that we are happy to have," Sebastian stated, letting the vamp know that Josh was protected by the pack.

"Whoever's successful," Josh continued, "bring the creature back here."

The vamps started toward the door when Josh declared, "You should pair up, vampire with were-animal."

The room grew quiet.

"Why?" Gabriella asked.

"With the were-animals, the creature shifts to match their appearance," he explained. "I assume it does the same with you all. Shifting, no matter how strong the magic is, can be difficult. If it has to shift quickly and too often, it will be easier to apprehend. We agreed to help each other," he said, cutting off several complaints, "which is an impressive sacrifice by both parties. Not much of a sacrifice if you never really deal with one another, now is it?"

"Of course," Gabriella said tersely.

"I think that's a grand idea," Michaela exclaimed with an impish smile. "Confuse the creature. One could only imagine how it would respond if we complicated the equation even more. Perhaps adding a human would improve our chances." Her mischievous regard shifted from Chris to Demetrius, who seemed indifferent.

Chris gave no reaction, either. She wanted to be a part of the hunt, but she had to know Michaela was putting her out there as bait, punishment for Demetrius's interest. Michaela was looking for revenge. I wondered if he would object, but she'd really left him no choice.

"That is a strategy worth considering." He nodded.

"Or perhaps adding her would further endanger whoever she's with," I said gruffly, earning a sharp glare from Chris that I ignored. "This isn't her fight."

"Ethan, you're insulting her as well as underestimating her skills," Michaela said. "If nothing else, she is efficient in wiggling herself in and out of all types of complicated situations, aren't you?"

Chris answered with a forced, polite smile and a perfunctory nod.

I scowled at the two women, irritated to be drawn into Michaela's game, but there was nothing I could do to stop either of them. "Fine," I conceded, "then she partners with me."

"If I am not mistaken, the last time she *partnered* with you, her shoulder was dislocated," Demetrius snapped. "Perhaps she would fare better if she was partnered with someone more capable of making sure she isn't harmed."

"Well, if your comfort with the situation is of utmost importance, perhaps I should demonstrate how capable I am of keeping her safe." I pushed myself from the wall.

"Perhaps you should," he declared, walking toward me.

"Gavin," Chris shouted, drawing our attention, "do you mind if I tag along with you?" Her face was flushed with anger.

"There aren't too many things that would make me happier," he agreed, glancing in my direction.

"Look at that," Michaela said, pleased as punch. "It's settled then. Josh, would you care to do the honors of pairing us off?"

"I don't think it really matters. I asked that you invite your strongest and most skilled. Pair as you like."

"Then I choose Gabriella," Gavin announced. Chase bared his fangs, drawing a smug smile from Gavin. He knew the vamp had a notorious temper.

"I choose Michaela," I declared, surprising everyone. She noted Demetrius, fuming, and gave me an intrigued nod.

The pairing off continued with some groans and complaints. When finished, the vamps left to feed before the hunt. As they departed, Gabriella guided Sable toward the door. Her attention remained transfixed on Gavin, as had been the case the entire meeting, until she reached the door. She turned away and was halfway through the door before she twisted from Gabriella's grip and lunged at him. As if expecting the outburst, he calmly stepped around her lunge and grabbed her from behind. One of his hands wrapped around her throat while the other wrapped around her forehead, pulling her head back into his chest. One simple gesture would snap her neck.

The room stilled. Every gaze focused on the pair—none more frightened than Gabriella and Chase.

"She attacked me," Gavin stated, a calm thrill in his voice. He'd gotten what he'd wanted. He looked to Sebastian, daring him to stop him. As Alpha, Sebastian could intervene, but he would appear weak before the vamps as well as the other were-animals. His hands were tied. That didn't mean there wouldn't be consequences for Gavin later. He was putting the pack's safety at risk to satisfy his own desires.

"Do as you see fit," Demetrius declared, surprisingly indifferent to Sable's fate.

That's one way to get rid of a problem child. The rumors that Sable had been turned without his approval seemed to be true.

"Please don't," Gabriella pled softly, her concern genuine. Chase stood next to her, his expression fearful as they waited in horror for Gavin's judgment. He wasn't known for mercy. It wasn't often those two faced a fear they couldn't kill.

He held her close, enjoying every moment of their despair. Chase remained relatively calm next to Gabriella, who was near hysterics. The tense standoff seemed to last forever before Gavin surprised everyone by releasing his hand from Sable's neck. His stared hard at Gabriella and Chase as he purposefully turned his wrist, offering it to Sable.

"Go ahead," he encouraged her.

She hesitated, suspecting a trap.

He brought his wrist to her lips. "Do it," he urged.

Cautious at first, she wrapped her fingers around his forearm, parted her lips, and sank her fangs into his flesh. He allowed her to feed, seemingly bored despite the pain.

"Sable, that's enough," Gabriella anxiously insisted after a long moment.

"She's okay," he said softly. "I'll stop her if I need to."

Sable continued greedily for another moment, then reluctantly withdrew her fangs, giving Gabriella a gleeful, bloody smile.

"Don't leave me marked," he instructed her. She happily sealed the wound, bathing his wrist with her tongue for much longer than was required. He released her, matching her steady gaze as she walked backward toward Gabriella.

"You've had a were-panther now," he calmly proclaimed. "Don't attack me again, because if you do, it won't end so favorably next time. I will kill you. It will be the most painful thing you will ever experience. And if you *call* me at any point, you will suffer the same fate."

Sable answered with a demure smile, her lips still bright with his blood, clearly more enamored than before. Gabriella nodded graciously.

"Sable," Demetrius snapped, disappointed. "Do you understand?"

She tore her attention from Gavin just long enough to acknowledge Demetrius, then was hustled out the door by Gabriella.

CHAPTER 11

The search areas were determined according to locations where the creatures had previously attacked or been spotted. Michaela and I strolled the woods near Thaddeus's home. She paused, as if noticing something for the first time, then lifted her chin and took a long, leisurely sniff of the night air. Her lips spread into a delighted smile.

"Hmm. Death."

"Thaddeus," I said matter-of-factly. His body remained in the house, the scent of decomposition drawing the predators who would eventually pick the bones clean of flesh.

"A friend of yours?" she asked, slyly hopeful.

"Gloria's son."

"How disappointing."

We continued for some time, silently traipsing between the trees, deliberately snapping twigs and crunching leaves to draw as much attention as possible. The Mistress of the Seethe walked beside me in a delicate t-shirt that clung to her thin frame and worn jeans that hung from her hips.

"If I don't have something to kill soon," she said, "I just might die of boredom."

"We're not here to kill," I chided her. "If you draw blood from a creature, it will disappear and we'll lose our chance to capture it."

"You're no fun." Her lips twisted into a mocking pout. "If this goes on much longer, I might need a snack."

"You *ate* before the search began."

"Did I?" She frowned. "I suppose I won't find much out here, anyway. Nothing I'd enjoy. It's a shame playgrounds don't have late-night drive-throughs."

Michaela's appetite for children was notorious. For a moment, I considered killing her.

"If it hadn't been for your little wolf," she continued, "Demetrius would've completed his ritual and I'd be able to visit any playground I wished in the middle of the day, when all the little darlings are laughing and playing their sweet little hearts out."

"I would never allow it," I growled.

"Oh, you would. Even if you could stop me. All you wolves care about is yourselves. As long as your precious pack remained outside human purview, you'd tolerate anything. You're not much different than we are. You like a bloody steak just like we do; you just buy yours at the grocery store."

I ground my teeth. "We are nothing like you."

Thankfully, for a few minutes she remained silent, the corners of her lips progressively drooping into a bored frown until she sighed audibly.

"Just how long must I endure this?" she asked.

"This alliance represents the Seethe's interests as much as the pack's," I reminded her.

"When vampires hunt with dogs, they use leashes," she said with an acerbic tone.

"You don't approve."

"Nothing personal. You're an inferior species. It's certainly not your fault. Demetrius simply spends too much

183

time with your kind, as well as the fae. And his human. He forgets himself. He was glorious, once; feared by all," she said wistfully. A malignant, secretive smile spread across her lips. "One day he'll remember. He just needs a little … motivation."

I remained silent for a moment while I weighed the cost of snapping her neck. She was baiting me. She didn't want our alliance any more than Gavin did. I needed to be careful.

"I selected you for a reason," I said, eventually.

She placed a hand on a broken tree branch as she steered around it. "For my waifish charm, I assume."

"We have a shared problem."

"Do we?" she asked, genuinely surprised. "Finally tired of your fellow were-animals, or just your little wolf? I wish you would've told me before dinner."

I answered with a baleful glare as I stepped on a twig, snapping it in two. "She and your creation have an *unhealthy* fascination with each other."

Michaela thought for a moment, her head bobbing slightly as she stepped around a large rock. "He sees something in her. I admit I am at a loss as to what. When I see that lovely little heart-shaped face I want to crush it between my palms and drink from her skull. Perhaps you could enlighten me. What is it about her that makes men stupid?"

I stopped to glare down at her, balling my hands into fists and squeezing until my knuckles cracked. "Tell him to stay away from her."

"Quell is free to do as he wishes, just as he's free to incur my displeasure. Honestly, I don't know why you don't just keep that pup of yours in a kennel."

As my jaw clenched, I felt my teeth grind together until I tore my gaze from her. In her, every quality I despised about vampires was on display. More than their passion for senseless violence, they loved their games. I didn't need her to deal with Quell, but her cooperation would simplify matters. I decided to try a different tack. "He abhors blood. That doesn't bother you?"

"It's part of his charm. I allow his plant because his choice fascinates me."

"He favors human life over his own kind."

She scoffed. "Quite the opposite, I assure you. My Quell is an accomplished killer."

"But he doesn't take part in the usual … pleasure."

Her lips clamped together in a thin smile. "If you have a point, I'd be delighted for you to make it."

I smiled, pleased at finally getting under her pale skin. "It would be in our mutual interest to discourage their acquaintance."

"You're worried that he'll break his vow to foreswear blood and kill your little wolf. Allow me to put your mind at ease. None of our vampires will harm your little wolf."

"You think I'm going to accept your word?"

"When the time comes, her blood is mine, silly," she said cloyingly, sending a cold chill down my spine. "Everyone knows that I've claimed her."

I stopped, but she continued ahead of me, oblivious as I drew a knife from the sheath at my thigh. Taken by a sudden rage, I couldn't stop myself as I strode toward her, knife poised to strike up into the back of her skull, scrambling her brains and incapacitating her while I sliced off her neck, but I didn't get the chance.

A creature burst from the darkness on my right and tackled me to the ground. Fighting from my back, I managed to evade the initial stab of its claws, then kicked the creature back a step. Before it could answer, Michaela leapt onto its back. It threw her off easily, dropping her back-first onto an exposed boulder. She let out a stifled cry as she landed, but gathered herself in time to roll away from a rake of claws that scraped stone. I drew the tranq pistol from its holster but hesitated as the creature pressed her, forcing her to dodge and counter from the ground as it relentlessly attacked.

Let her die. I considered it for just a moment, but I doubted Demetrius would believe that I didn't have a hand in her death. I growled as I fired two of the darts at the creature, striking it in center mass with both. It stumbled back toward me, giving Michaela a chance to rise to her feet. The cloying sweetness was gone from her expression, leaving nothing but a raging killer eager for vengeance.

"No!" I shouted, but too late.

As the creature fell back, succumbing to the tranquilizer, she grasped one of its massive hands between her own, twisted the wrist, then drove its claws into its own chest. It disappeared instantly, leaving her growling over a flattened patch of dirt.

"Dammit!" I shouted at her.

She glowered up at me and then disappeared, leaving me to vent my fury to the trees in a string of expletives.

When I returned to the retreat, I found Chris in the main room, sitting on the edge of a chair, absently hunched over a steaming cup of coffee between her palms. Her cheeks were drawn, her visage gaunt as she blankly stared at a wall, oblivious to my arrival. I'd never seen her so lost. Before I could approach her, Gavin walked into the room, offering her a nasty scowl.

She drew herself upright, prepared to answer some unspoken accusation, but her mouth snapped shut when she noticed me on the other side of the room. She glanced at the coffee, then set it down and strode out of the room.

I turned on Gavin for an explanation.

"Your girlfriend lost her shit out there," he snapped.

"Explain."

His scowl deepened. "One of the creatures morphed into

something she didn't like. She froze. If it wasn't for me, she'd be dead."

"Morphed," I said tightly, "into what?"

"A man with black hair. Had a scar." With a finger he traced a line down his right cheek.

Ryan? How is that possible? Are the creatures reading our thoughts, now? Up to then, they had appeared to morph into whomever they were attacking, often confused by the presence of more than one target. Had their abilities evolved?

I started out of the room when Gavin called after me, "When we hunt tomorrow, I suggest she stays home, unless you want to babysit her. I don't need that crap."

After a quick search I realized that Chris had left the retreat. Not surprisingly, she didn't return my call.

Still no response from Dennis. Before the meeting with the vamps, I had left him a message to stop following Chris until further notice. I didn't want him following her onto the retreat grounds, and I didn't want him anywhere near Demetrius and the Seethe. He didn't respond to me, either. Once again, I wasn't surprised.

The next night, Michaela didn't show up for the hunt. I continued without her, but gave up shortly after midnight. By the time I returned to the retreat, Sebastian had returned as well. Gavin had not, which meant Chris was still out there. For all his bluster, he hadn't complained when she'd joined him.

I walked the grounds, calming my nerves as I waited for their return. *She's a professional,* I reminded myself. I worried for Chris, anyway. That she could be so shaken by a reminder of her old mentor was another sign that her effectiveness as a Hunter was slipping. *She loved him.* She'd never confessed her feelings to me, but I suspected it. I knew she blamed herself for his death.

Gavin called an hour later. "We've got one," he announced. "On our way." He hung up before I could ask if any of them had been hurt.

At the house, I found Josh had fallen asleep in the library with his boots on a table and a book in his lap, snoring obnoxiously. I knocked his boots from the table, waking him. "They're coming," I said, then found Sebastian.

When the SUV parked in the driveway a few minutes later, I hurried outside with Sebastian and Steven, while Josh held open the front door. His excitement was palpable. The doors to the SUV swung open. Gavin and Chris emerged to join us at the back of the vehicle while Gabriella slipped away to watch from a distance.

Growling and grunting could be heard from the back, followed by the metallic thump of flat feet pounding the inside of the hatch. Peering through the window alongside Chris, I saw the creature was bound at the ankles, its wrists bound behind its back.

"So much for sleeping beauty," Chris said, drawing her tranquilizer pistol as she took a step back, waiting for me to open the hatch. I raised an eyebrow at her. *Ready?* She nodded, bracing the pistol with both hands in front of her.

"Don't draw blood," Sebastian warned her.

"I'll try not to shoot it in the eyeball. Other than that, I can't make any promises."

I snatched the hatch open and she fired two darts in quick succession, striking the creature twice in the chest. The tranquilizer took effect almost immediately. Once the creature was asleep, Gavin pulled it toward the edge of the hatch, then reached beneath its arms and wrapped his arms around its chest. I reached for the legs, but Chris brushed me aside to do the job herself.

"I got it," she snapped.

I could hear the gleeful racing of Josh's heart as they carried the creature past him into the house. Sebastian, Steven, and I followed closely, wary of trouble. The dosing of the tranquilizer was a guess, at best. We had no idea how long the effect would last, or how deeply. Any jarring motion might wake it. Fortunately it remained unconscious as Chris and Gavin jostled it downstairs to the cage reserved for just such an occasion that occupied a large portion of the cellar. The creature was too strong for the locked rooms upstairs. I wasn't entirely sure the bars of the cage would hold, either, but if the creature escaped, it would be surrounded, and contained.

"Good job," I said as I stepped in to help guide the body through the open cage door. Once the thing was placed inside, Chris reached in with a knife and cut its bonds. I didn't like the idea, but she acted too quickly for me to stop her.

Josh locked the cage door, and Gavin wasted no time jogging up the stairs. "I'm out," he announced, then disappeared past Gabriella, who watched scowling at us from the top of the stairs, clearly uncomfortable alone in a house filled with were-animals.

"I'll take my leave as well," she said politely, then followed him.

Josh immediately set to preparing his magic, distracted only by Sky when she appeared on the stairs. He gave her a welcoming smile. Of course he did. If the creature managed to escape, Sebastian, Steven, Chris, and I were there to contain it. Sky's presence only served to put her at risk, but there was little I could do to deny her. Sebastian had included her in the hunt, and then Josh thoughtlessly invited her to witness the ritual he was about to perform.

I positioned myself between her and the creature, standing next to Chris, who didn't notice as she stared into the cage. Chris's eyes grew distant and the corners of her mouth bent into a frown as she seemed increasingly absorbed in her thoughts. Glancing between her and the creature, I wondered if she was waiting for it to once more morph into Ryan.

Eventually, she noticed Sky, scrutinizing her and glancing between her and me. My agitation only piqued Chris's curiosity as she gave Sky a long, searching look. *Another reason to get her out of the room.* The less she attracted Chris's attention, the better. I was pretty certain that she'd noticed Sky's terait on at least one occasion. The small orange mark in the corner of her eye was an indicator of bloodlust in a vampire—an unusual occurrence in a were-animal. Chris wasn't the type of person to let such oddities go unexplored.

The two women held each other's gaze for a long moment before Sky, shifting uncomfortably, turned her attention to Josh and the slumbering creature.

"What happened last night?" I asked Chris. It was a conversation I'd intended to save for a private moment, but I figured a room full of ears would only piss her off, which was one way to get her attention from Sky. "Gavin told me you froze when the creature morphed into Ryan." She gave me a hard, weighted look, then turned back to Sky with an intensified curiosity. Sky, meanwhile, pretended not to notice, but I saw the uncomfortable shift in her posture. So did Chris.

A groan from the cage distracted us. Chris drew the tranq pistol and checked to make sure it was loaded, while I checked the lock on the door, but the creature remained on the floor, dazed. I looked to Josh, encouraging him to speed up his efforts. When he began his spell a moment later, the creature was jarred alert. In a desperate bid to reach him, it leapt to its feet and charged, rattling the cage as it struck the bars. Both arms shot between the bars and slashed at him, but Josh was well out of reach. His concentration remained unbroken as he continued the spell.

Grunting and growling in frustration, the creature

gripped the bars in its massive claws and tried pulling them apart. The cage seemed to be holding, but I moved closer to my brother just in case, careful to remain out of reach of the creature's claws.

Eventually, it noticed Sky. Its struggles ceased in an instant as it stared at her, almost disbelieving. After a moment, it let out a hissing sigh, then morphed into a humanoid creature with scaled, jet-black reptilian skin. From its dark, gaping maw it hissed, "Maaayyyyaaaa."

Josh remained unfazed, while Sebastian and I exchanged wary looks.

"Maaayyyyaaaa," it hissed once more, this time in a high, whining pitch.

I could see the curiosity burning in Chris's eyes as she stared, fixated on Sky.

Sky took one sideways step down the stairs, as if drawn to the creature, then hesitated. Her fingers were splayed at her side, twitching as she seemed to struggle.

"Maayyaa!" the creature screamed in a joyous, desperate plea, then stepped back, raised both hands, and stabbed its claws into its stomach. A moment later, it yanked its claws free, drawing out a spurt of blood that streaked the floor of the cage.

"No!" Josh yelled, finally distracted from his spell. Before I knew it, he was unlocking the cage.

"What are you doing?" I yelled, reaching for him too late as he charged inside the cage to somehow prevent the creature from disappearing. "Get the hell out of there!"

Before I could reach Josh, the creature slashed his arm. Oblivious to the wound, he gripped its arm and began to chant. His eyes became opaque. The lights in the cellar blinked erratically. A moment later, they shut off altogether, leaving us in perfect darkness for a few seconds until some of the lights blinked back on.

Reaching inside the cage, I gripped Josh's t-shirt collar

and yanked him backward out the door. Once he was out, Chris leapt into the cage brandishing a knife. Whether she intended to injure it or somehow prevent its escape, I wasn't sure, but the creature vanished just as she struck. Any trace of the creature's blood disappeared as well.

Josh thrashed himself free from my grip, cursing at the empty cage as Chris emerged. It took him a long string of furious expletives before he noticed with surprise the blood dripping from his wound.

I gripped his arm, assessing the gaping wound that bled profusely, then clamped my hands over it to staunch the bleeding. He needed medical attention soon. Fortunately, the poison wouldn't be a complication, since it only seemed to affect supernaturals.

My brother frowned at the sight of his blood on my hands. "Whoever is involved in this is stronger than I am," he admitted, swallowing his pride.

The few remaining lights still flickered, the rest blown out by the power of his magic. *Not by much.* "You did what you could," I consoled him, "more than you should have. Don't do anything like that again, okay?"

Josh frowned. "You're doing it again."

"You asked me to give you room. I'm doing what I can." I sighed, restraining the urge to yell at him for being so reckless and charging into the cage. *You're not invulnerable. What were you thinking?* "I am just asking that you be more careful." I gave him a tight, half-smile. "You're going to need stitches —several."

He grinned as he unwrapped my hands and clutched his arm to his chest. "I guess I should get it over with. You want to bet I get to hear another one of his speeches?" He accepted the inevitable with a shrug. "This should be fun."

You'll listen to Dr. Baker, but not to me? I chuckled, giving my brother a forced smile as I led him up the stairs.

CHAPTER 12

"I didn't have enough time," Josh lamented, then winced as Dr. Baker began stitching the wound together while Sebastian, Chris, and I watched. A badly shaken-up Sky was in her room, guarded by Steven. Sebastian had placed him there to make her feel comfortable, and to keep Chris from interrogating her.

She frowned. "We should've anticipated that." When we didn't respond, she asked, "What now?"

"We need another creature." Josh shrugged.

Her piercing stare shifted between him, Sebastian, and me, calculating. She wanted answers. *Who or what was Maya, and what did it have to do with Skylar?* had to be the question on her mind, but she knew better than to ask. That wouldn't stop her from finding out on her own, eventually.

"Is that what you want me to tell Demetrius?" she asked, skeptical.

Josh appeared about to offer an apology when Sebastian spoke first. "Yes. The hunt continues tomorrow, with or without the vampires," he stated with an obvious finality.

After a final round of suspicious glances, she nodded and left.

"It's my fault," Josh said.

Sebastian waved off his apology. "The creatures have never displayed the kind of awareness required for self-immolation."

"It recognized Maya," I said, stating the obvious. "How is that possible?"

"She's supposed to be dormant." Sebastian scowled.

Josh chewed at his nails before answering. "Its entire demeanor changed once the spell began. That was the witch, I'm sure. The genums aren't just empowered by him; he can control them directly. The real question is: what's the link between the witch and Maya?"

"He called to her," I said warily.

"Why?" Sebastian asked.

Josh shook his head, wearing an expression that blended frustration and disappointment. "Until we learn more about the witch, I don't have any answers." After a moment, he added, "What do we do about Chris?"

I scowled. As if her curiosity about Sky hadn't been enough motivation to dig into her past, now Chris had Maya's name to investigate as well. "She'll find out about Maya and Sky eventually."

"Can you put some roadblocks in her way?" Sebastian asked.

"Some," I said, "but she has too many resources, most of which she keeps to herself. The best thing we can do now is keep her away from Sky, which is going to be difficult while she's representing the vampires."

"We should keep Sky away from the creatures as well," Josh added.

"Can your ward protect her?" Sebastian asked.

Josh nodded, certain.

I grunted, amused as I imagined how she would react when told she needed to sit home and wait while the rest of us hunted.

"I'll talk to her," Sebastian stated.

I was more than happy to leave the task to him. Surprisingly, she agreed, though I doubted I would've received the same cooperation. She claimed she was falling behind in her job—Sky worked from home as a healthcare auditor for a private company—but I suspected she was more worried by her encounter with the creature than she let on. Perhaps focusing on something other than pack business would remind her of the safety and relative peace of mundane life. I could only hope. Knowing that she was safely tucked away behind Josh's ward gave me a peace I hadn't felt since before the attacks began.

The vamps didn't take well the news that Josh had failed to source the creature. Accusations of incompetence were bandied about, but they couldn't offer an alternative strategy. We had no choice but to return to the hunt and capture another creature to source, but we'd learned from our first failure. Once tranquilized, it would be hog-tied to ensure it could not injure itself. As an added precaution, the claws and feet would be splinted by specially cut wood blocks. So that it couldn't bite its tongue or cheek, a mouth guard would be inserted and the jaw taped shut. This time, we weren't taking any chances.

Unfortunately, the witch knew our strategy. Over the next two evenings, the hunt failed to draw a single attack. Most likely the witch was adjusting his tactics to accommodate ours, and his discovery of Maya, whatever that meant. We had the unfortunate circumstance of waiting to react to our enemy's change of tactics, but the hunt continued. For the moment, it was our only course of action.

Having returned from another fruitless search alone, I was surprised to find the library empty. I was going to look for Josh when I decided to take advantage of the moment. Having spent a great deal of time with him there, I knew how he organized the sections on magic.

At every turn, the witch seemed to reveal an increasing amount of power. Josh was doing his best, but he was overwhelmed, which said a great deal about the threat this witch represented. I had access to power Josh didn't have, but I'd spent little time learning how to use it. I could dismantle wards and fields, but that was largely an intuitive effort. More complicated magic required rituals and spells. Only Sebastian knew what I was capable of. If I were to reveal myself, it would put me, Josh, and the pack in danger, but an opportunity to exercise my power unnoticed might arise. If we couldn't turn the tables on the witch soon, I might not have a choice.

I quickly found the section I wanted, but it took a while to sort through and decide which books might be of most use to me. Judging by the wear on the bindings, I chose three books Josh was least likely to miss. After stashing them in my room, I returned to looking for him.

I was walking past the entryway when the front door was kicked open and Quell, wearing an intense, anxious look, entered carrying an unconscious Sky in his arms. His lips were stained with blood and his eyes, once bright green, were now jet-black. From the two of them, I heard only a single, faint heartbeat.

Anger and fear drew the air from my lungs. I gently took Sky from his arms as Steven, Sebastian, and Gavin rushed into the room. The heartbeat was hers, I realized. Her breathing was shallow—almost nonexistent. Suddenly oblivious to anyone but Sky, I shouted for Dr. Baker as I ran with her in my arms to the clinic. He arrived just as I laid her onto a table.

"What happened?" he asked, examining her.

"Vampire bite," I growled as he found the marks on her wrist, which appeared unusually clean, as if she hadn't offered any resistance. But the jagged bite wound on her neck told another story, as did the bruise forming on the back of her neck.

He listened briefly to her heartbeat through a stethoscope. When Kelly hurried into the room, he pulled the tool from his ears and gave instructions to begin a blood transfusion.

"Ethan, I need some room to work."

I backed out of the way. "Will she be okay?"

"As long as I work quickly," he said, his tone unusually tense as he worked with Kelly to save Sky.

I berated myself as I strode back toward the entryway. *I should've killed the vamp at the farmhouse that first night.* My prediction had come true. He'd lost control and fed from Sky. He hadn't drained her dry—this time. But Quella Perduta was never going to get another chance.

Each step became faster, until I reached the entryway at a full run, propelled by pure animal rage. Quell stood in the entryway like a repentant statue waiting for judgment while Sebastian questioned him. I could see in the rigidity of Sebastian's posture that he was controlling his rage, doing a better job than Steven, who stood on his toes as if he were going to pounce at any moment. Gavin, on the other hand, seemed unusually calm, almost enjoying himself.

Quell observed my charge with a sad, resigned expression, making no effort to stop me.

"Ethan!" Sebastian shouted. "Stop!"

I roared, a barely human sound, as I leapt past Sebastian, kicking the vamp in the chest and sending him flying several feet backward into a wall, leaving a deep impression. Shocked by the impact, he stumbled onto his feet, but made no move to protect himself as I unleashed a flurry of punches to his chest and torso and drove him back against the wall. Unsatisfied, I picked him up by his shirt, swung him around, and flung him across the room. A leather chair collapsed beneath him with a splintering crash.

I thought I heard Sebastian call my name again as I picked up an end table on my way toward Quell. The vampire managed to climb to his knees, but once more made no move to defend himself as I raised the table above my head. He watched unblinking as I smashed it over his skull, driving him back down to the hardwood floor. Picking up a jagged splinter of wood, I loomed over him. Before I could drive the stake through his heart, Sebastian slammed into me. The stake fell from my grip and the air fled from my lungs as he drove me, unbalanced, into a nearby wall, pinning me there with his forearm against my chest.

I tried unsuccessfully to push him off, then tried to slip sideways out of his grip, all the while glaring at Quell, but Sebastian was an unrelenting mountain. Suddenly his face was in mine. Amber sparks of his wolf flashed in his eyes and I could feel the heat of his breath as he yelled repeatedly.

"Ethan!"

Unable to break free, I roared in frustration. For a moment, I shifted enough to catch another glimpse of Quell as he slowly climbed to his feet, facing me with a forlorn expression. Still, he made no move to escape. Even if he tried, Gavin had moved in front of the door, and Steven had positioned himself to stop the vamp from fleeing into either of the neighboring rooms.

Sebastian slid me along the wall until he had me in trapped in a corner. "Enough!" he bellowed, blocking my view of Quell so that I had no distraction from his wrath. "Ethan! Stop!"

"He fed from Sky!"

"Not yet! Ethan!" He relaxed the pressure on my chest just enough to slam me back into the wall, shocking me. "Ethan!" I stared back at him, blinking in disbelief. "There are protocols."

"No!" I roared. I didn't give a damn about his sense of decorum.

"Before we punish Quell, Demetrius must be involved. He must see the evidence. When Sky recovers, she will tell her story. Then, and only then"—he slammed me back into the wall once more—"will we pass judgment."

I shook my head, but my resistance was cracking. As much as I hated to admit it, Sebastian was right. This wasn't just a matter of decorum. Had I witnessed the attack on Sky, I could've killed the vamp on the spot. But I hadn't. The only witness to the attack was Sky. Until she told her story, and Quell had a chance to refute it, killing him might not only end our alliance but trigger a war. I would be giving Michaela what she wanted. For the sake of the pack, I had to calm myself.

Sky will live, I repeated like a mantra until I slowly brought my rage under control. After a moment, Sebastian relented, releasing me from the wall.

"I will call Demetrius," he announced. "No harm is to come to Quell without my authority. Steven"—he singled out the young coyote who still struggled with his own fury—"go to Sky. Stay with her until I call for you."

He answered with a tense, defiant gaze, but only for a moment before turning away to obey. On his way out of the room, he punched a hole in the wall next to the doorway.

In a matter of minutes, Demetrius and Michaela transported to just outside the front door, accompanied by Chase, Gabriella, and a vampire known as Eros. He was new to the Seethe, someone we had spotted only recently but knew nothing about. Seeing him for the first time, it was apparent that while he was new to the Seethe, he was not a young vampire. He was a wild card that needed to be watched, carefully.

Demetrius's gaze was intense, his jaw clenched as he accepted Sebastian's invitation to enter the house. Demetrius understood the gravity of the situation, and I suspected he didn't appreciate being drawn back to the retreat to answer for the misbehavior of one of his own. I wondered what horror Quell would suffer from his Master if he managed to leave the house alive. Vampire punishments were notoriously brutal, often involving coffins and boxes that might remain locked for decades. But there was no chance I would surrender Quell's punishment to Demetrius, or anyone else.

Michaela's lips were drawn into a thin, flat line as she seemed to struggle between fury and fear. The other vamps were mostly curious, as if they'd come to see a show, but they remained alert in case the proceedings should turn violent. Or perhaps they believed Sebastian would violate the alliance and attack them. If so, they were mistaken.

As the vamps entered the house, their eyes were drawn to Quell, who met their judgment with stiff resolve. Demetrius's expression hardened until he turned away, as if the mere sight of Quell was an inconvenience. Michaela eyed his bloodstained lips, then turned to give me a narrow, suspicious look. Recalling our discussion during the hunt, I couldn't blame her for suspecting my role in Quell's assault on Sky.

Sebastian led the entourage into the main room, drawing the rest of us in his wake. From behind Quell, I noticed an obvious, jagged hole in his shirt, in the exact location I would strike to stake his heart. Though the skin beneath seemed undamaged, the surrounding material was stained with blood.

Quell chose to sit alone near the center of the room, his back rigid, on the edge of an ottoman. Demetrius and Michaela sat together on a couch on one side of the main room, with Chase and Gabriella sitting nearby. Eros stood near the door, as did Gavin.

"Where is Skylar?" Demetrius demanded, glancing about the room.

"With Dr. Baker," Sebastian answered sharply. "She required a blood transfusion."

"We shall examine her wounds, and hear her version of events."

Sebastian's eyes narrowed. "When she regains consciousness, she will have the opportunity to explain what happened."

Demetrius responded with a slight tilt of his head, then directed his attention at Quell. "Did you feed from the girl?"

"Yes," he answered simply.

Gavin smiled.

"A very unfortunate occurrence," Michaela announced, "but as I understand it, the young woman isn't part of your pack. While she has every right to defend and even avenge herself, Quell's poor taste is none of the pack's business. The alliance has not yet been broken. Not unless you intend to harm him, of course."

"Skylar has the protection of the pack," Sebastian stated.

Michaela's eyes widened as she laid a palm over her chest. "Was there an announcement? I certainly had no idea."

"She was at the table when the alliance was made," I answered. "No reasonable argument can be offered that she was anything other than a full participant of our party."

Michaela answered with a cloying smile.

"Explain yourself," Demetrius commanded of Quell.

"A hunger overcame me and I fed from her."

Demetrius scowled. "You confess?"

"I do."

Michaela remained skeptical. "After nearly seventy years, you finally tired of your Hidacus?"

"Yes."

"He has been stalking her," I interjected. "He spends hours outside her home, watching her."

Demetrius glanced aside, disgusted.

"He has confessed," I said. "His life is forfeit."

"We have his story," Demetrius proclaimed. "We shall hear Skylar's version before we pass judgment."

My fists clenched as I glared at Quell.

"She should regain consciousness at any moment," Sebastian said. "You are welcome to wait here—"

"We will be present when she awakes."

The vamps didn't trust us. They wanted to be certain that Sky's version of the story wasn't tainted. I scowled at the insult, but Sebastian nodded agreement.

From his place at Sky's side, Dr. Baker eyed his vampiric visitors with a dark glare, angry gold sparks flashing in his eyes as they filed into one side of the clinic. He reserved his harshest judgment for Quell. Steven and Taylor rose from their seats. I caught a glance from Steven and nodded to Eros, letting him know to keep a particular eye on the mysterious vampire.

At a nod from Sebastian, Dr. Baker scowled, then retrieved a syringe and a small bottle from his medicine cabinet. After injecting the solution into Sky's shoulder, he hovered over her, watching closely as she blinked awake.

"How do you feel?" he asked, a smoldering anger marring his usual bedside manner. "You lost a lot of blood. I had to give you a transfusion. Sit up, slowly." He gently guided her to sit on the edge of the table.

She noticed Sebastian and me, first, visibly confused as she tried to read the anger in our expressions. A question formed on her lips, but then she noticed the vampires glaring at her from the other side of the room—all but Quell. As she held his gaze, her expression softened.

She pities him! Even now, after he nearly killed her. I shook my head in disgust, barely able to look at her.

Her gaze shifted to the floor.

"Skylar," Demetrius said sharply, his accent thickening with his anger. "What happened between you and Quell?"

She blinked back at him, then glanced about the room. Did she really not understand? *Does she not remember that he fed from her?* Slowly, the gravity of the situation seemed to sink in as she once more regarded Quell.

"Someone tried to break in," she explained to Sebastian, choosing her words carefully. "They were forcing down the ward when Quell showed up. Quell tried to grab him when he was staked. I didn't think Quell deserved to die because he wanted to make sure I was safe, so I made sure he didn't," she announced proudly.

What Sky described was impossible. A were-animal's blood couldn't stop a reversion. Yet I knew by her respiratory and heart rates that she wasn't lying, and the bloody hole in the back of Quell's shirt seemed to corroborate her story. Was this some new, unexpected ability granted by Maya? If it was, this was a fucking bad time to find out.

Sebastian stoically accepted Sky's story. I did my best to do the same, but Steven and Taylor made no bones about their confusion. Gavin scowled and shook his head in loathing and disbelief. The vamps took their cue from Demetrius, who leaned forward with a renewed, but subdued curiosity.

"He refused at first," she continued, even more cautiously than before, "but I made him feed."

Steven scoffed. "You made him?"

She turned to Sebastian with a pleading look. *She has no idea what she's done,* I realized. The muscles of his neck were thick cords as he constrained his anger. Sparks of amber flashed in his eyes. She wasn't lying, but she wasn't telling the entire truth, either. The clean nature of the wound on her wrist indicated that she hadn't resisted, but the jagged wound on her neck was another matter. Most likely she'd offered her blood as she described, but Quell, experiencing the taste of human blood for the first time in his long life, had lost control. When she'd denied him more, he'd taken it.

Still she defended him.

"I couldn't let him die," she explained.

I shook my head, resisting the urge to cross the room and tear Quell's head from his shoulders. Everything I'd predicted had come to pass, yet her belief in him remained unbroken. If she was so determined to get herself killed, was it really my place to stand in her way?

Sebastian struggled with his anger as well. His entire upper body was a clenched knot. After a long, tense moment, he finally nodded—not an acceptance, but an acknowledgment. The wrong of what she'd done would be drilled into her later. I knew then that Quell was going to escape punishment—for the moment. Nothing was going to prevent me from dealing with him later. Eventually I would find him alone in the dark.

"Hmm," Michaela mused. "Why is that, Sky-lar?" she asked with a particular venom.

She had claimed Sky, I remembered with disgust. Not only had Sky robbed Quell of the very oddity that made him intriguing to Michaela, but he'd taken something his maker had claimed exclusively for herself—at Sky's urging. As if Michaela needed another reason to hate Sky.

"If the roles had been reversed, I believe Quell would have done the same."

"I would have," he promised her, drawing baleful glares from everyone in the room, vamp and were-animal alike. Disgust at the sickness of their relationship filled my gut like a poison.

"Sebastian, your reaction was unnecessary," Demetrius announced. "There wasn't a need for me and mine to be called here. I can assure you that Quell hasn't become so besotted by your precious little pup that he would abandon his way of life."

The other vamps seemed to relax—except for Michaela, who seemed to be stewing in her anger, her vengeful glare fixed on Sky.

Quell rose abruptly, starting toward Sky. I strode forward

to intercept him, but Steven got there first, blocking his path. Quell quickly raised his hands in surrender, clarifying that his intentions, whatever they were, weren't to cause her harm. Steven growled a warning. Instead of backing away, Quell turned to Sebastian for approval.

"I am going to remove her marks," he said. "I believe it would be best if there weren't any reminders of what has occurred."

I didn't want him anywhere near her. Perhaps the marks might prove a potent reminder of her folly, but they would also be a constant source of contention to the rest of the pack. Very likely, they would no longer accept her. I didn't want her to join the pack, but I didn't want the choice forced upon her by a vamp.

At a nod from Sebastian, Steven reluctantly stepped aside, his hard gaze following Quell's every move as he cautiously approached Sky and gently took her wrist. Slowly, carefully he raised her wrist to his lips. I uttered a warning growl, joined by Steven and Taylor. Even Gavin tensed. Despite his loathing of Sky, he wasn't going to stand by in our own house and watch a vampire bite one of our own. Now that Quell had tasted human blood, could he stop himself from biting her again? If he drew even a drop of blood, I would kill him first, then join the slaughter as war between pack and Seethe broke out in our clinic.

Delicately, he pressed his lips against her skin and laved his tongue across the marks there, filling me with disgust. He seemed to take his time before finally pulling away. Sky examined her wrist, then raised it to show us that the bite marks had vanished. Only the barest hint of a bruise remained, but I could see the glint of light reflecting from the vampire's saliva that still coated her skin.

"Why didn't you do that in the first place?" Steven snapped.

"Hiding the evidence of what was done would not have

helped in exonerating me," Quell stated softly. He leaned in to the crook of her neck, surprising even Sky as he licked the marks there.

A chorus of growls erupted, starting with my own as I clenched my fists in front of me, barely restraining myself.

Once again, he lingered, the two of them seemingly transfixed by each other. I found myself inching toward them, as did Steven, but then Quell gave a slight nod and backed away. I wasn't sure if I wanted to beat him more than I wanted to smash the smug smile on Demetrius's face.

"That will be enough, Quell," Michaela snapped. "I believe you have entertained yourself with her enough for the day."

"Very well," Sebastian stated in a barely restrained voice. "The matter is handled."

Get out, I thought. The sooner the better. I would have Josh revoke their invitation at the first possibility. *After you,* I gestured toward the double doors, then followed the vamps out. After Demetrius transported away with Chase and Gabriella, Michaela turned back to me, drawing something from the pocket of her faded jeans.

"I almost forgot," she said with a mischievous smile as she handed me a small card smeared with dried blood. A driver's license. "He was just lingering outside Demetrius's home," she chuckled. "Can you believe it?" I hesitated for a moment before wiping the blood that shrouded the picture, but I already knew it would be Dennis McDuffy. The expression in his photo was fittingly grim. I examined his blood that now stained the tip of my thumb.

"At first, I just thought he was a toy. I had barely started playing when he gave me your name. He even mentioned Sky," she mused, adding as an afterthought, "and Chris. Imagine my surprise. Well, we just played and played but turns out he'd already told me everything he knew. Does Sebastian know about your little spy? I know Chris doesn't. I wonder what she'd say." Her smile grew devilish just before she vanished, leaving me with my anger and guilt.

I should've sent Dennis away the moment he'd informed me that he'd followed Chris to Demetrius's house, but I'd let my anger cloud my judgment. Dennis didn't belong there. He didn't have the skill set required to evade the leader of the Seethe, or his Mistress, even if he had known what they were. In my anger, I'd left him to be slaughtered. Painfully. And slowly.

I carefully slipped the ID into my pocket and strode back into the house. On my way back to the clinic, I passed a glowering Gavin leaning against a wall with his arms folded over his chest, waiting for me. "She's in Sebastian's office. She just opened a whole shit storm and doesn't even know it," he scoffed as he pushed himself from the wall and unfolded his arms. "What do you think Demetrius is going to do once this alliance ends, now that he knows her blood can stop a reversion?" He glared at me, judging.

"It doesn't matter," I lied, glaring back.

"Demetrius knows she was the only were-animal who could be used to complete his ritual last year, and he knows she is the only were-animal that can stop a reversion. You think he doesn't want to find out what else she can do?"

"If he does," I growled, "we will deal with him."

"Will we? She's not a member of this pack."

"She hasn't made her choice," I stated. Sky's latest revelation changed everything for her, and she didn't even know it. I'd thought I could protect her on my own. Now that she'd drawn increased interest from Demetrius and Michaela, joining the pack might be the only way to keep her safe. In saving Quell, she might well have closed the door on the life she wanted.

"You've changed your mind, then." Gavin shook his head in disgust. "You were never interested in protecting the pack. You just wanted to protect her."

"She will always have my protection," I warned.

"She's a threat!" he snapped. "We have no idea what she is capable of. Letting her live puts the entire pack at risk. The only sensible move is to kill her. Kill the risk. If she were anyone else, you'd agree with me!"

I squared up to him, my arms ready at my side and my fists clenched. "Leave."

"Your obsession with her puts this pack at risk, and so does your obsession with Chris."

I glared down at him. "If you feel I am not able to fulfill my responsibilities as Beta, then challenge me."

The temptation played across his expression like a dance, until he finally smirked and walked away. I stayed there a moment, focusing on my breath as I worked to bring my anger under control. Punching a hole in the wall helped, so I punched another. I was on the verge of creating several more when Sebastian emerged from his office.

I strode to the door, but he stopped me, physically barring my path. "Not now."

"I need to talk to Sky."

"Come with me."

He closed the door behind him and walked away, leaving me there. For a moment, I considered barging through the door and demanding Sky explain what the hell she'd been thinking, but pack hierarchy was deeply ingrained into my being. I slowly eased myself back from the door, swallowed my frustration, then followed him to the kitchen where he was busy pulling leftovers from the fridge. He put a bowl of mac and cheese into the microwave, then placed a cold steakburger next to it. While that cooked, he retrieved a bun and some condiments from the refrigerator. Since Sebastian didn't eat mac and cheese, I assumed he was gathering a meal for Sky.

"How could she stop the reversion?" I asked.

"The only possible answer is Maya," he said, a hint of

frustration in his tone. "Ethan," he said as he added condiments to the bun, "how did you know that Quell had been stalking her?"

"Their fascination with each other was a threat," I announced, unrepentant. "Sooner or later he was going to tire of his plant. Sky made herself vulnerable to him. It was only a matter of time before he attacked her." Following Quell wasn't exactly a violation of our alliance with the vamps. Had I been caught, it would've been a source of contention.

Sebastian sighed. "The best way to protect Sky is for her to join the pack," he said matter-of-factly.

"Maybe," I admitted reluctantly, then changed the subject. "Quell will call her." New vampires struggled to control the intoxication of human blood. If anything, Quell's seventy years as a vamp would make his bloodlust even more difficult to control. That he hadn't killed Sky was a testament to his will, but that would fail eventually, once the hunger got to him. Having freshly fed from her, he had the power to call her. She wasn't strong enough to resist. For the next three days, she would need around-the-clock supervision.

"Sky will be staying with us until the danger passes. She'll need clothes and some of her belongings."

"I'll take her."

"No," he said definitively, meeting my gaze.

I growled.

"Ethan, you're no good to Sky right now. You're angry. You're overprotective. You're barely in control of yourself. Even on your best behavior, we both know how she will respond to you. I will take care of her myself."

I turned from him, suppressing a growl, but I knew he was right. I acknowledged his decision with a faint nod, then left the room.

. . .

I was in the gym, sparring with Taylor, when Joan informed me that Marko was awake. I didn't bother to clean up. When I arrived in his room, Dr. Jimenez was checking his vitals. He was pale and obviously weak as he lay supine, but he was awake.

He smiled at my arrival. "Ethan," he said in a strained voice, then retrieved a cup of water from the neighboring table and sipped from the straw. "That poison was a bitch, wasn't it?"

"You heard."

"The doc gave me the lowdown. Just give me an hour. I'll be back into the fight."

"Rest." I grinned, relieved. "You're going to need more than an hour."

"You're not going to deprive your number six, are you?"

"There'll be plenty more fights before this is over, I promise you." I studied him for a moment, my smile fading. "I shouldn't have gotten you into this. You had no business taking that trip with me."

He waved my confession aside with a weak gesture. "From what I hear, these creatures have been attacking our best fighters. I would've been the first one attacked, anyway. No shame in getting hit protecting one of my weaker companions." His sudden laugh was interrupted by a cough, but the smile remained.

"Right." I chuckled. "Good to have you back. Anything you need?"

"A steak? Winning lottery numbers would be convenient." He thought for a moment. "Fresh underwear."

"I'll see what I can do—about the underwear."

For security, Sky spent the night in Sebastian's room. The only entrance, protected by a sophisticated security lock, was through his office. Even if Quell called her, she wouldn't have the combination to escape. Sebastian retired to a nearby guest room, while I placed myself on a couch that gave me an unobstructed view of his office door.

When I woke in the morning, they had already left to retrieve Sky's clothes from her home. When they returned an hour later, Sebastian was furious, taking her and her bag of belongings directly to his room and locking her inside.

"What happened?" I demanded, prepared for a fight.

"Josh?" he asked.

"He's in the library."

"We need to talk."

We found Josh at a table in the library, studying from a handful of open books.

"Our silver-haired witch has made an appearance," Sebastian said. "At Sky's, while I was in the next room."

"You left the ward down?" I asked, irritated.

"No. The witch took it down effortlessly."

Looking at Sebastian from head to foot, I didn't see any sign of a fight.

"What happened?" Josh asked, slowly rising to his feet.

"He transported away before I interrupted them. According to Sky, he wanted to talk to her. She said he called her 'my amphora.'"

I turned to Josh, anxious. "Could this witch break your field here without you knowing?"

"No." He frowned, then asked Sebastian, "Are you sure he said 'amphora'?"

"Yes."

Josh ran a hand through his hair as he thought, pacing a small line along the side of the table. "It's a word for an ancient Roman jar with two handles. But it has a magical context as well. The handles of the vessel each exert an opposing force in an effort to control it. It's an allegory for the conflict between good and evil."

I felt a sense of dread pressing on my chest. "Sky is the vessel for Maya."

"You need to stay at the retreat until this is resolved," Sebastian said to Josh, drawing a quick nod in response. "I want you on hand if the witch attempts to break your field. I can't keep her in my room, but we need to make sure she is under constant watch."

"I'll take care of it," I said through gritted teeth.

"If he wanted to take Sky, he would have," Josh insisted. I gave him a warning look as Sebastian waited for him to continue. "He could've simply touched her and transported her away. Could it be that he just wants to talk?"

I grunted. "That's why he's sending his creatures to kill were-animals and vampires, just so he can *talk* to Sky?"

"Maya is a wrinkle in his plans. He obviously doesn't see us as a threat, but he might see her as one."

"You don't know that," I snapped. I didn't like where this was headed.

Josh paced, lost in thought for a moment. "Whatever he wants from her, he needs her cooperation."

"No," I declared.

He dismissed me with an irritable look, concentrating instead on Sebastian. "He didn't kill her and he didn't capture her. I don't think she's in danger."

"We're not using Sky as bait," I snapped.

There was a long, tense moment as I watched Sebastian weigh the risks and rewards. *He won't put her at risk.*

"Could you guarantee her safety?" he finally asked Josh.

The sudden urge to throw a nearby bookshelf to the ground was nearly impossible to control.

Josh considered carefully, bringing his hands together by threading his fingers between the knuckles. "If there's trouble, I can transport directly to her, as long as I know where she is."

My eyes narrowed at him. "You said this witch is more

powerful than you. If you show up, what's going to stop him from just killing you?"

"He is more powerful," he admitted, "but I'll have surprise on my side, and I've got a few tricks up my sleeve to create a diversion. I can get her back, Ethan." It was a brave and reckless offer. I shook my head at my brother, but I couldn't deny that the witch had had his opportunity to take or hurt Sky and had turned it down. And after a week of attacks and several casualties, we still knew nothing about him. If he was willing to talk to Sky, we could learn a great deal. One slip of the tongue by the witch, one seemingly small detail given away, might bring this war to a sudden and victorious conclusion.

"It has to be her choice," Sebastian said.

"She'll want to do it," Josh stated.

I sighed. *Of course she will. That doesn't make this right.* "We'll need to track her, in case he transports her somewhere." I didn't want to explain that I already had the means to track her phone. "If she agrees to do this, I'll give her a GPS device to carry. It has an audio transmitter as well."

Sebastian nodded. "Bring it to my office. I'll ask her when the time is appropriate."

I preferred to ask myself, but she would know I didn't want her to. She might agree just to spite me. Sebastian would make the risks clear. I half turned from the window and nodded once. "I'll take care of the security arrangements," I said, then left the library to round up a handful of were-animals Sky didn't generally pay much attention to. Their instructions were clear. Each of them had an hour block to watch her and instructions to hand her off to another if she became overly suspicious. I would drop in periodically and check on her. Anyone who lost contact with her for longer than it took Sky to use the bathroom was going to answer to me.

It didn't take her long to notice that she was being

watched. Rather than take our efforts as a personal affront, she turned it into a game. At times she moved spontaneously from one room to the next, seemingly on a restless whim. Other times she spent hours in the entertainment room, obliging her shadows to watch nonstop reality television and pretend to enjoy it; she seemed particularly fond of watching a show about wealthy women who screamed at one another.

Winter woke late in the afternoon. The entire house seemed to utter a sigh of relief. I was on my way to visit her when I saw Sky had gotten there before me.

"Why do I have fucking pigtails in my hair?" Winter playfully snapped at Sky. "When someone is unconscious, it doesn't give you permission to play dress up with them."

Sky smiled back as she answered.

Seeing the surprising camaraderie between them as they caught up, I decided to let them be. I smiled as I walked away, but the smile was short-lived as my mind went through all the risks of using Sky as bait. We would be putting Josh at risk as well. One misstep and I could lose them both.

CHAPTER 13

That night, I drifted in and out of a restless slumber as I lost Sky or Josh or both in a seemingly endless parade of nightmares that reflected my concerns. By the time the sun rose, I wasn't sure I'd slept at all, but I'd made a decision; I was going to present the choice to Sky. No matter who explained the risks to her, she was going to say yes. I needed to look into her eyes and know that she understood her choice, and I would do everything I could to convince her not to.

I rolled out of bed and did a few repetitions of one-handed push-ups until my mind was clear, then dressed and went to find Sky. Her belongings were already stripped from her room, and the bed made. She was gone. I found Sebastian in his office, waiting for me.

"It was her idea, Ethan," he said once I'd closed the door. "She approached me. I made sure she understood the potential consequences of her decision."

I turned from him, stifling my anger. *I should've gone to her last night.* That Sky had come up with the idea on her own didn't surprise me. She was brave and strong-willed and naïve enough to voluntarily put herself in harm's way for the sake of the pack. If I had my way, she would've been locked in a cell for her own good, but I couldn't help but admire her will.

I sighed, rubbing the stubble on my chin. "She has the GPS?"

"Yes. In addition, I gave her a phone pre-programmed with your number, mine, and Steven's."

"She has those numbers."

"The phone also has a tracking app running in the background." Sebastian gestured to his phone on his desk. "I can track it at all times."

I considered parking myself outside her house for the next week, or however long it took, but I doubted I could lurk within sight of the house without the witch spotting me. His attacks had been highly targeted, which suggested he had a means of tracking us individually when he wanted to.

"Who took her home?" I asked, but I had my suspicions.

"Steven."

I scowled.

"I've instructed him to find other living arrangements," Sebastian added with a half- smile. "She'll be alone at the house, but Steven will keep himself in the general vicinity. Josh is prepared to transport to her at a moment's notice."

He'd considered everything, but that still didn't ease my concern for Sky.

The next two days were tense as we waited for the silver-haired witch to make an appearance. I spent much of my time obsessively checking the location of her personal phone and her tracking device. As an added precaution, Sebastian and Josh called her throughout the day to make sure she was safe. I preferred to make the calls myself, but Sebastian reasonably pointed out that she might interpret my protectiveness, however justified, as stalking. *Yet she's okay with Josh calling her repeatedly?*

When I wasn't stalking Sky, I spent my time in the gym, working out and sparring.

Sebastian called an end to the hunts. We didn't bother explaining why. If Chris or Demetrius knew we were using Sky as bait, I doubted either would be content to sit back and wait for our call. She didn't need them showing up at her home while the witch was there, potentially triggering a violent response.

Marko and Winter were finally getting out of their beds, taking brief walks about the house as they grew stronger. Joan was continuing to grow stronger as well.

On the third day, I was sparring with Taylor when Sebastian informed me that Sky hadn't answered her phone. The GPS tracker indicated she was in her house, as did the tracker on the phone that Sebastian had given her, but that wasn't good enough for me. I needed to hear her voice. I called the pre-programmed phone. Again, no answer. I called her personal phone. No answer. The last time this had happened, I'd sped to her house only to get a lecture on how she was entitled to her privacy while in the bathroom.

"I'm sending Steven to check on her," I announced, calling his number.

He answered on the first ring. "Yeah?"

"Check her. Now."

"I'm on it."

It was a long, tense wait for his report as every possible negative scenario played out in my mind. He called when he arrived at the house and I put him on speakerphone. Her car was gone but the ward was intact. Josh instructed him how to break the ward and get inside. There was no sign of struggle, and no Sky.

Sebastian grunted. "Wait there."

I disconnected the call. While Sebastian paced, I stepped

out of his office, then out of the house before I opened the tracking app on my phone, relieved to see that she was carrying her personal phone. She appeared to be driving into a rural area that looked familiar. *Quell's farmhouse. He called her.* My hand squeezed around my phone until I thought I might crush it.

A short time later, I was speeding along the rural road that led to Quell's. As the farmhouse came into sight, I intended to race up the driveway, kick down the front door, and kill the vamp on the spot, but I needed to be careful for the sake of the pack. If possible, I needed to catch him in the act. I drove just past the driveway and parked on the side of the road. In an effort to control my rage, I punched the dash twice, then slipped out of the SUV and ran through the cornfield toward the house. Mindful of the wind carrying my scent, I circled around the back of the house for a look inside.

I was surprised to find the vamp's precious greenhouse nearly destroyed. Glass had been broken and in some cases blown out by fire. Inside, the Hidacus plant was a smoking ruin, reeking now of sulfur and burned flesh. Some of the neighboring plants were destroyed as well, but clearly the Hidacus had been the target of the attack. *Michaela*, I realized. I'd considered destroying the plant as well, but after Sky had fed Quell there was no point. Where my intention had been strategic, to force him to reveal his true self, this attack had been punitive. Retribution for feeding from Michaela's claimed prize. His preferred source of food gone and unable to venture out to hunt for hours, he'd called Sky to feed him.

She should've done us both a favor and just killed him.

I crept up to the house for a closer look. Peering through a window, I saw Sky seated on the other side of a couch, gazing down with a pitying look—at Quell, I was sure, but the back of the couch obscured him and most of her.

"I can help you," she stated softly, a slight tremble in her voice. "But what happened the other day can't happen again." She shifted closer, extending her arm toward him. "Just do it," she insisted.

He didn't call her, I realized, scowling. *She came here by choice.*

I saw the crown of Quell's head as he propped himself up and brushed her arm aside. "You're the reason for this."

"You were punished because of me?"

He said something so soft it was unintelligible, but then I heard, "I shouldn't have fed from you."

Sky scoffed. "It was to save your life!"

"It doesn't matter."

"Well, why don't you just tell that psychotic bitch I would sooner slit my wrists and bleed out before I would share a drop with her. You let her know that if she ever comes near me there isn't anything I will not be willing to do to make sure she never does it again and make sure it's the most painful thing she has ever experienced in her existence."

"Is there someone else who can feed you?" She stared pityingly at him, her expression heavy with guilt. "It's because of me this happened. Let me make it right." Once more, she raised her arm to him. "Take what you need to be strong enough to hunt at dusk. This is between us. No one will ever know. I prom—" She gasped, and I knew he'd bitten her.

I turned from the window in disgust. *What are you doing?* I kept asking Sky, but there would be no answer. Once again, she was feeding him of her own free will. If I killed Quell, it would be a violation of the pack's alliance with the Seethe. It would be a betrayal. Sebastian would have no choice but to forfeit my life. Yet I wanted to kill Quell for daring to test her blood.

Sky would never forgive me.

If he loses control, as he did last time ... I peered through the window just as Quell rose. She examined her wrist as he walked into the kitchen, opened a refrigerator, and returned to her with a glass of what appeared to be orange juice.

"How can you not be angry with her?" Sky asked, accepting the drink.

Unable to bear their camaraderie further, I tore myself from the window. *There's nothing I can do here. Not now.* I strode deep into the cornfield and proceeded to tear plants from the ground until I had vented enough of my fury, then paused to gather myself. Sky's choice to trust Quell was noble and foolish. It might yet lead to her demise, but I had to leave her to make her own choice.

I walked begrudgingly back to the SUV and waited, monitoring her on my phone until I saw a few minutes later that she'd left the house. I drove off before she emerged from the driveway, then circled back and followed her from a discreet distance. Once assured that she was returning to her home, I returned to the retreat.

Sebastian was on the phone when I walked into his office. "Skylar, I didn't give you this job—you requested it. If you want to bail, fine, but don't just flake. Honor your obligation as we always have with you." He waited for her brief answer, then disconnected the call.

I wondered how often my interactions left me with that same infuriated, perplexed look he had then.

"Where were you?" he demanded.

"Out looking for Sky." I wouldn't lie to Sebastian, but I saw no need to share the full truth with him if I didn't have to.

He scrutinized me for a long moment, assessing whether he wanted to know more and decided the better of it. He gestured irritably at paperwork on his desk and I left him to it.

. . .

If I'd thought the first three days of waiting were difficult, my sparring partners for the next two days probably had more to say on the matter. After sending Gavin to the clinic to have a rib put back into place, I checked my phone for messages, then took a quick shower. By the time I'd dried myself, there was a message from Sky, a group text sent to Sebastian, Steven, and me.

"He's here."

I grabbed my clothes and charged out of the room, practically running into Steven, who had come looking for me. Together we hurried into Sebastian's office. He was behind his desk, his phone faceup in front of him. Josh stood over the side of the desk, his hands gripping the corners as he stared intensely at the phone.

Steven tapped my shoulder as I dressed. Getting my attention, he gestured to his lips, then the phone.

"They can't hear us," I said, then gestured for him to be silent, anyway.

A man's voice, arrogant and theatrical like a game show host's, spoke. "Finally, we meet again."

"We've met before?" Sky asked, trying to sound casual.

I moved closer to Josh. If anything went wrong and he was going to transport to Sky, I was going along for the ride.

"Am I that forgettable, *amphora*?"

I could almost hear the smirk on the witch's face.

Our phones vibrated simultaneously with the message, "I'm okay."

"How could I forget the werewolf that snatched my magic from one of my servants and nearly forced me out as though I were powerless?" the witch said. "I enjoyed being linked to such untapped power."

Josh straightened as if he'd been jerked upright. His eyes

flicked side to side as if he didn't quite believe what he'd heard. "Ethos," he whispered.

The four of us traded anxious glances. Sky was in more danger than we could've imagined. When it came to dark magic, there was no more powerful practitioner than Ethos. Little was known about him other than he shared his power with his worshippers, like Pala. Last year, she'd betrayed Josh, attempting to absorb his power until Sky had intervened. In all our musings as to the identity of the silver-haired witch, it had never occurred to us that Ethos had come for revenge.

I put my hand on Josh's shoulder and gave him a look to let him know, *I'm ready when you are.* He nodded, his expression grim but determined.

Each of us leaned toward the phone, waiting for some sense of what was happening in Sky's home. For a long, anxious moment, there was only silence, then Ethos chuckled.

"If I wanted you hurt, rest assured, you would have known this by barely being alive. Please, have a seat. We have a great deal to discuss. You are quite the complex little vessel of magic. I can only imagine your potential. Good potential that I plan to use."

Don't show him your fear.

"What do you want?" she asked, irritated.

"I want you to have a seat and stop being rude," he snapped. After a moment he sighed audibly. "That Josh has quite a temper. You should have seen how scared my poor little Pala was. She was nearly in tears when I asked her to return my magic. She actually refused me because she needed it to protect herself from your boyfriend."

"I can't believe Josh would get riled over a little thing like Pala betraying him, attempting to steal his magic, and then trying to kill him. How dreadful, a clear overreaction."

I bowed my head, letting out a slow, tense breath. If she

survived this encounter, we were going to have a long talk about the difference between bravery and recklessness.

Ethos's tone shifted toward irritation. "She was quite ambitious, always wanting more. She was my most talented servant.

"My little run-in with you was quite an eye-opener," he continued. He was a talker. Why not? He thought himself invincible, but I intended to demonstrate otherwise, somehow. "I was expunged by a novice. It was quite embarrassing. I had spread myself too thin, sharing my gifts with so many. Over the years, I traded reverence and worship for my power. You helped me realize that I can be celebrated and adulated without the sacrifice.

"The were-animals and vampires are like overactive children, running around aimlessly, fighting and vying for dominance. Sebastian is limited by his rules and structure, Demetrius by his impulses and desires. They need direction and a real leader."

Now we know what he wants. Finally.

"And you think you should be that person?" Sky asked, incredulous.

"Of course. I should be revered for what I am, and they need to be controlled. A logical choice, don't you think?"

"And you think the way to gain that is by killing their people? Did you consider that would just really enrage them? I can assure you that showing you reverence is the furthest thing from their minds."

"The first ones were to make a point."

"Ever tried an Edible Arrangement? Those things really get your attention. They're fruit carved into cute little flowers. For a little extra, they can dip them in chocolate. They're the best. I just love them."

The rest of us held our breaths until we heard Ethos chuckle.

"On any given day, who is the most feared is a toss-up

between the were-animals and the vamps, and they are a force. Sebastian, unlike Demetrius, could turn to the South for assistance. I took care of that, and now they are on equal playing fields. I've destroyed the Southern Pack and killed a substantial number of the Northern Seethe. They are weakened. If I continue, how feared do you think they will be when they don't have the numbers to make them a threat? Do they think they will continue to enjoy the luxuries of their power?

"The elves and witches are considering an alliance, are you aware of that? How hard will it be for them to subjugate a fractured power? The vampires are immune to fae and elven magic, the were-animals to the witches'. Apart, they are at a disadvantage. Together they are a force that most will not deny. But they are too foolish and arrogant to form a lasting alliance that will be invincible. They are in need of direction and a real leader."

Sky released a nervous chuckle. "Again, you think it should be you? For argument's sake, let's say they submit, and you become … president, prime minister, CEO, king, the big cheese, or whatever of the otherworld—"

"Lord."

I could almost hear the laughter in her voice as she asked, "Then what?"

"Everyone else will follow. With them under my control, the elves wouldn't stand a chance, and the faes would submit without much of a fight. Then the witches will have no choice but to follow. I need them because they have something that belongs to me that I would like back."

"Why are you talking to me? Go call Demetrius and Sebastian and tell them your plan," Sky said, making no effort to disguise her sarcasm. "Perhaps they will think it's a good idea and submit upon request. Clearly they would see that you are more qualified to lead than they are."

"I would like to keep you alive because you will prove to

be very useful to me, but I will accept the loss if you can't control your tongue."

I heard a sharp intake of breath from Sky, and my heart skipped a beat. Judging by Josh's pale expression, Ethos could kill her quicker than we could react. Even if we transported in time, would it be a suicide trip for my brother? I had no problem putting my own life at risk, but I wouldn't do the same with his. I'd have to attack Ethos immediately, and hope I could buy him a few seconds to escape with Sky.

When she spoke again, her tone was cautious. "What do you want with me?"

"You will serve as my representative. Make them see that surrender is their only choice. I know you can do this. Although you consort with them, you are not part of their pack and you seem to have established a working relationship with the vampires as well." Steven lowered his head, as if in defeat, while Josh and Sebastian turned their gazes on me. "You are bonded to both. They know your power, and they will listen. You have three days. If they don't concede willingly, then ..." his voice trailed off.

"They will not listen to me," she insisted, almost laughing. "Coming from me, it will be ignored. You want it to be considered, then you should meet with Demetrius and Sebastian."

Ethos laughed. "You know a meeting between us would not be nearly as pleasant. How would anything be addressed with them looking for any and every opportunity to destroy me? No, I would rather not deal with such unpleasantness during a meeting."

"They'd rather die than be led by anyone other than themselves. They don't continue to fight for their leadership to hand it over to someone like a candy bar on Halloween. They would consider a brutal death more admirable than being considered a feckless and superable leader by submitting to you."

"It would be an easier transition if they did, but I am fine with getting rid of them if necessary," he said as if it were a small matter. "You have three days."

"I will need more time."

When he spoke again, his voice was further away. "No, three days. They either concede willingly or by force."

After a tense moment, Sky texted us, "He's gone." Josh brushed my hand from his shoulder and then disappeared. A moment later, he reappeared near the office door with a badly shaken Sky.

CHAPTER 14

I found it difficult to meet Sky's gaze as she described in a trembling voice her harrowing experience with Ethos, detailing his demands and threats. Now that she was safe, her bravado was gone, replaced by fear. At any moment of their encounter, he could've instantly killed her on a simple whim. *How could I just dangle her out there as bait? If anything had happened to her...* I could never have forgiven myself. At the same time, I felt immensely proud of Sky. I knew very few were-animals who could comport themselves with such bravery in the face of such a capricious and unassailable threat.

Sebastian and Gavin remained reticent as they absorbed her story. Informing her that we had bugged her GPS and had heard the entire conversation would only upset her unnecessarily. She was far too shaken to find our lack of shock suspicious. After she'd told her story, she announced that she needed a shower and left.

Sebastian picked up his phone and dialed a number. "Expect Demetrius and his vampires in a few hours." For once, Gavin made no complaint. Instead, he acknowledged the news with a sober nod. Now that we understood the threat that faced us, we were going to need all the help we could get. Once the meeting was arranged, I made the rounds, informing the others that the final fight was close at hand. The activity level in the gym, particularly the sparring room, increased immediately as the pall of futility that had been hanging over the pack since the attacks began was finally lifted.

I wanted to check on Sky, but I couldn't bring myself to face her.

A few hours later, I escorted Chris, Demetrius, and Michaela into the living room. Sebastian emerged from his office, while Josh brought Sky downstairs, directing her to an ottoman in the middle of the room. She took the seat with some trepidation as the vampires lined up on one side of her, and the were-animals lined up on the other.

"You say you have important news to share," Demetrius said, his tone bored. "Perhaps your witch would like us to catch all of the creatures for him, in the hope that at least one won't escape."

I saw my brother's jaw clench. He glared at Demetrius, who never bothered to meet Josh's gaze after insulting him. Despite his defiance, I could see the vamp had touched on some doubt by the way he began to fidget—subtle gestures like rotating his wrists, flicking his fingertips, and shifting his weight, but I knew them well. That Josh had failed to anticipate the creature's ability to injury itself as a means to escape had reflected badly on the pack, and on him.

Sebastian crossed his arms over his chest. "The silver-haired witch has made contact with Skylar."

I grunted as Demetrius turned to her with a raised eyebrow. *Interested in this conversation now, aren't you?* Chris leaned forward intently, while Michaela crossed one knee over the other and lazily reached over it with one hand, impatiently tapping her knee as she gave Sky a doubtful smile.

"It is Ethos," Sebastian stated.

I grinned as Michaela's smile melted into a general look of shock.

At Sebastian's urging, Sky told her story, leaving out that she had been held out by us as deliberate bait. As far as Chris and the vamps needed to know, Ethos's arrival at Sky's home was an entirely unexpected turn of events. She also left out the part about Ethos referring to her as an *amphora*.

At the time that Ethos had initially issued his demands, I'd been far too concerned about Sky for them to sink in. As she repeated his demands then, I felt an indignant fury fill my chest. Demetrius jumped to his feet, repeatedly shouting "Outrageous!" I found myself edging protectively closer to Sky as all three of the vamps paced and cursed as she carefully repeated every detail. By the third telling, Gavin, Sebastian, and I were equally incensed by Ethos's audacity. Only Chris took the news quietly, her attention fixed on Sky, who appeared increasingly uncomfortable in the room.

"Three days?" Michaela shouted, stomping a path back and forth through the room. "I want him dead. Now."

Sebastian turned to Josh. "How do we kill him?"

Josh's eyes widened. "You want to know how to kill one of the rulers of dark magic who has existed longer than anyone in this room?"

"Doesn't mean he can't be killed," Demetrius barked. "Just means no one has figured out how."

Josh gaped in stunned silence.

"He's no longer sharing his magic," Sky interjected, warning Demetrius. "He's at his strongest."

"Josh," I said, drawing my brother's attention. "Can his magic be taken?"

"If it was that easy, don't you think it would have been done years ago?" he snapped, venting his frustration at me. "Ethos has more enemies than the pack and the Seethe combined. There's a reason people don't screw with him."

"Then kill his creatures and the magic dies with him," Demetrius said, determined.

Josh rolled his eyes. "Are you even paying attention? At the first sign of fatal injury, he retrieves his creatures for the magic to be returned. We are not dealing with an amateur here."

The vampires began a fresh tirade of indignation, proclaiming the myriad of ways they intended to torture Ethos for an almost indefinite period before finally granting him permission to die. Eventually, Chris rose and left the room. Judging by her direction, she was either looking for a bathroom or headed to the library. A few minutes later, Sky had had enough and followed Chris, escaping the room with her head down to avoid drawing attention to departure.

"We have three days to come up with a plan," Sebastian stated, drawing a hard look from Demetrius. "We'll find a way."

Demetrius cast a sideways look at Josh. "Do you think your witch is up to the task?"

I growled, stepping forward to knock some manners into the vamp when Josh barred my path with his arm. His eyes darkened as he glared at Demetrius.

"Since you have no ideas of your own," he said sternly, "I guess I'll have to be."

Demetrius scoffed as he turned away.

"Then we are agreed," Sebastian said, drawing everyone's attention. "We fight Ethos to the death."

"You say that as if you considered surrender," Michaela said, as if tossing alcohol into a fire.

This time it was Gavin who strode forward, but Sebastian stopped him. "We will never submit," he stated coolly.

"We shall see," Demetrius answered, then stormed out of the house with Michaela on his heels.

Once they'd left, I turned to Josh. "Can you find a way?"

"Sure," he answered. "I'm sure I'll just open a hundred

books and the answer will just fall right out." He ran a hand through his hair as he blew out a tense breath. "I'll see what I can do," he said, then left for the library.

After a few final arrangements were made with Sebastian, I went to join Josh in the library. Instead, I found Chris and Winter having a glare-off. Winter's jet-black hair was pulled into a ponytail, revealing that her sun-kissed skin had finally returned to its usual hue. The bruising, from what I could see, had vanished, but she still wasn't a hundred percent. There was a fatigue there, and her posture, while defiant, lacked the flagrant confidence that she'd exuded before her injuries. She'd been defeated in a way that none of us—especially Winter—had thought possible. There was a certain caution that every fighter obtained once they'd been soundly beaten—it was difficult to see in Winter, but she would be stronger for it, eventually.

Their gazes locked together as the tension-filled room came to a boiling point. I glanced between them, wondering what I'd missed, but I knew a fight was coming. Neither of them was going to back down. I glanced at Sky's horrified expression, then at Josh, who watched over a pile of books on the table in front of him. Winter had been in a coma for days. What could Chris have done that made the were-snake so angry? I was going to intervene when Kelly appeared in the doorway, her usual smile and cheerful demeanor unswayed by the pall of impending violence.

"Here you are," she said, facing Winter. "Dr. Baker was about to send out a search party. You may be back to your old self, but he will not give up the chance to mother hen you some more. Just go humor him for me, will you? If not, I'll have to endure his ten-minute speech about how no one in this pack appreciates how hard he works and how everybody takes his talents for granted. Please don't make me listen to that speech again."

I watched Winter's expression as she slowly made up her

mind to kill Chris another day. When she turned to follow Kelly, her gaze fell to me. She hesitated. Her expression clouded with anger and her hazel eyes briefly became slits as her snake rose to the surface. In any other were-animal, I would've taken that steady, judgmental stare as a challenge, but I had known Winter a long time. Behind her surprising anger was ... disappointment? I stared back at her, waiting for an explanation. After a long moment, she rolled her eyes and followed Kelly out of the library.

I stared after her. *What did I do?*

Chris half-smiled as she sauntered out a moment later. Josh followed, clutching books under his arm and shaking his head at me. After they left, I turned to Sky for an explanation. Instead, she pursed her lips as if suppressing a grin, shrugged, then left me alone.

Later that evening, I locked myself in my room with the books I'd taken from the library. Dense reading. Much of it was either was either too dry or lacked any practical application that I could conceive of, but there were a few interesting spells, the kind Josh had never mentioned before. I wanted to ask him questions, but that wouldn't be possible without revealing more than was safe for him to know.

Thinking of my brother, I called him to check on his progress. He had a tendency to get lost in his work when focused, so the first time he didn't answer, I assumed he was hard at work. When he didn't answer the next three calls, I started to worry. I was halfway to his condo when it occurred to me that I might be overreacting. Up until then, the creatures had limited their targets to the vampires and were-animals. I had no reason to worry that my brother had been attacked. My showing up at his condo in the middle of the night was likely to start a fight. I'd promised to give him space, but he could be more considerate. I grumbled as I made a U-turn at a slow intersection and drove home instead.

The next morning, he called me, sounding as if he hadn't slept. "Ethan, you asked me earlier about the Aufero. Turns out, Marcia didn't destroy it after all. She's been using it to punish other witches."

I scowled. While I didn't think the Aufero was a direct threat to the pack, Marcia might be. "Sebastian has enough on his plate. We'll fill him in after we kill Ethos."

"I think I've found a way to do just that. Come over as soon as you can."

"On my way."

I disconnected the call and smiled. *I knew he'd find something.* But then came the worry. If I knew Josh, he was going to put himself at risk somehow.

A short time later, I knocked on the door of his condo. When he appeared, his eyes were bright with excitement. He eagerly welcomed me inside, where I found Sky sitting on a couch. A silver rod with a gentle, smoky glow sat on the coffee table next to her.

"Ethos killed Gloria and Thaddeus," Josh said in an excited rush. "It's their blood that's allowing the genums to morph into creatures larger than themselves. It's the only way the genums could operate the way they are," Josh said. "I should've figured it out myself."

I gestured to the rod.

His smile broadened. "A gift from London. It's called a *capsa*. You were right about taking Ethos's magic. The capsa is designed to do just that."

As I approached the rod, I felt the distinct heaviness of dark magic emanating from it. "It holds dark magic?"

"It holds Ethos's magic," Josh emphasized.

I gave him a skeptical look.

"It belonged to Pala. I think it was something she was working on to prevent him from taking back the magic he'd loaned her. Or perhaps she intended to steal more."

"Pala is dead." I waited, but Josh seemed to miss my point entirely. "How did London have the capsa?"

"Before Pala became obsessed with Ethos's magic, she and London were close. Maybe she was holding it for Pala. Maybe she was keeping it from her. Whatever the reason, we're lucky to have it. When the genums die, their magic goes back to Ethos—unless the capsa is closer. We can weaken him, Ethan. He's spending a lot of energy powering his little army. If we capture enough of his energy, we might be able to kill him."

"We'd have to know in advance where the genums are going to attack, to have the rod present." As unlikely as that was, I saw another problem. I shook my head. "It won't work. They disappear the moment they're injured. You'd have to have the rod present wherever it is they return to, which could be anywhere."

Josh grinned. "Even Ethos can't get around the limitations of a transportation spell. They're local. And I think I can use the capsa's affinity toward his magic to find them, but we need to test it, first. If I'm going to present my plan to Sebastian and Demetrius, I want to be sure that it'll work."

I was going to ask more when there was a knock at the door. When Josh answered, Chris slipped past him into the apartment, bringing with her the foul stench of Demetrius that wafted from her pores and quickly diffused throughout the entire condo. Watching her unusually lithe gait, I knew immediately that she had recently traded blood with the vamp. I shook my head, scowling in disgust.

Josh shot a cold look after her that she promptly ignored as she walked into the room. I stepped in front of the coffee table, blocking her view. Behind me I heard the faint scrape of the rod against the wooden table that indicated Sky had removed it from view.

Chris did her best to ignore my disapproving scowl as she announced, "London's gone."

"And?" Josh responded.

She smiled. "You visited her last night—now she's gone. A less cynical person would believe that was just a coincidence." She looked between myself and Josh. When neither of us bothered to answer, she turned to Sky. "What's going on?"

Sky shrugged.

"Chris," Josh said, crossing his arms over his chest, "I don't mind sharing information with you. In fact, you may be quite helpful in the matter. At this time, I have no new information for Demetrius. Are you here on your own or for Demetrius?"

I wasn't so sure she could distinguish between the two.

She smiled, giving Josh a full measure of her casual, disarming charm as she sauntered toward him. "I'm just a friend, stopping by. There's no harm in that, is there?"

"We're hardly friends. Chris, if you betray me—"

"You have my word."

He scrutinized her, unconvinced. When his gaze finally met mine, I gave a subtle shake of my head. When it came to Demetrius and the vamps, she couldn't be trusted anymore.

"Okay," he told her.

Before he could say more, I took her by the elbow and led her into the next room. She followed, gaping at me in disgusted disbelief. Once in the room, she snatched her elbow away. As she tried to walk out, I grasped her arm and threw the door shut, but it bounced off the frame and swung back open. She rounded on me with red-faced fury.

"Don't touch me!"

I stared back at her, wondering what in the world I could say this time that would get through to her. When it came to exchanging blood with Demetrius, she was like a drug addict amped up on her high. *This is the worst time to talk to her,* I realized, but it was too late. On an impulse, I'd already passed the point of no return. If I was to get through to her, I'd have to walk a very fine line. Frustrated, I rubbed my hands over my face and then through my hair, willing an answer that didn't come. Finally I surrendered in a long exhale.

"I know you well," I started. "Whatever you're sacrificing, tolerating, or dealing with to receive such considerations from Demetrius will eventually outweigh its benefits. I'm not sure when it will happen, but until then, don't you ever come around me, reeking of him. Do you understand?"

She reared back in offense. "You don't know me as well as you think, or you would know I didn't enter this foolishly or without considering the consequences. I can't keep having this discussion. I'm tired of it, and I'm sure you are, too. Make your decision now: either you deal with it and we don't have this discussion again, or you don't and we're through. Those are the only two options you have."

I leaned close to her, feeling the heat radiating from her body as my lips brushed against her ear. "I'm not the one who needs to make the decision—you are."

She pushed me back hard enough to bounce me off the wall. "You're such a selfish bastard. I came to you first. I asked you to change me."

"I refused." *And I was right to.*

"So don't bitch to me because you're not happy that I went to Demetrius. That's on you."

"You didn't know what you were asking. You still don't."

"You told me I can't keep hunting and expect to stay on top. And you know what? You're right," she said through gritted teeth. "Happy now? But there's nothing else for me out there. Can you understand that? I'm a Hunter. I belong in this world, not out there"—she gestured—"stamping bingo cards with a bunch of Q-tips. I can't keep this up without getting killed. Not unless I get a leg up. You turned me down. Fine, but just remember, I asked you first. You think I want to be involved with Demetrius and the vampires? I loathe every second of it, but at least he's offering."

"What are you offering in return?"

Her arm was a blur as it swung out and slapped me, knocking me a step to my left. I resisted the urge to touch my jaw, even though it ached from the blow; I didn't want to give her the satisfaction, but she'd surprised me. Without *his* blood, that wouldn't have happened. "I know you think changing you is a simple matter," I said carefully, "but it's not."

"What's so hard about it? Apparently I just need to growl a lot and lose my temper."

I turned my head and gave her a sideways look. "I was born a were-animal. Your body isn't designed for the change. The first time you change, nearly every bone in your body will break. Your muscles won't just expand like mine, they'll be shredded and re-formed. You think everyone survives the change, but they don't. Sometimes the body just breaks apart and fails to pull itself back together. Sometimes the shock and pain are so much the heart fails. I've seen it go wrong too many times."

"I can take it," she insisted, puffing out her chest.

"You're strong. But you can't will yourself through that kind of pain. Even if you did survive, there's the constant struggle with your animal nature."

"You all do just fine," she snapped.

"It's not the same. Everything will be harder for you."

"Steven was changed."

"He had Sebastian and Joan to guide him. And he was young. His body was more malleable."

"Screw you," she snarled.

I felt my fists clench and forced them open. *Please understand.* "I can't. Do that to you."

"It's not your choice," she said softly. "I've got a job to do. And whatever you have planned, I'm going with you whether you want me or not."

I remained on the other side of the living room, fuming, while Josh filled her in on the capsa and what we intended to do. I did have one option Chris hadn't accounted for; I could've tied her up and left her in her BMW, but if Josh was right we might be walking into a hornet's nest. We might need her skills before the night was through.

Once she understood the plan, we left together, climbed into my SUV, and began to scour the city while Josh held the capsa in his hand, waiting for some sort of signal that the rod was reacting to Ethos's energy. After an hour of driving, I was about to give up when Josh straightened in the passenger seat, his excitement palpable as he brought the tip of the rod level with his eyes. Glancing from the driver's seat, it seemed the glow of the rod had brightened slightly.

Swiveling in the passenger seat, he slowly swung the rod in an arc, first to the right, then to the left, until he finally stopped and pointed. Following his direction, I turned at the next intersection. For the next hour we followed the glow of the rod as it waxed and waned, obliging me to double back and retrace our steps several times. Eventually, we found ourselves parked on the road, staring at a well-lit white farmhouse. As we sat parked at the end of the driveway, the smoky glow of the rod was strong enough to light the cab of the SUV.

"We're about twenty miles from the retreat," I said.

"That's within range," Josh said to me.

In the backseat, I saw Chris was armed with two pistols holstered at her hips, and a knife sheathed to her thigh. Sky was on the edge of her seat, her eyes bright with anger. She was ready for revenge, but she was also weaponless. I reached across Josh to open the glove compartment, drew out a knife that I kept there, and handed it to her.

"Let's just hope we didn't find Ethos himself," Josh said.

At my direction, he tucked the rod inside his jacket, muting the light. I turned off the vehicle lights and backed the SUV up the driveway to the house.

"What are you doing?" Sky asked.

My attention remained fixed on the front door, via the rearview mirror, until I stopped about twenty meters out and left the engine running. "Leave your doors open," I said as we emerged from the SUV. The edge of the soybean fields on either side of us provided at least a hundred feet of open, uneven ground, mostly parched grass and weeds. At least we'd have some warning if the genums tried to surprise us, but an attack in force could prevent our escape by the SUV.

Most of the rooms in the house were lit, on both floors, but the curtains were drawn. We were going to have a hard time getting a look inside. The windows were closed, and there was no sign of movement.

"Remember," Josh whispered, "we're not here to fight. We just need to verify the genums are there. Then we come back with reinforcements."

I glanced at Sky and frowned. *I shouldn't have let her come.* If the genums were inside, there was a good chance we were going to get their attention. Depending on how many were there, the situation could deteriorate quickly.

"If I tell you to run," I said softly, "run to the SUV. Do not hesitate." I pointed out the cardinal points of the compass as I said, "North, south, east, west. If I tell you to run in any of those directions, do it. Don't wait for clarification. Don't second-guess me. Just run, and don't stop running until I tell you."

We were about six feet from the porch when the front door gently swung open and six small, hairless monkeys spilled onto the porch to scrutinize our arrival. Genums, I assumed, but they had a simian appearance, with long hands and feet, and walked on their knuckles as they slunk toward us.

"Well, that's confirmed," Josh whispered, raising the rod in front of his chest.

They were too close to us to run for the SUV. I crouched, drawing a knife from my boot sheath. Sky crouched with her knife held in front of her, while Chris laid her palms over the grips of her pistols.

Three of the creatures sprang toward me, nearly quadrupling in size as they rose onto their feet. Their short noses extended into long snouts and their canine teeth grew to unnaturally long fangs. Mangy gray fur burst from their skin, completing the disconcerting impression of large bipedal wolves.

I shifted, putting my back to my brother and forcing two of the genums to come around the third to reach me. The lead genum leapt snarling. I brought one hand up and caught its throat mid-leap, then drove my knife into its chest. The genum instantly disappeared, only to reappear on the ground in front of us, seemingly dead. I felt Josh shift away from me toward the motionless figure as I sidestepped again to position one of my remaining two genums in front of the other.

The popping of gunfire erupted behind me, and I heard Sky's frustrated growl, but I didn't dare risk a glance as the next genum swiped its claws at my head. I pivoted on my heel, positioning myself on the outside of its extended arm, then drove the knife up into the neck and into the brain. The last genum leapt just as its partner disappeared. I ducked, narrowly missing its fangs, and jabbed the knife up beneath its ribs toward its heart. The genum disappeared before it hit the ground.

Turning back to the porch I saw it reappear next to the other five, all seemingly dead—three of them with gunshot wounds to the forehead. A dark, thick ether rose like a roiling steam from the creatures as Josh gathered it with the capsa, moving from one corpse to another.

I glanced to Sky, relieved that she appeared unharmed, as did Chris.

"Ethan," Josh said, backing from the house as another fourteen genums emerged from the door.

"I think we should leave," Sky urged.

One genum emerged from the others, rising onto its back feet as it strode toward Sky. Like the first group, it transformed into a large mangy wolf. Almost immediately, it transformed again, this time into a distorted human figure. The genum hesitated, seemingly confused, as it continued to change. Sky gaped at a grotesque scaled humanoid with jet-black reptilian skin. It screamed as scales peeled away from its body, revealing a bright inner light that seemed to be burning its way out from the inside until the dirt around it was littered with smoldering scales and the thing became a humanoid body shaped by light.

The other creatures stared at Sky, seemingly in awe.

Horrified, she began backing her way toward the SUV.

"Run to the car," I said calmly. She broke into a run and Chris and Josh followed. I jogged backward at first, making sure the genums weren't on our heels, but their attention was absorbed by the light creature. When I heard car doors slamming, I turned and ran the last dozen feet, jumped into the driver's seat, then raced the SUV down the driveway to the street and sped away. I assumed the creatures couldn't drive, but that didn't stop me from keeping an eye on the rearview mirror.

The drive back to the condo was quiet as we all tried to grapple with what we had seen. Josh frequently glanced over his shoulder at Sky, at times with awe, at other times with an intense curiosity. I did the same. *What are you?* The question kept going through my mind, and I had no answer. The mystery that was Sky had only gotten deeper. Judging from the look of shock on her face, she didn't have any answers.

I looked to Chris, who appeared equally confused. Worse, she was curious. When I dropped them off at the condo, I wanted to pull Sky aside, but she went straight to her vehicle, ignoring our stares as she drove away.

I returned home and poured myself a Scotch, hoping to soothe the questions that now played on an endless loop through my mind, leaving no room for answers. I was pouring my third drink when my phone vibrated. Stacy.

"It's late," I answered.

"Yup. Are we doing criminal cases, now?" she asked in a nervous tone. "Or doing research for some as yet unannounced paranormal TV show?"

I scowled. "If you're going to drunk dial, call someone who isn't your boss."

"Well," she sighed heavily, "I e-mailed you my research on those names you gave me. And then I took a muscle relaxer and a sedative. If you need anything else, call me. I'll get back to you as soon as I wake up, about twelve hours from now."

I ended the call and opened the e-mail app on my phone.

It had been a long time since I'd first learned that my godmother was a Moura. It had been the only time she'd offered an explanation. Much of the history of their tradition had been lost over generations, but the Mouras were always women with supernatural abilities, which meant they could be elven or fae as well as witches. Whatever they were, they took human form in order to better disguise themselves in the world. In the beginning, there were five Mouras Encantadas, each assigned to protect one of five powerful mystical objects. When a Moura died, her responsibilities fell to the next female in her family line.

The first name in Stacy's report was the last protector of

the Gem of Levage. I already knew she was dead, but I wasn't prepared for what appeared to be a police photo of her body. It showed a woman who had died in a moment of severe terror, her arms frozen in an outstretched position as if forever reaching out in a desperate plea for help that would never come. According to the baffled coroner's report obtained by Stacy, the body showed no visible signs of direct damage. I assumed she'd died at the hands of some sort of magic—or from pure terror. Demetrius had obtained the Gem last year, though I doubted he'd been the one to kill her.

The Moura protecting the *Clostra* had been living in Texas before she disappeared from any public records over two decades ago. I made a mental note to follow up with her, then remembered my promise to Claudia. I would ask my godmother about the *Clostra* later. The Moura protecting the *Fatifer* had only a brief record of visiting the country a decade ago, traveling to and from Holland. Presumably she'd immigrated there.

That the Moura protecting the Aufero was deceased was hardly a surprise, considering it had eventually been destroyed by Marcia. This Moura had been known by several names, although Claudia had only given me one. I rubbed the tension from my eyes and read the names again. I'd read correctly the first time. The Moura had emigrated from Portugal over thirty years ago, then changed her name a number of times, as if running from someone. Her final name, the name she was using when she was murdered, was Senna Nunes. She was Skylar's biological mother.

I drank my Scotch, then carried my phone into the living room and dropped into a leather recliner. According to Sky's family, Senna had estranged herself. Whether that was before or after she came to the United States wasn't clear. Apparently, she hadn't surrendered the Aufero to them. I knew because they'd come looking for it. They had a duty to perform, but Sky was Senna's only daughter, which made her first in line to take on the role of Moura. Thanks to me, her family now knew of Sky's existence. Their interest in her was hardly passive, and no amount of threats from me would stop them from finding her unless they chose to accept her as Moura. *Hardly a safe bet. They know nothing about her.* They did know about Maya, who had to be involved with the Aufero as well. Was she dormant, or was she playing a role now?

The only thing I hated more than questions was not having answers.

The family was the least of Sky's concerns. The orb was protected for a reason. Sky was more mysterious and in more danger than I'd ever imagined. *Does she know? Has she been lying this entire time?* I found that hard to believe. How could she even know, unless Senna had passed on the knowledge of Sky's heritage through her adopted mother. Or Sky could've learned her heritage directly from Maya.

I brought the tumbler to my lips before realizing it was empty.

A few hours later I stood at Sky's door, calming myself by slowing my breath. She answered with an expectant smile that quickly faltered.

Who were you expecting?

"May I come in?" I asked as a formality, hoping to put her at ease. "Drop the ward."

"Why don't you do it?" she said with a defiant smirk.

I sighed and pressed my hand against the translucent barrier, triggering a sharp shrill. Sky watched with fascination as sparks of lavender and gold erupted across the ward, then quickly faded as it collapsed. I brushed past her into the house.

"We need to talk."

Frowning, she dropped down onto the sofa and waited. I

paced, organizing my thoughts. If she didn't know already, she was in for a hell of a shock. Would she give me an honest answer? Periodically I glanced to her for a clue and came up frustratingly empty.

"Where were you born?" I finally asked.

"Ohio," she offered, surprised. "I came to Illinois when I was six."

I gave her a speculative, sideways look.

"I am not you, Ethan. I have nothing to hide."

I strode across the room and knelt in front of her, catching her by surprise once more. "That's the problem. You have plenty you should be hiding, but you don't have the good sense to do so." I glanced aside and closed my eyes, dreading what came next. "What do you know of your birth mother?"

"This is getting old. Let's drop the BS. Obviously, you know something pretty big or you wouldn't be here. So why not just tell me?"

"Last year, you spoke with Maya. Four days you were with her. That's a long time. What did she talk to you about?"

Her expression became a defiant pout as she folded her arms over her chest. "Don't remember."

Then there's nothing I can do for you. Furious, I stood up and crossed the room to open the door. "I do believe you will be missed when you're dead."

"What is wrong with you?" she shouted. "Why do you think that's an acceptable thing to say to someone?"

I slammed the door and stared at her, wondering if there was any way I could save her from the same fate the Gem's Moura had suffered. *If she's not going to trust me, she's on her own.*

Sky hesitated, wrestling with something. "She told me that she was murdered and was forced to live this life as a spirit shade," she begrudgingly explained. "At first, she was only drawn to hosts with great power, but she soon learned that it was a miserable life because those with great power often possessed great evil. And she learned that those with power longed to host her because she enhanced their gifts. Then she showed me parts of my mother's life."

I didn't need to hear her vitals to know she was telling the truth. I saw it in her eyes. "You were born in Ohio," I explained with a sigh, "but your mother was born in Portugal, where she abandoned her responsibility as one of the five Mouras Encantadas. They guard mystical objects." Sky gaped at me as I slowly walked back into the room. "Her job was to protect the Aufero, the very orb that Marcia currently has in her possession. Your mother's death made her failure and responsibilities fall on the child she left behind. Right now, there are a select few that have this information, but I am the only one that cares whether you live past tonight. As I said before, you keep drawing attention to yourself, making it easier for the people she betrayed to find you. Your death will be no one's fault but your own."

I unfolded a printed photo from my pocket and handed it to her. "This is the Moura responsible for guarding the Gem of Levage."

She winced at the grotesqueness of the photo, then shook her head. "Why would you tell me this information like this?"

"My fire-and-brimstone warnings went ignored and friendly advice doesn't seem to work, either." I frowned at her. "How does a person get through to someone like you?" By the shocked indignation in her expression, I could see this conversation was going to descend into an argument about everything but the facts. I turned and walked out of the house, leaving her with the photo and hoping she would eventually come to her senses.

CHAPTER 15

The next day, I joined Steven, Gavin, and Josh in Sebastian's office. The capsa sat on his desk, drawing everyone's attention, though I doubted anyone felt the dark magic undulating within the blackened rod as intensely as I did. After Josh explained the rod's function, I described the encounter at the white farmhouse.

Gavin didn't approve. "You engaged them on your own?"

"We were conducting reconnaissance," I said stiffly, preferring to punch the scowl from his lips. "Unfortunately, we were discovered, but the rod has been tested." I turned my attention to Sebastian. "The capsa works."

Gavin scoffed. "And now Ethos knows our strategy."

"*Our strategy*," I snapped, "is to kill as many of the creatures as possible and claim his energy from them as a prelude to killing Ethos."

"But now he could move his creatures," Gavin complained. "He could disperse them all over the area. We'll have to find them all over again."

"He hasn't," Josh said. "This morning, I transported to the small woods outside the house. They're still there. In fact, I don't see any sign of them moving or even preparing for us."

He appeared mystified. "I don't think Ethos cares. He's supremely arrogant."

Sebastian sat on the corner of his desk. "Can you capture enough of his energy from the genums to make a difference?"

Josh considered the question carefully. "He's using a lot of energy on them, but I don't know his limits. I do know that tomorrow is his deadline. After that he'll come for us, and I don't think we can defeat Ethos at his full strength. The capsa is our best shot. It's our only shot."

"Will Demetrius show?" Gavin asked, doubtful.

"He will," Sebastian said confidently. "Ethos has made his intentions to destroy the Seethe perfectly clear. Demetrius needs our strength as much as we need his."

"What's the strategy?" Steven asked.

"We go tonight," I answered. "We make one approach, up the driveway."

"That's wide open. They'll see us coming," Gavin complained. "We should hit them from the woods and from the rear, simultaneously."

"Josh has to be as close as possible to the genums when they die. We need them all in one place where he can get to their corpses. If we have to clear the house, we'll miss a lot of bodies. We want them out and in the open."

"I should carry the capsa," Steven said to Josh. "We'll need you for the fight."

Josh shook his head. "The capsa requires a source of magic to provide a spark. I have to be the one to hold it."

I appreciated that he didn't mention Sky. She could wield the rod as well, but there was no chance I was going to let that happen. If he got into trouble, Josh could easily transport himself away. She didn't have that option.

"As Ethan said," he continued, "we can't afford to miss one body. There's going to be a lot of chaos. I can transport myself across the battlefield if I have to."

"That takes a lot of energy," I said.

Josh shrugged. "We're talking very short distances."

I gave my brother a stern look. "Your last transport is off the field. If you're running out of energy, you leave, regardless of the state of the battle. Understand?"

He rolled his eyes at me, but agreed with a repressed nod.

"I guess the next question," Steven said, suddenly anxious, "is who fights?"

Who stays behind, you mean.

He continued, "We have a lot of wounded who are still recovering."

"Winter will have to be locked into a cell," I said, only half joking. The same went for Marko and half a dozen others. I wasn't about to send them out as cannon fodder. Joan was questionable. As a superior species, she'd healed faster than the rest. I'd sparred with her yesterday. She still tired easily.

We waited silently while Sebastian considered, rubbing his chin as he thought. "Agreed," he said finally. "Joan will remain here with the others. They will assist Dr. Baker and Dr. Jimenez to receive the wounded."

Tension melted from Steven's body.

"I'll inform her and Winter," Sebastian said. I didn't envy him.

"I'd recommend Sky stay here as well."

"Why?" Sebastian asked, frowning.

"She's not a member of this pack," I reminded him. "This fight isn't hers."

Ignoring him, I waited for Sebastian's decision, expecting him to agree with me. In his own way, he cared about Sky. She'd been training hard over the last year. Her sword skills were decent, as was her defensive magic, but most of her experience came from training. She'd never experienced the chaos of a large-scale battle.

"Ethos has singled her out for attention," he said. "Ethan, her life depends on our success. She has the right to fight with us. If that's her wish, I'm not going to deny her."

"As long as she stays out of my way, I'm fine with it," Gavin declared, earning a dark look from Steven and me and a disapproving scowl from Sebastian.

"I'll present our plan to Demetrius, personally," he said. "No need to make this more complicated than it already is." He picked up his phone from his desk.

The rest of us took our cue to leave. *Better to break the news to Marko now.*

I found him at a bench in the gym, working his upper body with heavy dumbbells. Both the gym and the sparring room were alive with activity. I watched him as he struggled with weight that had been easy for him before his injury. His bicep trembled as he finished a set and placed the dumbbell on the floor. His body was slick with sweat, and he was breathing harder than he should be. Noticing my approach, he straightened and picked up the dumbbell, pumping it quickly up and down. After two reps, he returned the dumbbell to the floor, unable to continue his charade. He greeted me with a frown, then mopped the sweat from his face with a nearby towel.

I smiled. "Getting stronger."

"I'll be ready for the fight," he promised.

I squeezed his shoulder as he read my gaze, then quickly rose to his feet.

"You can't leave me behind," he insisted, posturing as if for a fight. "If you don't think I'm up for it, let's take it over to the ring and I'll show you."

The closest pack members quietly left their machines and weights and continued their workouts farther away.

"I need your honest assessment."

"Okay," he gave an emphatic nod. "I'm ready."

"Not you. Winter."

He pulled his head back and scowled, confused.

"Is she ready to fight Ethos? Your honest assessment," I stressed.

He glanced about the room as he struggled with his answer, then reluctantly admitted, his voice soft, "No. She'd put up a hell of a fight, but she's still too weak. Her reactions are slower than usual. Against an opponent like Ethos, she'd probably go straight at him and get herself killed."

"That's your honest assessment?"

He nodded. "That's my honest assessment, yeah."

"Do you think you're in better condition to fight Ethos than Winter is?"

Marko glared at me for a long moment, then finally lowered his gaze. "Crap."

"If we fail, the last stand will be here," I promised. "Then everyone fights."

He flipped his towel across his shoulder, sniffed, then walked away without returning my gaze. I watched him leave, then followed, stopping by the sparring room when I heard a familiar grunt. Inside I saw Winter and Sky in the ring. In the span of a few minutes I watched as she brought Winter to the mat three times. While not a pushover, she clearly wasn't her usual self. Sky noticed as well, refusing to gloat.

"Let's take a break," she suggested.

"You getting tired of kicking my butt?" Winter chided, wiping blood from her nose. "Now that I've lured you into a false sense of security, you're just going to quit?" She shook her head and dropped into an aggressive stance. Thirty seconds later she put Sky on the mat, only to join her a moment later when she countered with a predictable ankle sweep.

I left the gym before either of them saw me.

An hour later I heard Winter cursing from Sebastian's office, her angry objections carrying to the farthest corners of the house. I found Sky in the entryway of her room, listening with a sad expression. At my approach, her gaze become cold and angry. She leaned forward slightly, her body stiffening as if preparing for an argument she had no intention of losing.

"I'm not injured," she said. "There's no way you're keeping me from fighting with the pack."

"No," I agreed softly, scrutinizing her. Her body eased slightly, but she wasn't quite ready to trust my intentions. I wanted to talk her out of it, but that wasn't going to happen. The best I could do was prepare her. "You've worked hard. Winter is almost complimentary about your skills." Her lips cracked a hesitant smile. "It's going to be chaos out there."

She nodded. "I'm ready."

I frowned. *No one is ready for the first time.* "In training, you have one opponent to watch. Out there, they won't line up for you and take turns. Watch your flanks. Keep your head on a swivel. It only takes a moment to get killed. Stay close to one of us." *I'll be next to you the entire time.* "And don't let yourself get isolated."

She waited a moment, then asked, surprised, "Is that it?"

"In the heat of battle, that's enough," I said, then walked away before I begged her to change her mind.

Beneath the dull light of a waxing crescent moon, the pack gathered in the tall cornfield across the street from the white farmhouse. We arrived from several directions, careful not to draw the attention of prying eyes. I arrived with a sword in one hand, the flat of the blade resting against my shoulder. Sebastian gripped his sword in front of him, his free hand swinging over a dagger sheathed at his hip. Sky was armed with a sword as well, while Gavin carried a double-bladed battle axe in front of him with both hands. Josh stood beside me with the capsa, wearing an anxious expression. Our success hinged on defeating the genums before Ethos appeared. If he should lead them into the battle, or arrive before the bulk of them were killed, our chances of success were drastically diminished. Failure meant certain death, for those gathered here as well as those left behind at the retreat.

I was surprised to find Steven and Taylor arriving with Chris, a heavy caliber sniper rifle slung over her shoulder. Her hair was pulled back into a tight ponytail. Her jaw was set and her eyes burned with a smoldering fury. She loved a fight. Under normal circumstances I would expect to find her relaxed, even jovial, in anticipation. Sebastian had mentioned a tension between her and Demetrius that had bordered on violence when she'd appeared at the retreat during their strategy session. *Did he finally make it clear that he considers her his possession?* Scowling, she turned away from my questioning gaze. I wondered, but there was no obvious bruising or cuts on her arms or hands, no blood on her shirt like before, but her neck was conspicuously hidden beneath a high collar.

Before I could inquire further, Demetrius arrived with his Seethe in a single tight group. Tension rippled between vamps and were-animals as the two groups came together. It was only a year ago that the vamps had attacked us during the full moon, betraying an ancient agreement in the process. Judging by the growls and muttering arising from my pack, that betrayal was still a fresh wound. While much of our pack were weaponless, intending to fight in their animal forms, most of the vamps were armed with swords. Demetrius carried a long knife at his hip as well. His eyes narrowed at the sight of Chris, a slight sneer forming on his lips. Beside him, Michaela eyed Chris with a dreamy, murderous look.

Turning her back on them, Chris gestured to the copse of trees on the west side of the farmhouse. "I'll take a high position, there," she informed me, then walked out of the cornfield and across the road, cutting an angle that would take her around the house.

"Why did you bring her?" Demetrius snarled.

I stared down at him. "She's a good shot."

"I want her off this field. She does not belong here."

"You released her," Sebastian stated. "She is no longer in your employ. The choice is hers."

That was news to me, but welcome. "We're lucky to have her skill set," I informed Demetrius.

"Her safety is in your hands," he snapped, then walked away. Michaela gave me a crooked, almost empathetic smile, then followed him.

At Sebastian's signal, most of the pack stripped and transformed into their were-animals, sending a fresh ripple of anxiety among the vampires. *The sooner we get this battle started, the better.* As the Pack and Seethe advanced out of the cornfield in two separate groups, Sebastian and Steven positioned themselves on Sky's left while I appeared on her right. She acknowledged us with an appreciative half-smile, then focused her attention straight ahead as she steeled herself, her expression grim and determined. Gavin had my right, while Josh followed behind me with the capsa. Angry wolves trotted behind us.

We crossed the street, spreading out on either side of the driveway as we approached the two-story white house, making no effort to disguise our approach or mute our movements. Gazing at the copse of trees, it took me a moment to spot Chris perched on a thick branch about twenty feet off the ground, taking aim at the house.

As the front door swung open, I held my breath. The genums spilled out, transforming into their massive forms, but there was no sign of Ethos. I heard a sigh of relief from my brother behind me.

The head of one genum exploded unexpectedly, followed immediately by the sharp report of Chris's rifle. The rest of the creatures charged, baring fangs and dagger like claws. Growling barks and angry roars erupted around me as we charged to meet the enemy, with Sebastian and I getting a couple steps ahead of Sky to spare her the initial brunt.

The two forces met like stone walls colliding.

Roaring, I drove my sword two-handed through the skull of the first genum, turned the blade, then pushed the creature off with my boot. Josh slipped in behind me with the capsa as I stepped over the body to swipe at the next creature, forcing it back a step. I barely had time to notice the dark, cloud-like vapor that wafted up from the corpse toward the capsa.

Gavin directed a group of were-animals, while Sebastian wielded his sword and dagger with a deadly, efficient grace. Sky grunted next to me as she ducked under a raking swipe of claws, then drove the tip of her sword up into the underside of a genum's chin. It froze in shock, giving her the opportunity to grip her sword with both hands and drive the blade up into its skull. It fell backward, pulling the blade from her hand. As she recovered the pommel and yanked at the blade, trying to free it, I shifted to her side, hacking at the claws of a genum that tried to reach her. Screeching furiously, it lunged at me with its fangs and I drove the sword into its maw.

Sky finally yanked her blade free and strode forward to swing at the next genum in front of her. Beside her, Sebastian pivoted away to slice his sword into a charging genum's neck, then drove his dagger into its heart. Steven filled the gap at Sky's left flank, protecting her as she parried and attacked the genum in front of her.

I barely saw Josh running and sometimes transporting among the fallen before a lunging genum distracted me. Its deadly claws just missed my belly as I turned on my heel, slashing down across its shoulder with my sword. The genum jerked away, howling. Backing away as I pressed, it tripped backward over a dead wolf and landed on its back. I drove my sword down into its chest, feeling the satisfying crunch of bones through my blade. Before I could withdraw my sword, Gavin decapitated the genum with a single swipe of his axe.

I turned back to Sky and saw a pair of wolves and a dingo race past our ragged line, throwing themselves at the genums as they leapt for jugulars. They exposed their bellies in the process. The dingo and one of the wolves were quickly eviscerated, while the other wolf was knocked aside. Across the battlefield I saw several other were-animals had met the same fate. The rest had begun to shift their strategy, getting behind the genums and attacking their legs and ankles to bring them down, then swarming over them.

A thin layer of vapor was forming on the battlefield, rolling like a mist as it sought out the capsa, regardless of where Josh was. *He could've just planted the damn thing behind us,* I growled, but he wasn't taking chances. He was every-where, transporting himself to deliver the rod to every corpse, but he was having a hard time keeping up. I yelled at him to pay attention, but he disappeared and reappeared a dozen feet away, oblivious.

Fangs appeared to my right, rising toward my face. I pivoted, but hadn't seen the attack in time. A bullet ripped through the creature's head followed by the report from Chris's rifle. I didn't have time to acknowledge the shot before leaping to Sky's aid as two genums pressed her back-ward. I cut into the back of one while she sliced across the chest of the other, then parried the counterattack.

A glance across the battlefield revealed the vamps were fighting ferociously, none more entranced by the sheer carnage of the fight than Demetrius. He wore a fiendish grin, baring his fangs as he sliced and jabbed his way through the genums as they attempted to converge on him. In quick succession, bullets ripped through the skulls of two of them —expert shots taken dangerously close to Demetrius. A few inches off and Chris could've easily shot him in the head or neck.

Is she showing off, or trying to kill him? The rifle was powerful enough that a well-aimed shot might do enough damage to effectively decapitate him.

A nearby vamp screamed as a genum drove its claws into his heart, triggering a reversion that could only be stopped with fresh blood. I sure as hell wasn't going to oblige. Apparently the vamps had no strategy for saving their wounded, which was fine by me.

An angry shout from Sky focused my attention on her as she slipped on the blood-soaked ground nearby. The genum in front of her pressed for the kill. Before I could react, a were-dingo leapt to defend her, only to be eviscerated by a swipe of razor-sharp claws. I roared in white-hot fury as I charged to her aid. The genum backed away from my blade as it swept the air in front of its chest. Countering, it raised its claws to swipe across my face, but I caught it on the back-swing, slashing the dense gray flesh just above the genum's branch-like knee. The knee buckled. As the genum dropped, I sliced clean through its neck.

I spared a quick, anxious glance at Sky, relieved to see she had regained her balance and was uninjured. On the other side of her, Josh appeared next to a corpse. He had only begun to collect the escaping energy when a genum knocked him onto his back, tackling him and sending the capsa tumbling from his reach. As he wrestled with its arms, blocking its claws, I crossed the field in three strides and slammed into it with my body, sending it sprawling side-ways. I leapt over Josh, swinging down with all my strength as the genum rose. My blade cleaved down through its skull, slicing all the way through its torso. I roared in primal rage as the two severed halves collapsed away from each other.

From the ground beside me, Josh reached for the capsa. Sky snatched it from the dirt and held it over the creature, absorbing the dark vapor that arose from the corpse. I shielded her until she finished and gave the capsa back to Josh.

"Pay attention!" I shouted at him, then returned to the fight.

In the shifting battle, I found Demetrius fighting near us as he drove his sword through a genum's chest, the tip of his blade emerging from its back. It collapsed to its knees. Gloating, he placed his foot against its ribs and twisted his sword, completely unaware of another genum charging up behind him. Chase watched nearby, a cunning grin on his lips as he chose not to intervene. I looked up to Chris's perch to see she had the genum in her sights. What was she waiting for? The closer it got to Demetrius, the harder the shot. If she killed him by mistake—most likely the vamps wouldn't blame her for missing such a difficult shot. And if Demetrius died, Chase was the most likely successor. He'd probably reward her.

Catching motion out of the corner of my eye, I turned away to parry a blow from another genum. I fought on, expecting to hear the sound of Chris's shot at any moment, but it never came. After killing my genum, I turned to find Demetrius dismembering the genum that had tried to blindside him. Chase had already moved on to another fight. I glanced up at the tree to find Chris's perch conspicuously empty.

The battlefield became suddenly clear as I found no immediate enemy to kill. Glancing around me I saw the battle had all but ended, only a few scattered genums still fighting. As they quickly fell, Josh was there to capture their escaping energy. I felt a rush of relief to see he remained unscathed. Sky was safe as well, catching her breath as she leaned on the pommel of her bloodied sword protruding from the ground between Sebastian and Gavin. I started toward her until Gavin shook his head, letting me know she was alright. He turned to scrutinize her, allowing what appeared to be a hint of a smile.

Bodies and gore were strewn across the blood-soaked field. Steven and Taylor had survived, but a number of were-animals hadn't. Many of the vamps had died as well. Gabriella stood next to Chase, while Demetrius meandered across the battlefield with increasing agitation as he surveyed the bodies. Was he looking for Michaela, or Chris? Neither was in sight. I started toward the trees to look for Chris when I felt an oppressive wave of dark magic descend over the battlefield. Vampires and were-animals alike stood paralyzed by the overwhelming power that engulfed them.

Ethos.

CHAPTER 16

*D*ark magic pulsed across the field in stifling waves, leaving most of the Seethe and the pack frozen in terrified awe of its power. The darkness was so over-whelming that I wondered if our efforts had weakened Ethos at all. My sword in hand, I raced to Josh's side, assuming Ethos would target the capsa first in an attempt to regain his lost energy. Together, we stood back to back, waiting for the assault, while Gavin and Sebastian rallied the rest of the pack, drawing them out from their initial panic.

Sky was near Sebastian, but otherwise alone.

I shouted at her to run, but she seemed frozen. This fight was going to be too much for her. Ethos was more powerful than we'd imagined. Even if we succeeded in killing him, the casualties were going to be extensive. I wanted her as far from that field as possible, but I didn't dare leave my broth-er's side. When Ethos came, Josh was going to be the first target.

Before I could shout at Sky once more, Ethos appeared beside her. He was in his human form, the silver-haired witch with the purple eyes. His entire attention was focused on her.

Sebastian reacted first, lunging at Ethos, who cast him aside with a simple, effortless gesture. I charged, sword raised. Just before I was in range to strike Ethos down, a burst of copper sparks blinded me as I was repelled by a translucent protective field. I crashed to the ground a dozen feet away. Stunned for a moment, I heard violent roars and shouts interspersed with the crackle of electricity. Climbing to my feet, I saw Sebastian, Steven, and Gavin savagely attacking the field that surrounded Ethos and Sky, showering themselves in copper sparks as the field easily repelled their blows.

Seemingly unconcerned by the onslaught against his field, Ethos remained fixated on Sky, but the effort to maintain his field was draining his energy. As he slowly approached her, parts of his body began to shimmer, then flicker, briefly revealing oily black scales. She backed away from him, her eyes wide with terror, until he backed her up against the translucent barrier. She froze there, as if in a trance.

Electricity ran through my body as I felt my magic rising to the surface. Desperate to reach her, I picked up my sword and charged at the field once more, this time focusing my attention on a single point in the translucent wall just in front of me. His field was too powerful for me to bring down from the outside, but I could punch my way through. A ragged hole opened in the field, quickly sealing behind me as I landed between Ethos and Sky. I'd spent my entire life hiding my abilities from everyone, even my brother, but that didn't matter now. I didn't care about consequences. I probably wouldn't survive the day, but I was the only one able to stand between them.

He hissed in surprise, recoiling from me.

Hoping to escape the field with Sky, I reached out with my magic to push at the wavering walls of the field. They stretched, nearly to the breaking point, but I wasn't strong enough. The walls rebounded back to their original form. Ethos's eyes became a furious scarlet red. He flicked a hand toward me and I felt a crushing, unstoppable force slam into my chest, throwing me back through the field wall. I crashed to the ground a few feet away.

Ignoring the pain shooting through my body, I climbed back to my feet to find the vampires watching me with intrigued surprise. Sebastian and the other were-animals continued attacking the field at a furious pace, draining Ethos's power, while Josh positioned himself behind Sky and began to chant.

Once more, I crashed through the field. This time Ethos was prepared. He cast an arm toward me and I felt a force wrap around my torso, constricting my chest as it lifted me into the air and slammed me into the field wall. Again. And again. It battered me until I wasn't sure where I was. Pain exploded inside my skull like bursting fireworks. When I had nearly lost consciousness, Ethos swept his arm wide and I was flung back through the field to tumble several feet in the dirt. My head throbbed and pain stabbed at the back of my eyes as I once more picked up my sword and clambered to my feet.

I can do this all day.

Completing his chant, Josh gestured to the field. Inside, flashes of golden light burst between Sky and Ethos, knocking him to his knees and sending him sliding backward, but the effect was temporary. The golden light faded, and he rose unrestrained to his feet. Glaring at Josh, his eyes became black and lifeless like a shark's as he dropped a series of small pods to the ground. The pods quickly grew into small creatures that raced through the field toward my brother. Ethos smiled after them, eagerly anticipating his revenge, but he failed to notice that Josh had freed Sky from her trance.

She had crept around him. Drawing a knife from a sheath

at her thigh, she stabbed it deep into his neck. The creatures disappeared in a vaporous cloud as Ethos panicked, clawing at the knife. Blood pulsed in spurts from the wound. Judging by his gasps for breath I was certain that she had severed his trachea. Losing control of his power, he began to shift rapidly between human and his reptilian form that seemed marred by unnatural, disproportionate features.

I grinned at his efforts to remove the knife from his neck. With any luck, he'd succeed, hastening his blood loss. If he didn't suffocate first. Already he strained to remain on his feet. After a moment, he managed to grip the knife handle and pull it free. The expected spray of blood didn't follow. Instead, I felt a wave of magic that seemed to staunch the bleeding and repair his trachea. Able to breathe again, his recovery was nearly instantaneous. He grabbed Sky's cheeks with both hands and pulled her toward him until their noses touched. His eyes rolled into the back of his head as a thick fog emerged from his mouth, flowing into her mouth and nostrils. The green of her eyes disappeared as the vapor filled her pupils. Her mouth opened wide as if in a silent scream.

I lunged at the field, adding my fury to the others' as we desperately tried to wear the field down to get to her. Through the showering copper sparks, I saw his grotesque black form transform into a vaporous outline that drew itself into Sky until she had consumed it all. Ethos disappeared entirely.

The field collapsed.

As we ran to her, she collapsed to her knees, clawing at her throat as she choked. Josh reached her first and held a hand over her, chanting. I watched in helpless horror as she slowly strangulated while Josh tried one spell after another. *Not again!* I swore. I had watched her die once before—at my hands. I wasn't going to let her die again, but Josh was reaching the limits of his abilities. His expression became increasingly panicked.

My mind raced, grasping at anything. As I remembered the magic books I had taken from the library, the image of a single page appeared in front of my eyes as if it was being dangled before me. It wasn't a ritual I had the power to perform, but Josh could. As he pulled at his hair, I leaned into him and whispered the ritual.

He shook his head. "That's a myth. It will never work."

"Just do it," I urged, pushing him toward Sky. *Hurry.*

Still shaking his head, Josh leaned over her and began his chant. After a moment, he lowered his mouth nearly over hers. When he inhaled sharply, black vapor rose from her mouth to his. His cheeks swelled until they seemed about to burst, then he turned away and expelled the vapor that diffused harmlessly into the breeze. Sky's breathing eased slightly. I gestured for him to repeat the ritual, but he didn't need the encouragement. He bent down and drew more of the vapor from her. As he did, her eyes returned to normal. When he finished, turning to expel the vapor, she sucked in air in a panicked rush. Josh lowered himself to draw a third mouthful, but she pushed him away and sat up.

"I'm okay," she snapped. Her pupils remained dilated, her heart racing, as she rapidly sucked in breath, reassuring herself.

"It's all gone?" Josh asked, unconvinced.

It wasn't. I could feel a trace of Ethos's magic inside her still.

"I'm fine." She glanced evasively around the bloodied, body-strewn battlefield. "I'm fine."

Josh rose to his feet. "Of course you are."

Could he really not see that she was holding on to a splinter of power, or did he approve? I was about to challenge them both when Demetrius barked behind me.

"Where the hell is she?"

I turned to see him roaming the corpse-riddled field as

his Seethe looked on, reminding me that Chris still remained conspicuously missing.

"Find her now!" he commanded.

Vamps and were-animals alike quickly spread out. A few went straight to the trees, while most searched among the bodies.

I didn't expect them to find her there. She wouldn't have joined the melee, where being a lone human surrounded by powerful supernaturals would've put her at a disadvantage. She'd have stayed in her perch until she either ran out of ammunition or targets, and I knew she wouldn't run out of ammunition. I jogged to the copse of trees. When I found her rifle lying in the weeds, a sense of dread came over me.

"She's here," Josh called out from the center of the copse, his voice oddly strained. He stared down at the grass, his body slumped and his mouth agape. The strength drained from my legs as I rushed to his side, arriving just as Sky did. She gasped at Chris's mangled body lying in the grass, her figure barely more than a bloody pulp dotted with the dull white of jagged, protruding bones. She was still alive, but barely. Her heartbeat was feeble and faint. Each shallow breath was accompanied by a gurgling sound as she fought against the fluid building in her lungs. I stood next to Josh, frozen in horror.

Demetrius arrived, hissing at the sight of her. "How could you let this happen!" he screamed at me, enraged.

I turned on him with a fiery rage, my entire body suddenly as tense as a drum, my fists clenched into hammers. I stepped to him and shouted directly in his face, "You had no business getting her involved in the first place!"

"Do you think you own her?" he shouted back into mine, not backing up an inch. "I hired her because she is the best!"

The were-animals and vampires around us quickly chose sides, preparing themselves for another fight. More were arriving every moment from the battlefield.

I roared at him. "You used her!"

"I rescued her from a dog!"

Before I could wrap my hands around his throat, Sky appeared beside us, shouting fiercely, "This isn't helping!"

My gaze snapped to her, as did Demetrius's. In the same moment, we both realized that Chris's body was gone. Josh was gone as well. I quickly realized he must've transported her to Dr. Baker at the retreat. With her injuries, I couldn't imagine that she could be saved, but she shouldn't be left to die in a field. A rush of shame came over me. I'd let my rage get the best of me when I should've seen to Chris first.

Sky jabbed a finger a finger at my chest, her expression stern and furious. "You go to the house and see after Chris." She glared at Demetrius, then turned her wrath on the were-animals and vamps around us. "And the rest of you go home. It's over."

I stormed away from Demetrius without looking back. My anger was wound so tightly I wasn't sure I could keep from throttling his pale throat if I looked once more into those lifeless black eyes. I hurried across the neighboring field to where I'd left my SUV.

Speeding, I reached the retreat in record time. Dr. Jimenez was conducting triage in the entryway, though the number of injured were surprisingly few. The genums had shown a particular commitment to the kill, unwilling to settle for incapacitating their enemies. He was discussing the injured with Sebastian when I arrived.

"Ethan," Sebastian called to me, but I ignored him, striding directly to the clinic, where I found Josh anxiously waiting outside the double doors. Seeing my approach, he positioned himself against the seam of the doors, as if he could stop me.

"Out of my way," I commanded, but Josh held his ground.

"He needs the room to work, Ethan," Josh pleaded.

"Work?" I snapped. Was there even a chance he could save her? I stared at Josh, hoping and disbelieving.

"Ethan!" Sebastian called from the end of the hallway behind me.

I spun around, growling.

He gestured toward the front of the house. "We've got company," he said, then disappeared.

I turned to give the clinic doors a frustrated glare, then followed. Josh trailed behind me. Passing the windows in the entertainment room, I saw a number of vehicles parked haphazardly on the lawn at the front of the house, with more arriving. Demetrius had invited himself and had brought most of his Seethe with him.

Striding into the entryway, I found a cluster of furious were-animals agitating for a fight. At their head, Sebastian's large frame blocked the doorway.

"This is not acceptable," he said. "Take your people and go."

"Then I'll take her with me," Demetrius snapped.

I pushed through the crowd, finding Steven beside the door, next to Sebastian.

"I'm not leaving without her," the vampire insisted hotly.

"Then I'll make you!" I shouted, pushing past Steven. I'd nearly pushed past Sebastian before he held me back. The vamps behind Demetrius taunted me, hissing and snarling as I struggled to reach their Master.

"She is not yours to keep!" he spat.

Sebastian wrangled me around and pushed me back inside, where Steven and Josh got between me and door. Behind them I noticed a crouched Sky slip inside, angling herself past Sebastian. She gave me an irritated look, then squeezed past Josh and disappeared behind me.

"Ethan," Josh hissed at me, "We just fought a battle. We don't need another one. Look at them." He gestured to the were-animals behind me. Many of them had slight wounds. All of them appeared exhausted, but they were on their feet, shouting out the door and through the nearby windows at the vampires outside. My rage fueled them. I snarled, yanking myself free from Josh's and Steven's grips. For the sake of the pack, I did my best to contain my rage.

"Send them away and I will welcome you inside," Sebastian agreed at the door. "I will give you all the access to her that you require, if you agree to restrain yourself."

"And your dog?" Demetrius snapped, defiant.

Sebastian glanced over his shoulder to me. I growled, but nodded. Demetrius accepted the terms, dismissing his Seethe with an almost casual gesture before Sebastian stepped aside and invited him into the house. Demetrius entered, his expression a confused mixture of anger and sorrow.

"This way," I said tightly, leading Demetrius to the clinic.

We quietly eased inside, careful not to disturb Dr. Baker and Kelly as they worked intently on Chris. Their expressions were drawn, defeated, but they were doing everything possible for her. Sebastian and Sky filed in behind us.

After two hours, Dr. Baker had done everything he could to address Chris's wounds. While he stepped back, taking a moment to breathe, the rest of us remained silent. There were just the noises of the monitors and other equipment connected to her. Her breathing had eased, and Dr. Baker had pumped her full of pain medication. I could see the strain of failure in his eyes. Even if Chris had had the healing abilities of a were-animal, her injuries were likely too severe to survive.

After a moment I noticed Kelly glancing between Chris and the rest of us. With the backdrop of beeps and whirs from the machinery that monitored Chris and barely kept her alive, Kelly observed our silent grief with bewilderment. Slowly, steadily, her expression hardened into naked disgust.

"Whose genius idea was it to have her out there?"

Her accusation stung. Even Demetrius seemed taken aback. Before I could answer, the monitor sounded an alarm. Dr. Baker and Kelly reacted coolly, going straight to work.

"Cardiac arrest," he said to her as they worked to restart Chris's heart.

"Five minutes," Sky muttered beneath her breath, glancing at the clock on the wall.

After that, her brain will be damaged from lack of oxygen. I tensed, unblinking as I watched them work to get her heart beating. After what seemed an eternity, I realized I'd been holding my breath. The sudden beeping of her heart monitor brought a palpable relief to the room. Sky sighed aloud, expressing relief for both of us. I looked to her, admiring her strength. Nothing required her to be there, but she remained, resolute and strong and hopeful despite all odds.

Demetrius walked out of the room. A moment later his face appeared in the window, his expression hard and mournful as he watched. However twisted their relationship, he did care. But that didn't make him any less dangerous to Chris. He'd used his blood to lure her close. Without him, Chris wouldn't be lying on the hospital table, broken and dying.

While they tried to stabilize her, she went into another cardiac arrest. They revived her once more, only to have her heart fail again. By the time they finally got her stable, I had reached the limit of my endurance.

Once again, Kelly turned her wrath on us. "So guys, what's the endgame?" Her hard gaze passed over the others, then settled on me.

"I'll change her," I said. It was more likely to kill her than help her heal, but she was doomed anyway. There was no longer a reason to deny her what she wanted most from me.

Dr. Baker shook his head. "She will never survive it. Even a lesser species will be too hard for her body to endure. I don't think you realize how bad she is."

I know how bad she is. She's dying.

Josh appeared at my side, waiting in the silence as I battled my urge to run to Chris's crumpled form and change her anyway. If I didn't, she would die, but was I truly offering her mercy? Would I just be adding to her already unimaginable suffering?

"You have another option," Josh offered softly.

I gave him a questioning look, then followed his gaze until it stopped at Demetrius.

"No," I snapped, stiffening.

"Ethan." Josh's eyes were full of empathy as he held my gaze. "You'll regret it if you don't." Despite his dislike for Chris, it was impossible not to have compassion for the creature that lay in our clinic, broken into something barely human, suffering, but there was no chance I would condemn her to an eternity of evil depravity as a vampire.

I swallowed, turning away from his gaze. "I've learned to live with far worse." I wouldn't just hand her over to Demetrius to do what he would with her, forever.

"Ethan," Josh pleaded softly, but I ignored him.

Sebastian turned to Dr. Baker. "Don't let her suffer."

Kelly gaped, horrified and repulsed. "You're going to let her die?"

Sebastian ignored the accusation, frowning at Chris. I couldn't read his thoughts. Was he considering overriding my decision? He'd only deferred to me out of respect, but I knew his judgment wasn't clouded by my emotional involvement. To him, Chris was more liability than asset. Ultimately, that was all his decision came down to. As a human Hunter, she'd tried to kill Josh and conspired against our interests to capture Sky for the vamps. She had shown no compunction working against our interests when it had suited her. As a vampire, she could be highly dangerous.

Tears welled in Kelly's wide eyes. She gently laid a palm over her heart as she said, "Sebastian," as if he'd crushed her belief in him. If he knew, he didn't show it. Beneath his cold, steady gaze, she withered and sagged against the wall. Her eyes followed him as he turned and walked to the doors. He was halfway out of the clinic when he turned back to her, letting the doors swish shut behind him.

"Sometimes," he gently explained, "what seems like the cruelest thing is the best option."

Kelly's eyes passed over the rest of us once more, expecting one of us to take her side. When none did, her expression hardened into abhorrence. For the first time, she seemed to recognize that she was standing alone among monsters.

Behind her, Dr. Baker slowly turned off the monitors, then detached the multitude of lines that had connected them to Chris. My heart sank as I watched the slow, faint rise of her chest, expecting each to be her last. I listened to the faint, erratic beat of her heart as she stubbornly refused to die, but it was only a matter of moments.

"Ethan," Josh whispered beside me, adding urgency to his soft desperate plea.

I rounded on him with a harsh glower, daring him to press me further. I wanted her to live, but how could I damn her just to assuage my guilt? She'd taken Demetrius's blood because she'd wanted the abilities it granted her, but she'd never wanted to become a vampire. Whatever had happened between them in the end, I'd probably never know, but she'd walked away from Demetrius rather than let him own her. No. I would never surrender her to him. Stealing myself, I strode through the double doors and stood in front of Demetrius, glaring into his dark, heartless eyes. I didn't care about his pain. Her death was his fault. He'd used Chris's desperation for his own pleasure, and now she was paying the ultimate price. I didn't give a damn about his pain.

"Go home," I commanded.

Oblivious, he peered over my shoulder at Chris. When he

tried to step around me into the clinic, I shoved him back. His lips twisted into a vitriolic snarl. He bared his fangs in warning. Before I could tell him to go to hell, he pushed me hard enough that I stumbled across the hall and slammed into a wall, leaving a dent in the Sheetrock. *If that's how you want it.* I strode toward him, fists clenched, when Kelly suddenly appeared between us with her arms outstretched to keep us apart.

I glared over her head at him, letting him know I was ready to kill him at his convenience. He merely frowned, casually acknowledging Kelly, then turned back toward the doors with a forlorn look.

"Why can't he at least say good-bye?" she demanded of me. "Doesn't he at least deserve that much?"

He deserves nothing, I snarled, but she held her ground.

She was entranced by Demetrius's apparent grief, which did nothing to assuage his guilt. I was about to tell him so when I caught a look from Sebastian over the vamp's shoulder. My lips pressed together as I clamped my jaw shut. Reminding myself that this wasn't the time to fight a war, I did my best to suppress my anger. Though Sebastian wouldn't demand it of me, he wanted this crisis to end diplomatically. There was more at stake than my feelings. Our relations with the Seethe going forward depended a great deal on the moment at hand. If I were to deny Demetrius his chance to say good-bye, the consequences could affect our relations for decades. A little civility was all that was required. I ground my teeth, agonizing over my decision. *He couldn't change her,* I told myself. The battle had taken too much out of him, and I knew by the orange glow in his right eye that he'd not fed since before Ethos's defeat. Most likely he couldn't turn her, even if he wanted to. Allowing him to say good-bye to Chris was probably harmless, albeit offensive.

"Say your good-byes and leave," I grumbled, making a

show of glancing at my watch.

Demetrius disappeared. By the time I reached the doors, he was already at her side. At Sebastian's urging, Josh and Sky emerged from the room, followed by Kelly and Dr. Baker, to give Demetrius some privacy. Kelly remained at the doors, peering inside through the windows.

"What will happen to her when he is done?" she asked Dr. Baker next to her, her eyes glistening.

He sighed, choosing his words carefully. "She will be relieved," he promised.

His words were meant to be comforting. Instead, Kelly scoffed, horrified. "Relieved? You mean you will kill her."

Dr. Baker frowned, visibly wounded by her rebuke. "Yes."

Scowling, she shook her head in disgust as she peered back through the window. When he tried to touch her shoulder—meant to be a comforting gesture—she recoiled. He backed away, accepting her rebuke with a sad resignation.

After a few minutes of watching the disgusting image of a solemn Demetrius grieving next to Chris's broken body, I'd had enough. Sky stared at me, perplexed, as I stormed into the next room. I had one end of a couch off the floor before I stopped myself from throwing it. Why I didn't, I couldn't say. I could break every couch in the house and have them all replaced tomorrow.

Josh followed me into the room, wearing a pleading look. He just didn't know when to let up. "Ethan," he started.

I dropped the couch to the floor with a thud and growled a warning.

"You know it's what she wanted."

"Not. Him!" I shouted. "He doesn't get to have her like that!"

"Is that what this is about?" Josh shook his head, disappointed. "You're going to deny her a chance to live just because you can't stand seeing her with someone else?"

I reached under the couch and threw it one-handed

across the room. My brother had seen my temper too many times for it to faze him. I paced in front of him, scowling at the hall that led to the clinic. "She was trying to kill him."

"What? Demetrius?"

I continued pacing. "You didn't notice the way she looked at him before the battle?" He was sorting through his memories when I continued. "I said all along that he was going to go too far."

Josh frowned. "You think Demetrius did something to her?"

I stopped to jab a finger at his chest as I made my point. "If he turns Chris, he will have total control of her. Forever. She'll never have a choice. So, yeah, I'd rather see her die than become his."

I heard the bang of heavy metal doors slamming shut in the hall, followed by Sebastian's shout.

"Kelly!"

Josh and I ran into the hall to find Sebastian and Dr. Baker trying to force open the Alamo doors while Sky stood aside, shocked and horrified. Demetrius had no idea about the doors, let alone how to activate them. Kelly had done it. She'd locked herself and Chris inside the clinic—with Demetrius.

I ran to the door, adding my strength to Sebastian's, but it wouldn't budge.

"Kelly!" he shouted, banging the door with the bottom of his fist. "Open the door!"

Together, we assaulted the door, attempting to smash it in through sheer brutal strength. The metal whined and creaked and dented beneath the onslaught, but the locks didn't break—it had been designed to withstand just such an assault. I turned to Josh, expecting him to transport me inside.

"Iridium," he said with a defeated expression, gesturing to the doors.

Furious, I turned and slammed my entire body into the door. Iridium had been built into the door on my instructions, specifically to prevent a witch or vampire from transporting through it. There was nothing Josh could do because I'd made sure of it.

Gavin and Steven arrived, immediately adding their fury to the assault on the doors. After several minutes of throwing our bodies against it, the doors finally bent in at the center—enough that we could push the opening wider until the door finally broke in half and we all stumbled into the clinic, with Josh and Sky close behind. Apart from our arrival, the room was quiet. Chris and Demetrius were gone. Only Kelly remained, calmly cleaning up the mess left from the trauma of trying to save Chris. Fresh bruising was visible on her neck, surrounding a fresh vampire bite. She frowned at us as she straightened containers on a counter.

A growl rumbled from my throat as I glared at her.

"Where are they?" Sebastian demanded through clenched teeth, amber sparks flashing in his eyes, but she seemed oblivious to the danger as she removed the sheets from the hospital bed and began cleaning the vinyl table with a sanitizer. "Answer me!"

Kelly flinched. As she met his gaze, I saw fear finally gather in her eyes. He stepped closer to her, glowering. "I need you to tell me where they are."

She glanced at me, then the others, as if expecting help, shocked that we didn't understand the choice she'd made. Slowly, she backed away from him, guiding herself along the counter. Sebastian took several slow breaths, trying to calm himself, but he was in a rare anger, the kind of anger that could get Kelly killed if she wasn't careful. She'd betrayed the pack.

Unable to speak, he continued to glare down at her as he slowly advanced until she was forced to change direction to avoid being backed into a corner. She tried backing toward

Dr. Baker, looking for help, but he offered her no protection; he was just as furious as the rest of us. The only detail that might save her was that she didn't seem to fully understand the choice she'd made.

In her time working with Dr. Baker, Kelly had endeared herself to the pack. She was a skilled nurse and unfazed by our kind, which was rare among humans. Until then, she'd been fearless. But she wasn't ignorant of pack rules. Though she wasn't a member, the rules still applied to her. Did she think this was just a club house, and faced with her self-described *moral choice* we would all nod and agree to exempt her from punishment? Betrayal of the pack was the worst possible offense, and it was punishable by death. Sebastian was well within his rights to kill her. Judging from the depth of his anger, it was a very real possibility, one she was only now coming to grips with.

Finally, Sebastian turned his scowl to Dr. Baker. "You wanted her here, so you need to handle this." He started to walk out of the clinic, then stopped, turning to sneer at Kelly as if he might pass judgment on her after all, then abruptly went out of the broken steel doors.

Dr. Baker's hand trembled as he ran it through his silver hair. "Please excuse us," he said, glowering at Kelly. As she stared up into his disappointed face, I saw just an ember of remorse taking hold in her.

I glared at her while Steven left the room, followed by Josh. Sky remained, watching with an intense, anxious expression. Finally I tore my gaze from Kelly and strode out.

I found Josh and Steven in the next room. Steven had just started playing a console game, angrily slapping at the controls, while Josh paced, worrying the stubs of his fingernails as he gazed absently at the floor. I picked up the couch I had thrown earlier and returned it to its place. A moment later, an anxious Sky emerged from the hall, ignoring me as she was absorbed in her thoughts.

Ten minutes later, Dr. Baker entered the room with a subdued Kelly behind him, closely clutching her tote bag as she followed him to the front door of the house. She hesitated in the doorway. If Dr. Baker had dismissed her, it was probably for the best. We would miss her skills, but she couldn't flaunt pack rules without consequences. She was getting off easy. Eventually my anger would dissipate enough for me to appreciate Sebastian's restraint.

After a long, pensive glance back at us, she stepped across the threshold.

"Kelly." Sebastian's booming voice called to her from his office door.

She froze with her hand on the doorknob. I heard the frantic beating of her heart. After a long, tense moment, she slowly turned to meet Sebastian's stern gaze. Despite her fear, she still had the firm resolution of someone convinced they'd made the moral choice and would resist all accusations to the contrary.

"I'm sorry," she said.

I frowned at her insincerity, but her attention remained focused on Sebastian. He walked out of his office to stand in front of her, taking in everything about her as if she were a stranger he was meeting for the first time. His eyes fell to the bite mark on her neck, and I saw his jaw shift sideways.

"No, you're not, so you can keep your damn apology. If given the chance, you would do it again. That's why we have a problem."

She lowered her gaze to the floor. "I couldn't let her die."

"She's still dead!" he shouted abruptly, causing her to flinch, but she held her ground. "Let's just put aside your paramount betrayal of this pack," he continued. "You fed a vampire—a powerful one—who, less than two weeks ago, was so enthralled by you he had to restrain himself. Or have you forgotten that so quickly? I realize in your idealistic, naïve world, you believe that he wouldn't *call* you, strip you of your will, and force you to do whatever he desired. History has proven otherwise. He doesn't possess that level of control. He is and always has been a servant to his lusts."

"I couldn't let her die," she repeated matter-of-factly. When she looked up to meet his gaze, her disappointment became an accusation. "You should have felt the same way. I expected better from you."

"Then it's a good thing your happiness isn't predicated on me living up to your expectations. We can stand here all day and discuss how I have insulted your moral sensibilities, but I have neither the time nor the desire to do so. Since you didn't really think your little plan out, let me tell you what is going to happen now. For the next five days, you get Gavin as your guardian. By then Demetrius should have lost the ability to call you. Don't even consider sending Gavin away during this time."

She opened her mouth to object, but quickly thought better of it as Sebastian stepped close to her. She tried to turn away but he gripped her shoulders, obliging her to hold his gaze. "If you ever do anything like that again, it will not be as easily forgiven or as kindly handled. Are we clear?"

"What are you going to do," she said coolly, "kill me?"

Sebastian let go, allowing her to back away from him. "Are we clear?"

She answered with a faint nod. He turned, strode into his office, and closed the door. I understood the control he must've exerted not to slam it. Indignant and growing increasingly angry, Kelly strode after him. She was about to knock on his door when Sky intervened.

"I wouldn't," she warned, her expression an earnest appeal.

Kelly's lips pressed into a thin line as she pulled her bag close to her, then picked a couch and sat impatiently waiting for Gavin.

CHAPTER 17

*H*ours later, I waited at the white farmhouse while Josh used his magic to erase any evidence of the battle. We'd been fortunate in the number of losses suffered, but seeing the lifeless forms of several pack members in various states of gore was still difficult to endure. As many times as I'd seen death, it never got easier.

Thankfully, Sky was not among the dead. Despite her inexperience, she'd held her ground and fought to the end, impressing even Gavin. But I wasn't surprised. She'd shown her grit on several prior occasions: fighting off the genum that had attacked Winter; removing the silver bullet from my chest last year. Like Winter, Sky would always be underestimated by her opponents, and would make them pay for it.

One by one, Josh erased the bodies of my fellow were-animals. We did not bury our dead. Even in cases of natural death, which were rare, a medical examiner would likely raise questions about our unique physiology. Were-animals often came to violent ends, with the kind of wounds that would draw a homicide investigation. In order for the pack to maintain its obscurity, we used magic to dispose of bodies.

Nothing could be left to memorialize the were-animal's bravery or sacrifice.

The pack remembers.

Josh removed the genums as well, followed by any trace of blood in the soil and grass—even the piles of dust that were the remains of fallen vamps. While he worked, I kept an eye on the road for any unwanted visitors, but my thoughts drifted to Chris, her brutalized body appearing fresh in my mind.

For the sake of the relationship we'd once shared, dysfunctional as it had been, I'd tried to protect her. Demetrius had been right. She hadn't belonged on that battlefield. He'd cast her aside, trying to keep her out of the fight, but I'd welcomed her. It was a decision I regretted, but that didn't mean anything. She was dead. Her wounds were methodical, brutal, personal. She hadn't been killed by a genum. As much as I blamed Demetrius for taking advantage of her in the first place, it hadn't been his doing—not directly. He blamed me. Her death had nearly started a war between pack and Seethe, and there was only one person I knew who wanted such a war. Not a person. A vampire.

Michaela.

With one well-timed murder, she'd gotten rid of a rival and driven Demetrius into a vengeful fury, but she hadn't counted on Kelly. I could never condone what our nurse had done, but I couldn't deny that her actions had tempered Demetrius's rage in perhaps the only way possible. Did he suspect his Mistress's involvement? If so, Michaela appeared to have survived his wrath intact.

Chris is dead. She's a vampire, now—a bloodsucking, depraved murderer. My obligations to her were gone. Like all vamps, she was a potential threat to the pack, to be monitored and, if necessary, dealt with. If our paths crossed again, there would be no mercy.

When Josh had finished, the field was clear of bodies and

gore and blood. We spent the drive back to the retreat in somber silence.

I grieved in my own way, alone. Over the next few days, I made appearances at the retreat to carry out my duties and support those who struggled with loss, but I left my pain at my door.

A Scotch in hand, I sat on my sofa, glancing through one of the three magic books I had taken from the pack library. They were old and obscure. Judging by the dust on the covers when I'd first taken them, they hadn't been referenced for some time, but they'd proven invaluable. The ritual that Josh had used to draw Ethos's energy from Sky—most of it— had come from the book in my hand. It had been an impressive feat of magic, but not the magic that was on my mind in that moment.

Were-animals couldn't use magic. That had been the accepted norm. Sky was an exception—she was more than just a were-animal, and she had Maya, the spirit shade, whose powers and influence over her remained a mystery. My ability to use magic came from another source. I'd spent my entire life hiding my abilities, even from my own brother. But in the fight against Ethos—to save Sky—I'd put them on display, breaking through his field not once but three times, when Josh hadn't been able to do it once. The questions would come eventually. For the moment, he was respecting my grief, but it wasn't Josh's questions that concerned me.

I had graciously given the vampires an unobstructed view of my abilities. Only time would tell how that knowledge would provide value to them. Marcia was a much bigger concern. The witches considered magic their private domain. She wouldn't miss the chance to investigate—not that I had to cooperate, but there was my brother to consider. Though he was not a member of the Creed, they maintained a murky jurisdiction over him. Marcia had never approved of his alliance with the pack. She was looking for a reason to rebuke him. If she believed that Josh had knowingly hidden my abilities from the Creed, he could be punished. I was at risk as well; even if the origin of my abilities remained undiscovered, the mere fact that I was a were-animal who possessed magic, let alone powerful magic, was enough to invite intrigue—or worse. In the past, young were-animals who showed an aptitude for magic, however slight, had a tendency to die of unusual causes.

Sooner or later, Marcia was going to stick her nose in my business. Most likely, I'd have to deal with her.

I poured myself another Scotch.

I had just opened my laptop to distract myself when I heard a single set of footsteps approach my door, followed by a crisp knock. I frowned. Approaching the door, I peered through the peephole to find a determined Sky on my porch, waiting impatiently. I sighed at the inevitable.

When I opened the door, I noticed a book in her hand. Since this wasn't a conversation I wanted to have on the porch, I stepped aside and let her in, closing the door behind her. She stopped in the living room, her green eyes entranced by the three books lying on my sofa next to my laptop.

"What do you want?" I asked.

She turned to me with a mischievous smile. "Not going to offer me a glass of water or something?"

Let's just get to the point. "What. Do you. Want?"

Her eyes narrowed as she raised her chin to me. "Why do you care that I am a Moura? And how does it affect the pack? You've called me naïve and foolish more than once, yet I am not foolish or naïve enough not to realize that what I am affects the pack. I suspect that what I am affects you as well. So, what are you?"

"You know what I am."

"No, I know what you claim to be—a werewolf—just like

me. I know that you seem to have a lot of information about me that should otherwise be unimportant. I know that when Gloria met you, she wanted to get as much distance as possible from you, and so did Thaddeus. Ethos was repelled by you and couldn't get you away from him quick enough, but with Josh, he just wanted to play magical one-upmanship. Why?"

"A lot of people are afraid of me." I smiled. "I don't think that's cause for suspicion."

Her gaze softened as she monitored the rate of my respiration, listened to the beat of my heart. Frustration slowly settled on her face, cracking her confidence when she failed to detect any change whatsoever. She was learning, but I'd been at that game much longer than her.

"You effortlessly breeze through wards and fields that even Josh has trouble with."

"So?"

"I think there is more to you. A great deal more."

I smirked. "What, do you think I'm like you?"

"Yes"—she nodded—"something like that."

I didn't begrudge her her curiosity, but she didn't have a right to answers. Knowledge was dangerous, and I didn't need to put her at risk. I also knew I had little chance of steering Sky away without a significant distraction. Her eyes widened as I stepped closer to her, slowly leaning in until my lips nearly brushed her ear.

"What's the matter, Skylar?" I whispered. "Do you hate being alone—the only one of your kind in this big bad world? Do you need someone to hold your hand through it, coddle you, and tell you that you're a special little snowflake and everything is going to be okay?"

I watched the muscles in her neck tighten into cords before she backed a step away, scowling at me. "Yes, I hate knowing that when I stand in a room full of were-animals, I am still different. Sometimes it's thrilling, but most of the time, it's really scary to know what I can do with magic, and I can't help but wonder if it will help me or destroy me. And it sucks that the more I find out about myself, the more I feel like my birth mother sentenced me to something far worse than death by letting me live. So yes, I hate being out here alone."

I studied her for a moment. She was feeling sorry for herself. In our world, confidence mattered. She was strong and brave, but self-pity was a weakness that could get her killed.

"You and I are nothing alike. There is no one else like you," I admitted. "You're not about to be soothed, pampered, and told that everything's going to be okay, because it's not. Get over it. Grow a pair and deal with it. Let's just hope that when everything hits the fan, you are still breathing afterward, or at the very least, your death is simple and not some torturous revenge."

"Well, I don't think we're that different at all," she scoffed, but this time she refused the bait. "You can't be a witch, or at least you will never admit it. Is it because you are afraid of them, what they will do to you, or to Josh, for not exposing you?"

"One thing we don't do is underestimate the witches. If I had shown signs of being a witch, I would not be standing here with you. So no, I am not a witch."

She grunted her dissatisfaction. "In all the time I have spent with Josh, he's never mentioned the protected objects."

"Perhaps you two were so busy with other things that the subject just never came up."

Her jaw clenched as she scrutinized me. Her green eyes darkened. "I'm tied to the Aufero," she announced. "What are you linked to?"

I couldn't help a small smile. In the past, she'd been much easier to distract. When I didn't answer, she continued.

"The Clostra? The Fatifer?"

I glanced at the book in her hand as I crossed my arms over my chest. *Somebody's been a busy bee.*

"You said there were five Mouras Encantadas, which means there are five mystical objects in need of protection. I only found four, and since we destroyed the Gem of Levage, that makes only three. One is missing. What do you know about the elusive fifth object that even the books have no knowledge of?"

And this bee is full of surprises. I steadied myself, careful to mask my surprise, but she noticed. I heard it in the excited leap of her heart. I shrugged, my smile casual. "I made a mistake. Perhaps there were only four."

Sensing weakness, she moved in for the kill. "You have a lot of information and know a hell of a lot about me. What are you hiding?"

I didn't answer.

"I'm going to find out," she promised, jabbing a finger toward my chest.

Crap. "You do that," I chuckled. There was only one way I knew to get rid of Sky, or distract her entirely. Either way was fine with me. I took off my shirt on my way to the back door. "I'm going for a run. Unless you plan on joining me, you can let yourself out."

Her eyes turned longingly to the books on my sofa. I returned to pick them up, along with my laptop, and locked them in the neighboring den. "Are you joining me or not?" I asked as I unbuttoned and then slipped off my pants. She stared back at me, defiant as I took off my underwear. Her lips pressed together in annoyance as she tried not to express her frustration. After a moment, she averted her gaze, but then quickly turned back. Her eyes fixed like a lifeline on mine, but I saw the twitch in them as I slowly approached her. Finally, willfully, she allowed herself a full look. Her jaw remained set as she met my gaze once more.

"In or out, Sky?" I asked.

"I'll just wait here until you get back," she said with a sly smile.

"That wasn't an option."

"I'll pass."

Suit yourself. I walked to the back door, then stopped. "Ethos could have killed you at any time," I said over my shoulder. "Do you wonder why he didn't?"

She let out a long, slow breath before answering. "I'll let myself out."

CHAPTER 18

*T*he next morning, I found Dr. Yoshi sitting pensively on his bed, his breakfast mostly untouched. As I entered his cell, he met my gaze with an anxious look.

"Get your things," I barked.

After a moment's hesitation, he obeyed, but with the reluctance of someone who thought they might not survive their journey. Despite Ethos's apparent demise, the spell that prevented Dr. Yoshi from remembering his interactions with the silver-haired witch remained unbreakable. We had no means to verify whether he'd been forced to create the poison that had devastated us in the initial attack by the genums, but Stacy had confirmed Artemis's story of him. On ethical grounds, he'd quit a lucrative position creating biological weapons for the military, settling instead for a steady but uncompromising career as a chemistry teacher. He signed online petitions for liberal causes and made small but consistent donations to animal rights groups, usually in his wife's name. Nothing about Dr. Yoshi suggested the kind of greedy, amoral opportunist who would create such a deadly weapon for mere profit.

Not everyone agreed to letting him live. His skill set made him dangerous to us, but it also made him an asset in case we ever encountered another poison or a disease particular to our kind. He would have to be watched—carefully.

Riding in the passenger seat of my SUV, he remained withdrawn until he realized we were close to his home. I stopped in a grocery store parking lot a block away from his gated community.

"Here's what's going to happen," I said, glaring down at him.

"I'll leave town," he blurted. "You'll never see me again, I promise. I—"

"No. You're going to stay here and live your life exactly as you were before this mess started." I handed him a cell phone from my pocket. "If you leave the city limits, you text me where you're going, and for how long. You move to another house, you text me your new Chicago address. If I call you, you answer. Understand?"

He nodded emphatically.

"Dr. Baker took your blood sample," I stated. "Do you understand why?"

"No," he whispered.

"If you run, we can always find you."

"I understand."

"No more contract work."

He flinched as I reached over him to open the passenger door, but he didn't hesitate to scramble out of my SUV.

That evening I was on my way to the club to check on Josh when I received a text from Sebastian.

"She's in."

I nodded to myself. Admittedly, I felt relieved. Since our war with Ethos, the world had become a much more dangerous place for Skylar Brooks. I could no longer give her the life she wanted, but it was going to be much easier to protect her now that she was a member of the Midwest Pack. It would also be much easier to control her curiosity.

MESSAGE TO THE READER

Thank you for choosing *Darkness Unveiled* from the many titles available to you. Our goal is to create an engaging world, compelling characters, and an interesting experience for you. We hope you've accomplished that. Reviews are very important to authors and help other readers discover our books. Please take a moment to leave a review. We'd love to know your thoughts about the book.

For notifications about new releases, *exclusive* contests and giveaways, and cover reveals, please sign up for our mailing lists at www.emerson-knight.com.

www.emerson-knight.com
Author@Emerson-Knight.com